EX LIBRIS

VINTAGE CLASSICS

THEATRE

William Somerset Maugham was born in 1874 and lived in Paris until he was ten. He was educated at King's School, Canterbury, and at Heidelberg University. He spent some time at St. Thomas' Hospital with the idea of practising medicine, but the success of his first novel, *Liza of Lambeth*, published in 1897, won him over to letters. *Of Human Bondage*, the first of his masterpieces, came out in 1915, and with the publication in 1919 of *The Moon and Sixpence* his reputation as a novelist was established. At the same time his fame as a successful playwright and short story writer was being consolidated with acclaimed productions of various plays and the publication of *The Trembling of a Leaf*, subtitled *Little Stories of the South Sea Islands*, in 1921, which was followed by seven more collections. His other works include travel books, essays, criticism and the autobiographical *The Summing Up* and *A Writer's Notebook*.

In 1927 Somerset Maugham settled in the South of France and lived there until his death in 1965.

OTHER WORKS BY W. SOMERSET MAUGHAM

W. SOMERSET MAUGHAM

Theatre

VINTAGE BOOKS
London

Published by Vintage 2001

24

First published in Great Britain by William Heinemann in 1937

Vintage
Random House, 20 Vauxhall Bridge Road,
London SW1V 2SA

www.vintage-classics.info

Addresses for companies within The Random House Group Limited
can be found at: www.randomhouse.co.uk/offices.htm

The Random House Group Limited Reg. No. 954009

A CIP catalogue record for this book
is available from the British Library

ISBN 9780099286837

Penguin Random House is committed to a sustainable future for
our business, our readers and our planet. This book is made from
Forest Stewardship Council® certified paper.

Printed and bound in Great Britain by Clays Ltd, Elcograf S.p.A.

PREFACE

It is not very difficult to write a preface to a book that you wrote a long time ago, for the hurrying years have made a different man of you and you can look upon it with a stranger's eyes. You see its faults, and for the reader's delectation you can recall, according to your temperament with toleration or with dismay, the defects in your character as it was then which account for the defects of your book; or you can look back, maybe with the pleasure which distance lends the past, upon the conditions under which you wrote; you can draw a pretty picture of your garret or dwell with modest complacency on the stiff upper lip with which you faced neglect. But when, in order to tempt a reader to buy a book that has no longer the merit of novelty, you set about writing a preface to a work of fiction that you composed no more than two or three years back, it is none too easy to find anything that you want to say, for you have said in your book all you have to say upon the theme with which it deals and having done so have never given it another thought. As nothing is more dead than a love that has burnt itself out, so no subject is less interesting to an author than one upon which he has said his say. Of course you can quarrel with your reviewers, but there is little point in that; what such and such a critic thought of a novel that he read the year before last can only matter to an author of his susceptibility is really too tender for the rough and tumble of this queer world; the critic has long forgotten both the book and his criticism, and the generality of readers never trouble their heads with criticism anyhow.

When first I set up as a professional author I used to paste such reviews as I got in great scrap-books, thinking it would amuse me some day to read them again, and I would carefully head each one with the date and the name of the paper in which it had appeared. But in course of time these unwieldy volumes grew very cumbersome, and because for one reason and another I have seldom lived for long in the same house, I found it necessary at last to get the dustman to rid me of them. Since then I have contented myself with reading my notices, as time wore on with sufficient equanimity not to be unduly perturbed by those that were unfavourable nor unduly elated by those that were laudatory, and throwing them into my waste-paper basket. My recollection is that on the whole the criticisms of Theatre were pretty good. Some critics, however, complained that Julia Lambert, my heroine, was not a creature of high moral character, great intelligence and nobility of soul, and concluded from this that she was a mediocre actress. I have been given to understand that a number of leading ladies were of the same opinion. Indeed one old actress, celebrated for her acting when I was a boy, and still remembered by the middle-aged for the amusingly disagreeable things she so often said, chiefly at the expense of her fellow-players, was quite biting in her references to me; but I think her acrimony was due to a misapprehension. I took pains in my novel to make it clear that my heroine, whatever her other faults, was not a snob, and this naturally enough prevented the old person in question from recognising the fact that my Julia was a fine actress. We are all inclined to think that others can only have our virtues if they also have our vices.

Greatness is rare. During the last fifty years I have seen most of the actresses who have made a name for themselves. I have seen many who had eminent gifts, many who excelled in a domain they had made their own, many who had charm, beauty and knowledge, but I cannot think of more than one to whom I could without hesitation ascribe greatness. This was Eleanora Duse. It may be that Mrs. Siddons had it; it may be that Rachel had it; I do not know; I never saw Sarah Bernhardt till she was past her prime; the glory that surrounded her, the extravagance of her legend, made it difficult to judge her coolly; she was often mannered and she could rant at times like any player queen; at her best she may have had greatness, I only saw its appurtenances, the crown, the sceptre and the ermine cloak – the Emperor of China's new clothes, but no Emperor of China. With the one exception I have mentioned I have only seen actresses who could be good, sometimes very good, in certain parts. I have a notion that one's opinion in this matter depends a good deal on how much one is affected by the glamour of the stage. There are many people whom the theatre fills with an excitement which no familiarity can stale. It is to them a world of mystery and delight; it gives them entry into a realm of the imagination which increases their joy in life, and its illusion colours the ordinariness of their daily round with the golden shimmer of romance. When they watch the celebrated actress, her beauty enhanced by make-up, her significance emphasized by spot-lights, uttering her fine phrases as though they came out of her own head, undergoing remarkable experiences and suffering poignant emotions, they feel that they live more fully; and it is natural enough that they should make a somewhat excessive use of hyperbole when they seek to describe the sensations which the skilful interpreter has given them. It is natural also that they should overlook the fact that the performance which has filled them with rapture owes at least something to the costumier, the scene-painter, the electrician and the author.

Even in my early youth I was never stage-struck; but whether because I am by nature of a somewhat sceptical disposition or whether because my mind was filled with private dreams which satisfied my romantic yearnings, I cannot say; and when I began to have plays acted I lost even the few illusions I had. When I discovered how much effort was put to achieving the gesture that had such a spontaneous look, when I realized how often the perfect intonation which moved an audience to tears was due not to the actress's sensibility but to the producer's experience, when in short I learnt from the inside how complicated was the process by which a play is made ready to set before an audience, I found it impossible to regard even the most brilliant members of the profession with the same awed and admiring wonder as the general public. On the other hand I learnt that they had qualities with which the public is little inclined to credit them. I learnt, for example, that with few exceptions they were hardworking, courageous, patient and conscientious. Though dropping with fatigue after a long day's work, I saw them consent with cheerfulness to go through still once more a difficult scene that they had that very day rehearsed half a dozen times already; I saw them, in illness, give a performance when they could hardly stand on their feet rather than let the company down; and I learnt that for all the frills and airs they might put on, when it came down to the business of getting the best out of the play and themselves, they were as reasonable as anyone could desire. Behind their famous 'temperament', which is a combination of selfishness and nerves more or less consciously emphasized under the erroneous impression that it is a proof of artistic sensibility, there is far oftener than the public imagines an abundance of shrewd, practical sense. I have never known a child that didn't like to show off, and in every actor there remains something of the child; it is to this that he owes many of his most charming gifts. He has more than the normal exhibitionism which is common to all but very few of us, and if he hadn't he would not be an actor; it is wiser to regard this particular trait with humour than with disdain. If I had to put in a phrase the impressions I formed of actors during the long time of my connection with the stage, I should say that their virtues are more solid than they pretend and their failings incidental to the hazardous and exacting profession they follow.

Thirty years elapsed between the production of my first play and the production of my last and in that period I was thrown into intimate contact with a great number of distinguished actresses. Julia Lambert is a portrait of none of them. I have taken a trait here and a trait there and sought to create a living person. Because I was not much affected by the glamour of the brilliant creatures I had known in the flesh I drew the creature of my fancy, I daresay, with a certain coolness. It is this, perhaps, which has disconcerted those readers who cannot separate the actress from the limelight that surrounds her and vexed those actresses who have been so dazzled by the limelight that they honestly think there is no more in them than that. They do themselves an injustice. The quality of the artist depends on the quality of the man and no one can excel in the arts who has not, besides his special gifts, moral rectitude; I would not deny, however, that this may exhibit itself in a form that is surprising and fantastic. I think Julia Lambert is true to life. I should like the reader to notice that though her admirers ascribe greatness to her, and though she accepts the flattery greedily, I, speaking in my own person, have not claimed that she was more than highly successful, very talented, serious and industrious. I should add that for my part I feel a great affection for her; I am not shocked by her naughtiness, nor scandalized by her absurdities; I can only consider her, whatever she does, with fond indulgence.

Before I bring this preface to a close I must tell the reader that in the book which I am now inviting him to peruse I have made two errors in fact. The novelist tries to be accurate in every detail, but sometimes he makes a mistake, and there is generally no lack of persons who are prepared to point it out to him. Once I wrote a novel in which I had occasion to mention a beach called Manly, which is a favourite resort during the bathing season of the inhabitants of Sydney, and unfortunately I spelt it Manley. The superfluous 'e' brought me hundreds of angry and derisive letters from New South Wales. You would have thought that the slip, which might after all have been a printer's error, though of course it was due only to my own carelessness, was a deliberate insult that I had offered to the Commonwealth. Indeed one lady told me that it was one more proof of the ignorant superciliousness of the English towards the inhabitants of the English colonies, and that it was people like me who would be responsible if next time Great Britain was embroiled in a Continental war the youth of Australia, instead of flying to her rescue, preferred to stay quietly at home. She ended her letter on a rhetorical note. What, she asked me, would the English say if an Australian novelist, writing about England, should spell Bournmouth with an 'e'? My first impulse was to answer that to the best of my belief the English wouldn't turn a hair, even if it were incorrect, which in point of fact it wasn't, but I thought it would better become me to suffer the lady's stern rebuke in silence. Now in this book I have made two mistakes; I have made my heroine put down her failure in Beatrice to the fact that she was not at ease with blank verse, and I have made her, when she speaks of Racine's *Phèdre*, complain that the heroine did not appear till the third act. Instead of verifying my facts as I should have done, I trusted my memory, and my memory played me false. Beatrice speaks very little verse; all her important scenes are in prose; and if Julia failed in the part it was not for the reason she gave. Phèdre enters upon the stage in the third scene of the first act. I do not know why only two persons, one apiece, pointed out to me these inexcusable blunders; I like to think that most readers did me the credit of supposing that they were due, not to my ignorance, but to my subtlety, and that in making Julia Lambert speak in this casual and haphazard fashion I was adding a neat touch to my delineation of her character. But I may be unduly flattering myself, and it is just possible that my readers' recollection of the famous plays in which these characters appear was as hazy as my own, and they knew no better.

The door opened and Michael Gosselyn looked up. Julia came in.

'Hulloa! I won't keep you a minute. I was just signing some letters.'

'No hurry. I only came to see what seats had been sent to the Dennorants. What's that young man doing here?'

With the experienced actress's instinct to fit the gesture to the word, by a movement of her neat head she indicated the room through which she had just passed.

'He's the accountant. He comes from Lawrence and Hamphreys. He's been here three days.'

'He looks very young.'

'He's an articled clerk. He seems to know his job. He can't get over the way our accounts are kept. He told me he never expected a theatre to be run on such business-like lines. He says the way some of those firms in the city keep their accounts is enough to turn your hair grey.'

Julia smiled at the complacency on her husband's handsome face.

'He's a young man of tact.'

'He finishes to-day. I thought we might take him back with us and give him a spot of lunch. He's quite a gentleman.'

'Is that a sufficient reason to ask him to lunch?'

Michael did not notice the faint irony of her tone.

'I won't ask him if you don't want him. I merely thought it would be a treat for him. He admires you tremendously. He's been to see the play three times. He's crazy to be introduced to you.'

Michael touched a button and in a moment his secretary came in.

'Here are the letters, Margery. What appointments have I got for this afternoon?'

Julia with half an ear listened to the list Margery read out and, though she knew the room so well, idly looked about her. It was a very proper room for the manager of a first-class theatre. The walls had been panelled (at cost price) by a good decorator and on them hung engravings of theatrical pictures of Zoffany and de Wilde. The armchairs were large and comfortable. Michael sat in a heavily-carved Chippendale chair, a reproduction but made by a well-known firm, and his Chippendale table, with heavy ball and claw feet, was immensely solid. On it stood in a massive silver frame a photograph of herself and to balance it a photograph of Roger, their son. Between these was a magnificent silver ink-stand that she had herself given him on one of his birthdays and behind it a rack in red morocco, heavily gilt, in which he kept his private paper in case he wanted to write a letter in his own hand. The paper bore the address, Siddons Theatre, and the envelope his crest, a boar's head with the motto underneath: Nemo me impune lacessit. A bunch of yellow tulips in a silver bowl, which he had got through winning the theatrical golf tournament three times running, showed Margery's care. Julia gave her a reflective glance. Notwithstanding her cropped peroxide hair and her heavily-painted lips she had the neutral look that marks the perfect secretary. She had been with Michael for five years. In that time she must have got to know him inside and out. Julia wondered if she could be such a fool as to be in love with him.

But Michael rose from his chair.

'Now, darling, I'm ready for you.'

Margery gave him his black Homburg hat and opened the door for Julia and Michael to go out. As they entered the office the young man Julia had noticed turned round and stood up.

'I should like to introduce you to Miss Lambert,' said Michael. Then with the air of an ambassador presenting an attaché to the sovereign of the court to which he is accredited: 'This is the gentleman who is good enough to put some order into the mess we make of our accounts.'

The young man went scarlet. He smiled stiffly in answer to Julia's warm, ready smile and she felt the palm of his hand wet with sweat when she cordially grasped it. His confusion was touching. That was how people had felt when they were presented to Sarah Siddons. She thought that she had not been very gracious to Michael when he had proposed asking the boy to luncheon. She looked straight into his eyes. Her own were large, of a very dark brown, and starry. It was no effort to her, it was as instinctive as brushing away a fly that was buzzing round her, to suggest now a faintly amused, friendly tenderness.

'I wonder if we could persuade you to come and eat a chop with us. Michael will drive you back after lunch.'

The young man blushed again and his adam's apple moved in his thin neck.

'It's awfully kind of you.' He gave his clothes a troubled look. 'I'm absolutely filthy.'

'You can have a wash and brush up when we get home.'

The car was waiting for them at the stage door, a long car in black and chromium, upholstered in silver leather, and with Michael's crest discreetly emblazoned on the doors. Julia got in.

'Come and sit with me. Michael is going to drive.'

They lived in Stanhope Place, and when they arrived Julia told the butler to show the young man where he could wash his hands. She went up to the drawing-room. She was painting her lips when Michael joined her.

'I've told him to come up as soon as he's ready.'

'By the way, what's his name?'

'I haven't a notion.'

'Darling, we must know. I'll ask him to write in our book.'

'Damn it, he's not important enough for that.' Michael

3

asked only very distinguished people to write in their book. 'We shall never see him again.'

At that moment the young man appeared. In the car Julia had done all she could to put him at his ease, but he was still very shy. The cocktails were waiting and Michael poured them out. Julia took a cigarette and the young man struck a match for her, but his hand was trembling so much that she thought he would never be able to hold the light near enough to her cigarette, so she took his hand and held it.

'Poor lamb,' she thought, 'I suppose this is the most wonderful moment in his whole life. What fun it'll be for him when he tells his people. I expect he'll be a blasted little hero in his office.'

Julia talked very differently to herself and to other people: when she talked to herself her language was racy. She inhaled the first whiff of her cigarette with delight. It was really rather wonderful, when you came to think of it, that just to have lunch with her and talk to her for three-quarters of an hour, perhaps, could make a man quite important in his own scrubby little circle.

The young man forced himself to make a remark.

'What a stunning room this is.'

She gave him the quick, delightful smile, with a slight lift of her fine eyebrows, which he must often have seen her give on the stage.

'I'm so glad you like it.' Her voice was rather low and ever so slightly hoarse. You would have thought his observation had taken a weight off her mind. 'We think in the family that Michael has such perfect taste.'

Michael gave the room a complacent glance.

'I've had a good deal of experience. I always design the sets myself for our plays. Of course, I have a man to do the rough work for me, but the ideas are mine.'

They had moved into that house two years before, and he knew, and Julia knew, that they had put it into the hands of an expensive decorator when they were going on tour, and he had agreed to have it completely ready

4

for them, at cost price in return for the work they promised him in the theatre, by the time they came back. But it was unnecessary to impart such tedious details to a young man whose name even they did not know. The house was furnished in extremely good taste, with a judicious mixture of the antique and the modern, and Michael was right when he said that it was quite obviously a gentleman's house. Julia, however, had insisted that she must have her bedroom as she liked, and having had exactly the bedroom that pleased her in the old house in Regent's Park which they had occupied since the end of the war she brought it over bodily. The bed and the dressing-table were upholstered in pink silk, the chaise-longue and the armchair in Nattier blue; over the bed there were fat little gilt cherubs who dangled a lamp with a pink shade, and fat little gilt cherubs swarmed all round the mirror on the dressing-table. On satinwood tables were signed photographs, richly framed, of actors and actresses and members of the royal family. The decorator had raised his supercilious eyebrows, but it was the only room in the house in which Julia felt completely at home. She wrote her letters at a satinwood desk, seated on a gilt Hamlet stool.

Luncheon was announced and they went downstairs.

'I hope you'll have enough to eat,' said Julia. 'Michael and I have very small appetites.'

In point of fact there was grilled sole, grilled cutlets and spinach, and stewed fruit. It was a meal designed to satisfy legitimate hunger, but not to produce fat. The cook, warned by Margery that there was a guest to luncheon had hurriedly made some fried potatoes. They looked crisp and smelt appetizing. Only the young man took them. Julia gave them a wistful look before she shook her head in refusal. Michael stared at them gravely for a moment as though he could not quite tell what they were, and then with a little start, breaking out of a brown study, said No thank you. They sat at a refectory table, Julia and Michael at either end in very grand Italian chairs, and the young man in the middle on a chair that was not at all comfortable, but perfectly in character. Julia noticed that he seemed to be looking at the sideboard and with her engaging smile, leaned forward.

'What is it?'

He blushed scarlet.

'I was wondering if I might have a piece of bread.'

'Of course.'

She gave the butler a significant glance; he was at that moment helping Michael to a glass of dry white wine, and he left the room.

'Michael and I never eat bread. It was stupid of Jevons not to realize that you might want some.'

'Of course bread is only a habit,' said Michael. 'It's wonderful how soon you can break yourself of it if you set your mind to it.'

'The poor lamb's as thin as a rail, Michael.'

'I don't not eat bread because I'm afraid of getting fat. I don't eat it because I see no point in it. After all, with the exercise I take I can eat anything I like.'

He still had at fifty-two a very good figure. As a young man, with a great mass of curling chestnut hair, with a wonderful skin and large deep blue eyes, a straight nose and small ears, he had been the best-looking actor on the English stage. The only thing that slightly spoiled him was the thinness of his mouth. He was just six foot tall and he had a gallant bearing. It was his obvious beauty that had engaged him to go on the stage rather than to become a soldier like his father. Now his chestnut hair was very grey, and he wore it much shorter; his face had broadened and was a good deal lined; his skin no longer had the soft bloom of a peach and his colour was high. But with his splendid eyes and his fine figure he was still a very handsome man. Since his five years at the war he had adopted a military bearing, so that if you had not known who he was (which was scarcely possible, for in one way and another his photograph was always appearing in the illustrated papers) you might have taken him for an officer of high rank. He boasted that his weight had not changed since he was twenty, and for years, wet or fine, he had got up every morning at eight to put on shorts and a sweater and have a run round Regent's Park.

'The secretary told me you were rehearsing this morning, Miss Lambert,' the young man remarked. 'Does that mean you're putting on a new play?'

'Not a bit of it,' answered Michael. 'We're playing to capacity.'

'Michael thought we were getting a bit ragged, so he called a rehearsal.'

'I'm very glad I did. I found little bits of business had crept in that I hadn't given them and a good many liberties were being taken with the text. I'm a great stickler for saying the author's exact words, though, God knows, the words authors write nowadays aren't much.'

'If you'd like to come and see our play,' Julia said graciously, 'I'm sure Michael will be delighted to give you some seats.'

'I'd love to come again,' the young man answered eagerly. 'I've seen it three times already.'

'You haven't?' cried Julia, with surprise, though she remembered perfectly that Michael had already told her so. 'Of course it's not a bad little play, it's served our purpose very well, but I can't imagine anyone wanting to see it three times.'

'It's not so much the play I went to see, it was your performance.'

'I dragged that out of him all right,' thought Julia, and then aloud: 'When we read the play Michael was rather doubtful about it. He didn't think my part was very good. You know, it's not really a star part. But I thought I could make something out of it. Of course we had to cut the other woman a lot in rehearsals.'

'I don't say we re-wrote the play,' said Michael, 'but I can tell you it was a very different play we produced from the one the author submitted to us.'

'You're simply wonderful in it,' the young man said.

7

('He has a certain charm.') 'I'm glad you liked me,' she answered.

'If you're very nice to Julia I daresay she'll give you a photograph of herself when you go.'

'Would you?'

He blushed again and his blue eyes shone ('He's really rather sweet.') He was not particularly good-looking, but he had a frank, open face and his shyness was attractive. He had curly light brown hair, but it was plastered down and Julia thought how much better he would look if, instead of trying to smoothe out the wave with brilliantine, he made the most of it. He had a fresh colour, a good skin and small well-shaped teeth. She noticed with approval that his clothes fitted and that he wore them well. He looked nice and clean.

'I suppose you've never had anything to do with the theatre from the inside before?' she said.

'Never. That's why I was so crazy to get this job. You can't think how it thrills me.'

Michael and Julia smiled on him kindly. His admiration made them feel a little larger than life-size.

'I never allow outsiders to come to rehearsals, but as you're our accountant you almost belong to the theatre, and I wouldn't mind making an exception in your favour if it would amuse you to come.'

'That would be terribly kind of you. I've never been to a rehearsal in my life. Are you going to act in the next play?'

'Oh, I don't think so. I'm not very keen about acting any more. I find it almost impossible to find a part to suit me. You see, at my time of life I can't very well play young lovers, and authors don't seem to write the parts they used to write when I was a young fellow. What the French call a raisonneur. You know the sort of thing I mean, a duke, or a cabinet minister, or an eminent K.C. who says clever, witty things and turns people round his little finger. I don't know what's happened to authors. They don't seem able to write good lines any more. Bricks without straw; that's what we actors are expected to make nowadays. And are they grateful to us? The authors, I mean. You'd be surprised if I told you the terms some of them have the nerve to ask.'

'The fact remains, we can't do without them,' smiled Julia. 'If the play's wrong no acting in the world will save it.'

'That's because the public isn't really interested in the theatre. In the great days of the English stage people didn't go to see the plays, they went to see the players. It didn't matter what Kemble and Mrs Siddons acted. The public went to see them. And even now, though I don't deny that if the play's wrong you're dished, I do contend that if the play's right, it's the actors the public go to see, not the play.'

'I don't think anyone can deny that,' said Julia.

'All an actress like Julia wants is a vehicle. Give her that and she'll do the rest.'

Julia gave the young man a delightful, but slightly deprecating smile.

'You mustn't take my husband too seriously. I'm afraid we must admit that he's partial where I'm concerned.'

'Unless this young man is a much bigger fool than I think him he must know that there's nothing in the way of acting that you can't do.'

'Oh, that's only an idea that people have got because I take care never to do anything but what I can do.'

Presently Michael looked at his watch.

'I think when you've finished your coffee, young man, we ought to be going.'

The boy gulped down what was left in his cup and Julia rose from the table.

'You won't forget my photograph?'

'I think there are some in Michael's den. Come along and we'll choose one.'

She took him into a fair-sized room behind the dining-room. Though it was supposed to be Michael's private sitting-room – 'a fellow wants a room where he can get

9

away by himself and smoke his pipe' – it was chiefly used as a cloak-room when they had guests. There was a noble mahogany desk on which were signed photographs of George V and Queen Mary. Over the chimney-piece was an old copy of Lawrence's portrait of Kemble as Hamlet. On a small table was a pile of typescript plays. The room was surrounded by bookshelves under which were cupboards, and from one of these Julia took a bundle of her latest photographs. She handed one to the young man.

'This one is not so bad.'

'It's lovely.'

'Then it can't be as like me as I thought.'

'But it is. It's exactly like you.'

She gave him another sort of smile, just a trifle roguish; she lowered her eyelids for a second and then raising them gazed at him for a little with that soft expression that people described as her velvet look. She had no object in doing this. She did it, if not mechanically, from an instinctive desire to please. The boy was so young, so shy, he looked as if he had such a nice nature, and she would never see him again, she wanted him to have his money's worth; she wanted him to look back on this as one of the great moments of his life. She glanced at the photograph again. She liked to think she looked like that. The photographer had so posed her, with her help, as to show her at her best. Her nose was slightly thick but he had managed by his lighting to make it look very delicate, not a wrinkle marred the smoothness of her skin, and there was a melting look in her fine eyes.

'All right. You shall have this one. You know I'm not a beautiful woman, I'm not even a very pretty one; Coquelin always used to say I had the *beauté du diable*. You understand French, don't you?'

'Enough for that.'

'I'll sign it for you.'

She sat at the desk and with her bold, flowing hand wrote: Yours sincerely, Julia Lambert.

2

When the two men had gone she looked through the photographs again before putting them back.

'Not bad for a woman of forty-six,' she smiled. 'They are like me, there's no denying that.' She looked round the room for a mirror, but there wasn't one. 'These damned decorators. Poor Michael, no wonder he never uses this room. Of course I never have photographed well.'

She had an impulse to look at some of her old photographs. Michael was a tidy, business-like man, and her photographs were kept in large cardboard cases, dated and chronologically arranged. His were in other cardboard cases in the same cupboard.

'When someone comes along and wants to write the story of our careers he'll find all the material ready to his hand,' he said.

With the same laudable object he had had all their press cuttings from the very beginning pasted in a series of books.

There were photographs of Julia when she was a child, and photographs of her as a young girl, photographs of her in her first parts, photographs of her as a young married woman, with Michael, and then with Roger, her son, as a baby. There was one photograph of the three of them, Michael very manly and incredibly handsome, herself all tenderness looking down at Roger with maternal feeling, and Roger a little boy with a curly head, which had been an enormous success. All the illustrated papers had given it a full page and they had used it on the programmes. Reduced to picture-postcard size it had sold in the provinces for years. It was such a bore that Roger when he got to Eton refused to be photographed with her any more. It seemed so funny of him not to want to be in the papers.

'People will think you're deformed or something,' she told him. 'And it's not as if it weren't good form. You should just go to a first night and see the society people how they mob the photographers, cabinet ministers and judges and everyone. They may pretend they don't like it, but just see them posing when they think the camera man's got his eye on them.'

But he was obstinate.

Julia came across a photograph of herself as Beatrice. It was the only Shakespearean part she had ever played. She knew that she didn't look well in costume; she could never understand why, because no one could wear modern clothes as well as she could. She had her clothes made in Paris, both for the stage and for private life, and the dressmakers said that no one brought them more orders. She had a lovely figure, everyone admitted that; she was fairly tall for a woman, and she had long legs. It was a pity she had never had a chance of playing Rosalind, she would have looked all right in boy's clothes, of course it was too late now, but perhaps it was just as well she hadn't risked it. Though you would have thought, with her brilliance, her roguishness, her sense of comedy she would have been perfect. The critics hadn't really liked her Beatrice. It was that damned blank verse. Her voice, her rather low rich voice, with that effective hoarseness, which wrung your heart in an emotional passage or gave so much humour to a comedy line, seemed to sound all wrong when she spoke it. And then her articulation; it was so distinct that, without raising her voice, she could make you hear her every word in the last row of the gallery; they said it made verse sound like prose. The fact was, she supposed, that she was much too modern.

Michael had started with Shakespeare. That was before she knew him. He had played Romeo at Cambridge, and when he came down, after a year at a dramatic school, Benson had engaged him. He toured the country and played a great variety of parts. But he realized that Shakespeare would get him nowhere and that if he wanted to become a leading actor he must gain experience in modern plays. A man called James Langton was running a repertory theatre at Middlepool that was attracting a good deal of attention; and after Michael had been with Benson for three years, when the company was going to Middlepool on its annual visit, he wrote to Langton and asked whether he would see him. Jimmie Langton, a fat, bald-headed, rubicund man of forty-five, who looked like one of Rubens' prosperous burghers, had a passion for the theatre. He was an eccentric, arrogant, exuberant, vain and charming fellow. He loved acting, but his physique prevented him from playing any but a few parts, which was fortunate, for he was a bad actor. He could not subdue his natural flamboyance, and every part he played, though he studied it with care and gave it thought, he turned into a grotesque. He broadened every gesture, he exaggerated every intonation. But it was a very different matter when he rehearsed his cast; then he would suffer nothing artificial. His ear was perfect, and though he could not produce the right intonation himself he would never let a false one pass in anyone else.

'Don't *be* natural,' he told his company. 'The stage isn't the place for that. The stage is make-believe. But *seem* natural.'

He worked his company hard. They rehearsed every morning from ten till two, when he sent them home to learn their parts and rest before the evening's performance. He bullied them, he screamed at them, he mocked them. He underpaid them. But if they played a moving scene well he cried like a child, and when they said an amusing line as he wanted it said he bellowed with laughter. He would skip about the stage on one leg if he was pleased, and if he was angry would throw the script down and stamp on it while tears of rage ran down his cheeks. The company laughed at him and abused him and did everything they could to please him. He aroused a protective instinct in them, so that one and all they felt that they couldn't let him down. Though they said he drove

them like slaves, and they never had a moment to themselves, flesh and blood couldn't stand it, it gave them a
sort of horrible satisfaction to comply with his outrageous
demands. When he wrung an old trooper's hand, who was
getting seven pounds a week, and said, by God, laddie,
you're stupendous, the old trooper felt like Charles Kean.

It happened that when Michael kept the appointment
he had asked for, Jimmie Langton was in need of a leading
juvenile. He had guessed why Michael wanted to see him,
and had gone the night before to see him play. Michael
was playing Mercutio and he had not thought him very
good, but when he came into the office he was staggered
by his beauty. In a brown coat and grey flannel trousers,
even without make-up, he was so handsome it took your
breath away. He had an easy manner and he talked like
a gentleman. While Michael explained the purpose of his
visit Jimmie Langton observed him shrewdly. If he could
act at all, with those looks that young man ought to go
far.

'I saw your Mercutio last night,' he said. 'What d'you
think of it yourself?'

'Rotten.'

'So do I. How old are you?'

'Twenty-five.'

'I suppose you've been told you're good-looking?'

'That's why I went on the stage. Otherwise I'd have
gone into the army like my father.'

'By gum, if I had your looks what an actor I'd have
been.'

The result of the interview was that Michael got an
engagement. He stayed at Middlepool for two years. He
soon grew popular with the company. He was good-humoured and kindly; he would take any amount of trouble
to do anyone a service. His beauty created a sensation in
Middlepool and the girls used to hang about the stage
door to see him go out. They wrote him love letters and
sent him flowers. He took it as a natural homage, but did
not allow it to turn his head. He was eager to get on and

seemed determined not to let any entanglement interfere with his career. It was his beauty that saved him, for Jimmie Langton quickly came to the conclusion that, notwithstanding his perseverance and desire to excel, he would never be more than a competent actor. His voice was a trifle thin and in moments of vehemence was apt to go shrill. It gave then more the effect of hysteria than of passion. But his gravest fault as a juvenile lead was that he could not make love. He was easy enough in ordinary dialogue and could say his lines with point, but when it came to making protestations of passion something seemed to hold him back. He felt embarrassed and looked it.

'Damn you, don't hold that girl as if she was a sack of potatoes,' Jimmie Langton shouted at him. 'You kiss her as if you were afraid you were standing in a draught. You're in love with that girl. You must feel that you're in love with her. Feel as if your bones were melting inside you and if an earthquake were going to swallow you up next minute, to hell with the earthquake.'

But it was no good. Notwithstanding his beauty, his grace and his ease of manner, Michael remained a cold lover. This did not prevent Julia from falling madly in love with him. For it was when he joined Langton's repertory company that they met.

Her own career had been singularly lacking in hardship. She was born in Jersey, where her father, a native of that island, practised as a veterinary surgeon. Her mother's sister was married to a Frenchman, a coal merchant, who lived at St. Malo, and Julia had been sent to live with her while she attended classes at the local lycée. She learnt to speak French like a Frenchwoman. She was a born actress and it was an understood thing for as long as she could remember that she was to go on the stage. Her aunt, Madame Falloux, was 'en relations' with an old actress who had been a sociétaire of the Comédie Française and who had retired to St. Malo to live on the small pension that one of her lovers had settled on her when after many years of faithful concubinage they had parted. When Julia was a child of twelve this actress was a boisterous, fat old woman of more than sixty, but of great vitality, who loved food more than anything else in the world. She had a great, ringing laugh, like a man's, and she talked in a deep, loud voice. It was she who gave Julia her first lessons. She taught her all the arts that she had herself learnt at the Conservatoire and she talked to her of Reichenberg who had played ingénues till she was seventy, of Sarah Bernhardt and her golden voice, of Mounet-Sully and his majesty, and of Coquelin the greatest actor of them all. She recited to her the great tirades of Corneille and Raine as she had learnt to say them at the Français and taught her to say them in the same way. It was charming to hear Julia in her childish voice recite those languorous, passionate speeches of Phèdre, emphasizing the beat of the Alexandrines and mouthing her words in the manner which is so artificial and yet so wonderfully dramatic. Jane Taitbout must always have been a very stagy actress, but she taught Julia to articulate with extreme distinctness, she taught her how to walk and how to hold herself, she taught her not to be afraid of her own voice, and she made deliberate that wonderful sense of timing which Julia had by instinct and which afterwards was one of her greatest gifts.

'Never pause unless you have a reason for it,' she thundered, banging with her clenched fist on the table at which she sat, 'but when you pause, pause as long as you can.'

When Julia was sixteen and went to the Royal Academy of Dramatic Art in Gower Street she knew already much that they could teach her there. She had to get rid of a certain number of tricks that were out of date and she had to acquire a more conversational style. But she won every prize that was open to her, and when she was finished with the school her good French got her almost immediately a small part in London as a French maid. It looked for a while as though her knowledge of French would specialize her in parts needing a foreign accent, for after this she was engaged to play an Austrian waitress. It was two years later that Jimmie Langton discovered her. She was on tour in a melodrama that had been successful in London; in the part of an Italian adventuress, whose machinations were eventually exposed, she was trying somewhat inadequately to represent a woman of forty. Since the heroine, a blonde person of mature years, was playing a young girl, the performance lacked verisimilitude. Jimmie was taking a short holiday which he spent in going every night to the theatre in one town after another. At the end of the piece he went round to see Julia. He was well enough known in the theatrical world for her to be flattered by the compliments he paid her, and when he asked her to lunch with him next day she accepted.

They had no sooner sat down to table than he went straight to the point.

'I never slept a wink all night for thinking of you,' he said.

'This is very sudden. Is your proposal honourable or dishonourable?'

He took no notice of the flippant rejoinder.

'I've been at this game for twenty-five years. I've been a call-boy, a stage-hand, a stage-manager, an actor, a publicity man, damn it, I've even been a critic. I've lived in the theatre since I was a kid just out of a board school, and what I don't know about acting isn't worth knowing. I think you're a genius.'

'It's sweet of you to say so.'

'Shut up. Leave me to do the talking. You've got everything. You're the right height, you've got a good figure, you've got an indiarubber face.'

'Flattering, aren't you?'

'That's just what I am. That's the face an actress wants. The face that can look anything, even beautiful, the face that can show every thought that passes through the mind. That's the face Duse's got. Last night even though you weren't really thinking about what you were doing every now and then the words you were saying wrote themselves on your face.'

'It's such a rotten part. How could I give it my attention? Did you hear the things I had to say?'

'Actors are rotten, not parts. You've got a wonderful voice, the voice that can wring an audience's heart, I don't know about your comedy, I'm prepared to risk that.'

'What d'you mean by that?'

'Your timing is almost perfect. That couldn't have been taught, you must have that by nature. That's the far, far better way. Now let's come down to brass tacks. I've been making enquiries about you. It appears you speak French like a Frenchwoman and so they give you broken English parts. That's not going to lead you anywhere, you know.'

'That's all I can get.'

'Are you satisfied to go on playing those sort of parts for ever? You'll get stuck in them and the public won't take you in anything else. Seconds, that's all you'll play. Twenty pounds a week at the outside and a great talent wasted.'

'I've always thought that some day or other I should get a chance of a straight part.'

'When? You may have to wait ten years. How old are you now?'

'Twenty.'

'What are you getting?'

'Fifteen pounds a week.'

'That's a lie. You're getting twelve, and it's a damned sight more than you're worth. You've got everything to learn. Your gestures are commonplace. You don't know that every gesture must mean something. You don't know how to get an audience to look at you before you speak. You make up too much. With your sort of face the less make-up the better. Wouldn't you like to be a star?'

'Who wouldn't?'

'Come to me and I'll make you the greatest actress in

England. Are you a quick study? You ought to be at your age.'

'I think I can be word-perfect in any part in forty-eight hours.'

'It's experience you want and me to produce you. Come to me and I'll let you play twenty parts a year. Ibsen, Shaw, Barker, Sudermann, Hankin, Galsworthy. You've got magnetism and you don't seem to have an idea how to use it.' He chuckled. 'By God, if you had, that old hag would have had you out of the play you're in now before you could say knife. You've got to take an audience by the throat and say, now, you dogs, you pay attention to me. You've got to dominate them. If you haven't got the gift no one can give it to you, but if you have you can be taught how to use it. I tell you, you've got the makings of a great actress. I've never been so sure of anything in my life.'

'I know I want experience. I'd have to think it over of course. I wouldn't mind coming to you for a season.'

'Go to hell. Do you think I can make an actress of you in a season? Do you think I'm going to work my guts out to make you give a few decent performances and then have you go away to play some twopenny-halfpenny part in a commercial play in London? What sort of a bloody fool do you take me for? I'll give you a three years' contract, I'll give you eight pounds a week and you'll have to work like a horse.'

'Eight pounds a week's absurd. I couldn't possibly take that.'

'Oh yes, you could. It's all you're worth and it's all you're going to get.'

Julia had been on the stage for three years and had learnt a good deal. Besides, Jane Taitbout, no strict moralist, had given her a lot of useful information.

'And are you under the impression by any chance, that for that I'm going to let you sleep with me as well?'

'My God, do you think I've got time to go to bed with the members of my company? I've got much more important things to do than that, my girl. And you'll find that after you've rehearsed for four hours and played a part at night to my satisfaction, besides a couple of matinées, you won't have much time or much inclination to make love to anybody. When you go to bed all you'll want to do is to sleep.'

But Jimmie Langton was wrong there.

3

Julia, taken by his enthusiasm and his fantastic exuberance, accepted his offer. He started her in modest parts which under his direction she played as she had never played before. He interested the critics in her, he flattered them by letting them think that they had discovered a remarkable actress, and allowed the suggestion to come from them that he should let the public see her as Magda. She was a great hit and then in quick succession he made her play Nora in 'The Doll's House,' Ann in 'Man and Superman,' and Hedda Gabler. Middlepool was delighted to discover that it had in its midst an actress who it could boast was better than any star in London, and crowded to see her in plays that before it had gone to only from local patriotism. The London paragraphers mentioned her now and then, and a number of enthusiastic patrons of the drama made the journey to Middlepool to see her. They went back full of praise, and two or three London managers sent representatives to report on her. They were doubtful. She was all very well in Shaw and Ibsen, but what would she do in an ordinary play? The managers had had bitter experiences. On the strength of an outstanding performance in one of these queer plays they had engaged an actor, only to discover that in any other sort of play he was no better than anybody else.

When Michael joined the company Julia had been playing in Middlepool for a year. Jimmie started him with Marchbanks in 'Candida.' It was the happy choice one would have expected him to make, for in that part his great beauty was an asset and his lack of warmth no disadvantage.

Julia reached over to take out the first of the cardboard cases in which Michael's photographs were kept. She was sitting comfortably on the floor. She turned the early photographs over quickly, looking for that which he had had taken when first he came to Middlepool; but when she came upon it, it gave her a pang. For a moment she felt inclined to cry. It had been just like him then. Candida was being played by an older woman, a sound actress who was cast generally for mothers, maiden aunts or character parts, and Julia with nothing to do but act eight times a week attended the rehearsals. She fell in love with Michael at first sight. She had never seen a more beautiful young man, and she pursued him relentlessly. In due course Jimmie put on 'Ghosts,' braving the censure of respectable Middlepool, and Michael played the boy and she played Regina. They heard one another their parts and after rehearsals lunched, very modestly, together so that they might talk of them. Soon they were inseparable. Julia had little reserve; she flattered Michael outrageously. He was not vain of his good looks, he knew he was handsome and accepted compliments, not exactly with indifference, but as he might have accepted a compliment on a fine old house that had been in his family for generations. It was a well-known fact that it was one of the best houses of its period, one was proud of it and took care of it, but it was just there, as natural to possess as the air one breathed. He was shrewd and ambitious. He knew that his beauty was at present his chief asset, but he knew it could not last for ever and was determined to become a good actor so that he should have something besides his looks to depend on. He meant to learn all he could from Jimmie Langton and then go to London.

'If I play my cards well I can get some old woman to back me and go into management. One's got to be one's own master. That's the only way to make a packet.'

Julia soon discovered that he did not much like spending money, and when they ate a meal together, or on a Sunday went for a small excursion, she took care to pay her share of the expenses. She did not mind this. She liked him for counting the pennies, and, inclined to be extravagant herself and always a week or two behind with her rent, she admired him because he hated to be in debt and even with the small salary he was getting managed to save up a little every week. He was anxious to have enough put by so that when he went to London he need not accept the first part that was offered him, but could afford to wait till he got one that gave him a real chance. His father had little more than his pension to live on, and it had been a sacrifice to send him to Cambridge. His father, not liking the idea of his going on the stage, had insisted on this.

'If you want to be an actor I suppose I can't stop you,' he said, 'but damn it all, I insist on your being educated like a gentleman.'

It gave Julia a good deal of satisfaction to discover that Michael's father was a colonel, it impressed her to hear him speak of an ancestor who had gambled away his fortune at White's during the Regency, and she liked the signet ring Michael wore with the boar's head on it and the motto: Nemo me impune lacessit.

'I believe you're prouder of your family than of looking like a Greek god,' she told him fondly.

'Anyone can be good-looking,' he answered, with his sweet smile, 'but not everyone can belong to a decent family. To tell you the truth I'm glad my governor's a gentleman.'

Julia took her courage in both hands.

'My father's a vet.'

For an instant Michael's face stiffened, but he recovered himself immediately and laughed.

'Of course it doesn't really matter what one's father is. I've often heard my father talk of the vet in his regiment.

He counted as an officer of course. Dad always said he was one of the best.'

And she was glad he'd been to Cambridge. He had rowed for his College and at one time there was some talk of putting him in the university boat.

'I should have liked to get my blue. It would have been useful to me on the stage. I'd have got a lot of advertisement out of it.'

Julia could not tell if he knew that she was in love with him. He never made love to her. He liked her society and when they found themselves with other people scarcely left her side. Sometimes they were asked to parties on Sunday, dinner at midday or a cold, sumptuous supper, and he seemed to think it natural that they should go together and come away together. He kissed her when he left her at her door, but he kissed her as he might have kissed the middle-aged woman with whom he had played Candida. He was friendly, good-humoured and kind, but it was distressingly clear that she was no more to him than a comrade. Yet she knew that he was not in love with anybody else. The love-letters that women wrote to him he read out to Julia with a chuckle, and when they sent him flowers he immediately gave them to her.

'What blasted fools they are,' he said. 'What the devil do they think they're going to get out of it?'

'I shouldn't have thought it very hard to guess that,' said Julia dryly.

Although she knew he took these attentions so lightly she could not help feeling angry and jealous.

'I should be a damned fool if I got myself mixed up with some woman in Middlepool. After all, they're mostly flappers. Before I knew where I was I'd have some irate father coming along and saying, now you must marry the girl.'

She tried to find out whether he had had any adventures while he was playing with Benson's company. She gathered that one or two of the girls had been rather inclined to make nuisances of themselves, but he thought it was a terrible mistake to get mixed up with any of the actresses a chap was playing with. It was bound to lead to trouble.

'And you know how people gossip in a company. Everyone would know everything in twenty-four hours. And when you start a thing like that you don't know what you're letting yourself in for. I wasn't risking anything.'

When he wanted a bit of fun he waited till they were within a reasonable distance of London and then he would race up to town and pick up a girl at the Globe Restaurant. Of course it was expensive, and when you came to think of it, it wasn't really worth the money; besides, he played a lot of cricket in Benson's company, and golf when he got the chance, and that sort of thing was rotten for the eye.

Julia told a thumping lie.

'Jimmie always says I'd be a much better actress if I had an affair.'

'Don't you believe it. He's just a dirty old man. With him, I suppose. I mean, you might just as well say that I'd give a better performance of Marchbanks if I wrote poetry.'

They talked so much together that it was inevitable for her at last to learn his views on marriage.

'I think an actor's a perfect fool to marry young. There are so many cases in which it absolutely ruins a chap's career. Especially if he marries an actress. He becomes a star and then she's a millstone round his neck. She insists on playing with him, and if he's in management he has to give her leading parts, and if he engages someone else there are most frightful scenes. And of course, for an actress it's insane. There's always the chance of her having a baby and she may have to refuse a damned good part. She's out of the public eye for months, and you know what the public is, unless they see you all the time they forget that you ever existed.'

Marriage? What did she care about marriage? Her heart melted within her when she looked into his deep, friendly eyes, and she shivered with delightful anguish when she considered his shining, russet hair. There was nothing that he could have asked her that she would not gladly have given him. The thought never entered his lovely head.

'Of course he likes me,' she said to herself. 'He likes me better than anyone, he even admires me, but I don't attract him that way.'

She did everything to seduce him except slip into bed with him, and she only did not do that because there was no opportunity. She began to fear that they knew one another too well for it to seem possible that their relations should change, and she reproached herself bitterly because she had not rushed to a climax when first they came in contact with one another. He had too sincere an affection for her now ever to become her lover. She found out when his birthday was and gave him a gold cigarette case which she knew was the thing he wanted more than anything in the world. It cost a good deal more than she could afford and he smilingly reproached her for her extravagance. He never dreamt what ecstatic pleasure it gave her to spend her money on him. When her birthday came along he gave her half a dozen pairs of silk stockings. She noticed at once that they were not of very good quality, poor lamb, he had not been able to bring himself to spring to that, but she was so touched that he should give her anything that she could not help crying.

'What an emotional little thing you are,' he said, but he was pleased and touched to see her tears.

She found his thrift rather an engaging trait. He could not bear to throw his money about. He was not exactly mean, but he was not generous. Once or twice at restaurants she thought he undertipped the waiter, but he paid no attention to her when she ventured to remonstrate. He gave the exact ten per cent, and when he could not make the exact sum to a penny asked the waiter for change.

'Neither a borrower nor a lender be,' he quoted from Polonius.

When some member of the company, momentarily hard up, tried to borrow from him it was in vain. But he refused so frankly, with so much heartiness, that he did not affront.

'My dear old boy, I'd love to lend you a quid, but I'm absolutely stony. I don't know how I'm going to pay my rent at the end of the week.'

For some months Michael was so much occupied with his own parts that he failed to notice how good an actress Julia was. Of course he read the reviews, and their praise of Julia, but he read summarily, without paying much attention till he came to the remarks the critics made about him. He was pleased by their approval, but not cast down by their censure. He was too modest to resent an unfavourable criticism.

'I suppose I was rotten,' he would say ingenuously.

His most engaging trait was his good humour. He bore Jimmie Langton's abuse with equanimity. When tempers grew frayed during a long rehearsal he remained serene. It was impossible to quarrel with him. One day he was sitting in front watching the rehearsal of an act in which he did not appear. It ended with a powerful and moving scene in which Julia had the opportunity to give a fine display of acting. When the stage was being set for the next act Julia came through the pass door and sat down beside Michael. He did not speak to her, but looked sternly in front of him. She threw him a surprised look. It was unlike him not to give her a smile and a friendly word. Then she saw that he was clenching his jaw to prevent its trembling and that his eyes were heavy with tears.

'What's the matter, darling?'

'Don't talk to me. You dirty little bitch, you've made me cry.'

'Angel!'

The tears came to her own eyes and streamed down her face. She was so pleased, so flattered.

'Oh, damn it,' he sobbed. 'I can't help it.'

He took a handkerchief out of his pocket and dried his eyes.

('I love him, I love him, I love him.')

Presently he blew his nose.

'I'm beginning to feel better now. But, my God, you shattered me.'

'It's not a bad scene, is it?'

'The scene be damned, it was you. You just wrung my heart. The critics are right, damn it, you're an actress and no mistake.'

'Have you only just discovered it?'

'I knew you were pretty good, but I never knew you were as good as all that. You make the rest of us look like a piece of cheese. You're going to be a star. Nothing can stop you.'

'Well then, you shall be my leading man.'

'Fat chance I'd have of that with a London manager.'

Julia had an inspiration.

'Then you must go into management yourself and make me your leading lady.'

He paused. He was not a quick thinker and needed a little time to let a notion sink into his mind. He smiled.

'You know that's not half a bad idea.'

They talked it over at luncheon. Julia did most of the talking while he listened to her with absorbed interest.

'Of course the only way to get decent parts consistently is to run one's own theatre,' he said. 'I know that.'

The money was the difficulty. They discussed how much was the least they could start on. Michael thought five thousand pounds was the minimum. But how in heaven's name could they raise a sum like that? Of course some of those Middlepool manufacturers were rolling in money, but you could hardly expect them to fork out five thousand pounds to start a couple of young actors who had only a local reputation. Besides, they were jealous of London.

'You'll have to find your rich old woman,' said Julia gaily.

She only half believed all she had been saying, but it excited her to discuss a plan that would bring her into a close and constant relation with Michael. But he was being very serious.

'I don't believe one could hope to make a success in London unless one were pretty well known already. The thing to do would be to act there in other managements for three or four years first; one's got to know the ropes. And the advantage of that would be that one would have had time to read plays. It would be madness to start in management unless one had at least three plays. One of them out to be a winner.'

'Of course if one did that, one ought to make a point of acting together so that the public got accustomed to seeing the two names on the same bill.'

'I don't know that there's much in that. The great thing is to have good, strong parts. There's no doubt in my mind that it would be much easier to find backers if one had made a bit of a reputation in London.'

4

It was getting on for Easter, and Jimmie Langton always closed his theatre for Holy Week. Julia did not quite know what to do with herself; it seemed hardly worth while to go to Jersey. She was surprised to receive a letter one morning from Mrs Gosselyn, Michael's mother, saying that it would give the Colonel and herself so much pleasure if she would come with Michael to spend the week at Cheltenham. When she showed the letter to Michael he beamed.

'I asked her to invite you. I thought it would be more polite than if I just took you along.'

'You are sweet. Of course I shall love to come.'

Her heart beat with delight. The prospect of spending a whole week with Michael was enchanting. It was just like his good nature to come to the rescue when he knew she was at a loose end. But she saw there was something he wanted to say, yet did not quite like to.

'What is it?'

He gave a little laugh of embarrassment.

'Well, dear, you know, my father's rather old-fashioned, and there are some things he can't be expected to understand. Of course I don't want you to tell a lie or anything like that, but I think it would seem rather funny to him if he knew your father was a vet. When I wrote and asked if I could bring you down I said he was a doctor.'

'Oh, that's all right.'

Julia found the Colonel a much less alarming person than she had expected. He was thin and rather small, with a lined face and close-cropped white hair. His features had a worn distinction. He reminded you of a head on an old coin that had been in circulation too long. He was civil, but reserved. He was neither peppery nor tyrannical as Julia, from her knowledge of the stage, expected a colonel to be. She could not imagine him shouting out words of command in that courteous, rather cold voice. He had in point of fact retired with honorary rank after an entirely undistinguished career, and for many years had been content to work in his garden and play bridge at his club. He read *The Times* went to church on Sunday and accompanied his wife to tea-parties. Mrs Gosselyn was a tall, stoutish, elderly woman, much taller than her husband, who gave you the impression that she was always trying to diminish her height. She had the remains of good looks, so that you said to yourself that when young she must have been beautiful. She wore her hair parted in the middle with a bun on the nape of her neck. Her classic features and her size made her at first meeting somewhat imposing, but Julia quickly discovered that she was very shy. Her movements were stiff and awkward.

29

She was dressed fussily, with a sort of old-fashioned richness which did not suit her. Julia, who was entirely without self-consciousness, found the elder woman's deprecating attitude rather touching. She had never known an actress to speak to and did not quite know how to deal with the predicament in which she now found herself. The house was not at all grand, a small detached stucco house in a garden with a laurel hedge, and since the Gosselyns had been for some years in India there were great trays of brass ware and brass bowls, pieces of Indian embroidery and highly-carved Indian tables. It was cheap bazaar stuff, and you wondered how anyone had thought it worth bringing home.

Julia was quick-witted. It did not take her long to discover that the Colonel, notwithstanding his reserve, and Mrs Gosselyn, notwithstanding her shyness, were taking stock of her. The thought flashed through her mind that Michael had brought her down for his parents to inspect her. Why? There was only one possible reason, and when she thought of it her heart leaped. She saw that he was anxious for her to make a good impression. She felt instinctively that she must conceal the actress, and without effort, without deliberation, merely because she felt it would please, she played the part of the simple, modest, ingenuous girl who had lived a quiet country life. She walked round the garden with the Colonel and listened intelligently while he talked of peas and asparagus; she helped Mrs Gosselyn with the flowers and dusted the ornaments with which the drawing-room was crowded. She talked to her of Michael. She told her how cleverly he acted and how popular he was and she praised his looks. She saw that Mrs Gosselyn was very proud of him, and with a flash of intuition saw that it would please her if she let her see, with the utmost delicacy, as though she would have liked to keep it a secret but betrayed herself unwittingly, that she was head over ears in love with him.

'Of course we hope he'll do well,' said Mrs Gosselyn.

'We didn't much like the idea of his going on the stage; you see, on both sides of the family, we're army, but he was set on it.'

'Yes, of course I see what you mean.'

'I know it doesn't mean so much as when I was a girl, but after all he was born a gentleman.'

'Oh, but some very nice people go on the stage nowadays, you know. It's not like in the old days.'

'No, I suppose not. I'm so glad he brought you down here. I was a little nervous about it. I thought you'd be made-up and . . . perhaps a little loud. No one would dream you were on the stage.'

('I should damn well think not. Haven't I been giving a perfect performance of the village maiden for the last forty-eight hours?')

The Colonel began to make little jokes with her and sometimes he pinched her ear playfully.

'Now you mustn't flirt with me, Colonel,' she cried, giving him a roguish, delicious glance. 'Just because I'm an actress you think you can take liberties with me.'

'George, George,' smiled Mrs Gosselyn. And then to Julia: 'He always was a terrible flirt.'

('Gosh, I'm going down like a barrel of oysters.')

Mrs Gosselyn told her about India, how strange it was to have all those coloured servants, but how nice the society was, only army people and Indian civilians, but still it wasn't like home, and how glad she was to get back to England.

They were to leave on Easter Monday because they were playing that night, and on Sunday evening after supper Colonel Gosselyn said he was going to his study to write letters; a minute or two later Mrs Gosselyn said she must go and see the cook. When they were left alone Michael, standing with his back to the fire, lit a cigarette.

'I'm afraid it's been very quiet down here; I hope you haven't had an awfully dull time.'

'It's been heavenly.'

'You've made a tremendous success with my people. They've taken an enormous fancy to you.'

'God, I've worked for it,' thought Julia, but aloud said: 'How d'you know?'

'Oh, I can see it. Father told me you were very ladylike, and not a bit like an actress, and mother says you're so sensible.'

Julia looked down as though the extravagance of these compliments was almost more than she could bear. Michael came over and stood in front of her. The thought occurred to her that he looked like a handsome young footman applying for a situation. He was strangely nervous. Her heart thumped against her ribs.

'Julia dear, will you marry me?'

For the last week she had asked herself whether or not he was going to propose to her, and now that he had at last done so, she was strangely confused.

'Michael!'

'Not immediately, I don't mean. But when we've got our feet on the ladder. I know that you can act me off the stage, but we get on together like a house on fire, and when we do go into management I think we'd make a pretty good team. And you know I do like you most awfully. I mean, I've never met anyone who's a patch on you.'

('The blasted fool, why does he talk all that rot? Doesn't he know I'm crazy to marry him? Why doesn't he kiss me, kiss me, kiss me? I wonder if I dare tell him I'm absolutely sick with love for him.')

'Michael, you're so handsome. No one could refuse to marry you.'

'Darling!'

('I'd better get up. He wouldn't know how to sit down. God, that scene that Jimmie made him do over and over again!')

She got on her feet and put up her face to his. He took her in his arms and kissed her lips.

'I must tell mother.'

32

He broke away from her and went to the door.

'Mother, mother!'

In a moment the Colonel and Mrs Gosselyn came in. They bore a look of happy expectancy.

('By God, it was a put-up job.')

'Mother, father, we're engaged.'

Mrs Gosselyn began to cry. With her awkward, lumbering gait she came up to Julia, flung her arms round her, and sobbing, kissed her. The Colonel wrung his son's hand in a manly way and releasing Julia from his wife's embrace kissed her too. He was deeply moved. All this emotion worked on Julia and, though she smiled happily, the tears coursed down her cheeks. Michael watched the affecting scene with sympathy.

'What d'you say to a bottle of pop to celebrate?' he said. 'It looks to me as though mother and Julia were thoroughly upset.'

'The ladies, God bless 'em,' said the Colonel when their glasses were filled.

5

Julia now was looking at the photograph of herself in her wedding-dress.

'Christ, what a sight I looked.'

They decided to keep their engagement to themselves, and Julia told no one about it but Jimmie Langton, two or three girls in the company and her dresser. She vowed them to secrecy and could not understand how within forty-eight hours everyone in the theatre seemed to know all about it. Julia was divinely happy. She loved Michael more passionately than ever and would gladly have married him there and then, but his good sense prevailed. They were at present no more than a couple of provincial actors, and to start their conquest of London as a married couple would jeopardize their chances. Julia showed him as clearly as she knew how, and this was very clearly indeed, that she was quite willing to become his mistress, but this he refused. He was too honourable to take advantage of her.

'I could not love thee, dear, so much, loved I not honour more,' he quoted.

He felt sure that when they were married they would bitterly regret it if they had lived together before as man and wife. Julia was proud of his principles. He was a kind and affectionate lover, but in a very short while seemed to take her a trifle for granted; by his manner, friendly but casual, you might have thought they had been married for years. But he showed great good nature in allowing Julia to make love to him. She adored to sit cuddled up to him with his arm round her waist, her face against his, and it was heaven when she could press her eager mouth against his rather thin lips. Though when they sat side by side like that he preferred to talk of the parts they were studying or make plans for the future, he made her very happy. She never tired of praising his beauty. It was heavenly, when she told him how exquisite his nose was and how lovely his russet, curly hair, to feel his hold on her tighten a little and to see the tenderness in his eyes.

'Darling, you'll make me as vain as a peacock.'

'It would be so silly to pretend you weren't divinely handsome.'

Julia thought he was, and she said it because she liked saying it, but she said it also because she knew he liked to hear it. He had affection and admiration for her, he felt at ease with her, and he had confidence in her, but she was well aware that he was not in love with her. She consoled herself by thinking that he loved her as much as he was capable of loving, and she thought that when they were married, when they slept together, her own passion would excite an equal passion in him. Meanwhile she exercised all her tact and all her self-control. She knew she could not afford to bore him. She knew she must never let him feel that she was a burden or a responsibility. He might desert her for a game of golf, or to

34

lunch with a casual acquaintance, she never let him see for a moment that she was hurt. And with an inkling that her success as an actress strengthened his feeling for her she worked like a dog to play well.

When they had been engaged for rather more than a year an American manager, looking for talent and having heard of Jimmie Langton's repertory company, came to Middlepool and was greatly taken by Michael. He sent him round a note asking him to come to his hotel on the following afternoon. Michael, breathless with excitement, showed it to Julia; it could only mean that he was going to offer him a part. Her heart sank, but she pretended that she was as excited as he, and went with him next day to the hotel. She was to wait in the lobby while Michael saw the great man.

'Wish me luck,' he whispered, as he turned from her to enter the lift. 'It's almost too good to be true.'

Julia sat in a great leather armchair willing with all her might the American manager to offer a part that Michael would refuse or a salary that he felt it would be beneath his dignity to accept. Or alternatively that he should get Michael to read the part he had in view and come to the conclusion that he could not touch it. But when she saw Michael coming towards her half an hour later, his eyes bright and his step swinging, she knew he had clicked. For a moment she thought she was going to be sick, and when she forced on her face an eager, happy smile, she felt that her muscles were stiff and hard.

'It's all right. He says it's a damned good part, a boy's part, nineteen. Eight or ten weeks in New York and then on the road. It's a safe forty weeks with John Drew. Two hundred and fifty dollars a week.'

'Oh, darling, how wonderful for you.'

It was quite clear that he had accepted with alacrity. The thought of refusing had never even occurred to him.

'And I – I,' she thought, 'if they'd offered me a thousand dollars a week I wouldn't have gone if it meant being separated from Michael.'

Black despair seized her. She could do nothing. She must pretend to be as delighted as he was. He was too much excited to sit still and took her out into the crowded street to walk.

'It's a wonderful chance. Of course America's expensive, but I ought to be able to live on fifty dollars a week at the outside, they say the Americans are awfully hospitable and I shall get a lot of free meals. I don't see why I shouldn't save eight thousand dollars in the forty weeks and that's sixteen hundred pounds.'

('He doesn't love me. He doesn't care a damn about me. I hate him. I'd like to kill him. Blast that American manager.')

'And if he takes me on for a second year I'm to get three hundred. That means that in two years I'd have the best part of four thousand pounds. Almost enough to start management on.'

'A second year!' For a moment Julia lost control of herself and her voice was heavy with tears. 'D'you mean to say you'll be gone two years?'

'Oh, I should come back next summer of course. They pay my fare back and I'd go and live at home so as not to spend any money.'

'I don't know how I'm going to get on without you.'

She said the words very brightly, so that they sounded polite, but somewhat casual.

'Well, we can have a grand time together in the summer and you know a year, two years at the outside, well, it passes like a flash of lightning.'

Michael had been walking at random, but Julia without his noticing had guided him in the direction she wished, and now they arrived in front of the theatre. She stopped.

'I'll see you later. I've got to pop up and see Jimmie.' His face fell.

'You're not going to leave me now! I must talk to somebody. I thought we might go and have a snack together before the show.'

'I'm terribly sorry. Jimmie's expecting me and you know what he is.'

Michael gave her his sweet, good-natured smile.

'Oh, well, go on then. I'm not going to hold it up against you because for once you've let me down.'

He walked on and she went in by the stage door. Jimmie Langton had arranged himself a tiny flat under the roof to which you gained access through the balcony. She rang the bell of his front door and he opened it himself. He was surprised, but pleased, to see her.

'Hulloa, Julia, come in.'

She walked past him without a word, and when they got into his sitting-room, untidy, littered with typescript plays, books and other rubbish, the remains of his frugal luncheon still on a tray by his desk, she turned and faced him. Her jaw was set and her eyes were frowning.

'You devil!'

With a swift gesture she went up to him, seized him by his loose shirt collar with both hands and shook him. He struggled to get free of her, but she was strong and violent.

'Stop it. Stop it.'

'You devil, you swine, you filthy low-down cad.'

He took a swing and with his open hand gave her a great smack on the face. She instinctively loosened her grip on him and put her own hand up to her cheek, for he had hurt her. She burst out crying.

'You brute. You rotten hound to hit a woman.'

'You put that where the monkey put the nuts, dearie. Didn't you know that when a woman hits me I always hit back?'

'I didn't hit you.'

'You damned near throttled me.'

'You deserved it. Oh, my God, I'd like to kill you.'

'Now sit down, duckie, and I'll give you a drop of Scotch to pull you together. And then you can tell me all about it.'

37

Julia looked round for a big chair into which she could conveniently sink.

'Christ, the place is like a pig-sty. Why the hell don't you get a charwoman in?'

With an angry gesture she swept the books on to the floor from an armchair, threw herself in it, and began to cry in earnest. He poured her out a stiff dose of whisky, added a drop of soda, and made her drink it.

'Now what's all this Tosca stuff about?'

'Michael's going to America.'

'Is he?'

She wrenched herself away from the arm he had round her shoulder.

'How could you? How could you?'

'I had nothing to do with it.'

'That's a lie. I suppose you didn't even know that filthy American manager was in Middlepool. Of course it's your doing. You did it deliberately to separate us.'

'Oh, dearie, you're doing me an injustice. In point of fact I don't mind telling you that I said to him he could have anyone in the company he liked with the one exception of Michael Gosselyn.'

Julia did not see the look in Jimmie's eyes when he told her this, but if she had would have wondered why he was looking as pleased as if he had pulled off a very clever little trick.

'Even me?' she said.

'I knew he didn't want women. They've got plenty of their own. It's men they want who know how to wear their clothes and don't spit in the drawing room.'

'Oh, Jimmie, don't let Michael go. I can't bear it.'

'How can I prevent it? His contract's up at the end of the season. It's a wonderful chance for him.'

'But I love him. I want him. Supposing he sees someone else in America. Supposing some American heiress falls in love with him.'

'If he doesn't love you any more than that I should have thought you'd be well rid of him.'

The remark revived Julia's fury.

'You rotten old eunuch, what do you know about love?'

'These women,' Jimmie sighed. 'If you try to go to bed with them they say you're a dirty old man, and if you don't they say you're a rotten old eunuch.'

'Oh, you don't understand. He's so frightfully handsome, they'll fall for him like a row of ninepins, and poor lamb, he's so susceptible to flattery. Anything can happen in two years.'

'What's this about two years?'

'If he's a success he's to stay another year.'

'Well, don't worry your head about that. He'll be back at the end of the season and back for good. That manager only saw him in "Candida". It's the only part he's halfway decent in. Take my word for it, it won't be long before they find out they've been sold a pup. He's going to be a flop.'

'What do you know about acting?'

'Everything.'

'I'd like to scratch your eyes out.'

'I warn you that if you attempt to touch me I shan't give you a little bit of a slap, I shall give you such a biff on the jaw that you won't be able to eat in comfort for a week.'

'By God, I believe you'd do it. Do you call yourself a gentleman?'

'Not even when I'm drunk.'

Julia giggled, and Jimmie felt the worst of the scene was over.

'Now you know just as well as I do that you can act him off his head. I tell you, you're going to be the greatest actress since Mrs Kendal. What do you want to go and hamper yourself with a man who'll always be a millstone round your neck? You want to go into management; he'll want to play opposite you. He'll never be good enough, my dear.'

'He's got looks. I can carry him.'

'You've got a pretty good opinion of yourself, haven't

39

you? But you're wrong. If you want to make a success you can't afford to have a leading man who's not up to the mark.'

'I don't care. I'd rather marry him and be a failure than be a success and married to somebody else.'

'Are you a virgin?'

Julia giggled again.

'I don't know that it's any business of yours, but in point of fact I am.'

'I thought you were. Well, unless it means something to you, why don't you go over to Paris with him for a fortnight when we close? He won't be sailing till August. It might get him out of your system.'

'Oh, he wouldn't. He's not that sort of man. You see, he's by way of being a gentleman.'

'Even the upper classes propagate their species.'

'You don't understand,' said Julia haughtily.

'I bet you don't either.'

Julia did not condescend to reply. She was really very unhappy.

'I can't live without him, I tell you. What am I to do with myself when he's away?'

'Stay on with me. I'll give you a contract for another year. I've got a lot of new parts I want to give you and I've got a juvenile in my eye who's a find. You'll be surprised how much easier you'll find it when you've got a chap opposite you who'll really give you something. You can have twelve pounds a week.'

Julia went up to him and stared into his eyes searchingly.

'Have you done all this to get me to stay on for another year? Have you broken my heart and ruined my whole life just to keep me in your rotten theatre?'

'I swear I haven't. I like you and I admire you. And we've done better business the last two years than we've ever done before. But damn it, I wouldn't play you a dirty trick like that.'

'You liar, you filthy liar.'

'I swear it's the truth.'

'Prove it then,' she said violently.

'How can I prove it? You know I'm decent really.'

'Give me fifteen pounds a week and I'll believe you.'

'Fifteen pounds a week? You know what our takings are. How can I? Oh well, all right. But I shall have to pay three pounds out of my own pocket.'

'A fat lot I care.'

6

After a fortnight of rehearsals, Michael was thrown out of the part for which he had been engaged, and for three or four weeks was left to kick his heels about till something else could be found for him. He opened in due course in a play that ran less than a month in New York. It was sent on the road; but languished and was withdrawn. After another wait he was given a part in a costume play where his good looks shone to such advantage that his indifferent acting was little noticed, and in this he finished the season. There was no talk of renewing his contract. Indeed the manager who had engaged him was caustic in his comments.

'Gee, I'd give something to get even with that fellow Langton, the son of a bitch,' he said. 'He knew what he was doing all right when he landed me with that stick.'

Julia wrote to Michael constantly, pages and pages of love and gossip, while he answered once a week, four pages exactly in a neat, precise hand. He always ended up by sending her his best love and signing himself hers very affectionately, but the rest of his letter was more informative than passionate. Yet she awaited its coming in an agony of impatience and read it over and over again. Though he wrote cheerfully, saying little about the theatre except that the parts they gave him were rotten and the plays in which he was expected to act beneath contempt, news travels in the theatrical world, and Julia knew that he had not made good.

'I suppose it's beastly of me,' she thought, 'but thank God, thank God.'

When he announced the date of his sailing she could not contain her joy. She got Jimmie so to arrange his programme that she might go and meet him at Liverpool.

'If the boat comes in late I shall probably stay the night,' she told Jimmie.

He smiled ironically.

'I suppose you think that in the excitement of homecoming you may work the trick.'

'What a beastly little man you are.'

'Come off it, dear. My advice to you is, get him a bit tight and then lock yourself in a room with him and tell him you won't let him out till he's made a dishonest woman of you.'

But when she was starting he came to the station with her. As she was getting into the carriage he took her hand and patted it.

'Feeling nervous, dear?'

'Oh, Jimmie dear, wild with happiness and sick with anxiety.'

'Well, good luck to you. And don't forget you're much too good for him. You're young and pretty and you're the greatest actress in England.'

When the train steamed out Jimmie went to the station bar and had a whisky and soda. 'Lord, what fools these mortals be,' he sighed. But Julia stood up in the empty carriage and looked at herself in the glass.

'Mouth too large, face too puddingy, nose too fleshy. Thank God, I've got good eyes and good legs. Exquisite legs. I wonder if I've got too much make-up on. He doesn't like make-up off the stage. I look bloody without rouge. My eyelashes are all right. Damn it all, I don't look so bad.'

Uncertain till the last moment whether Jimmie would allow her to go, Julia had not been able to let Michael

42

know that she was meeting him. He was surprised and frankly delighted to see her. His beautiful eyes beamed with pleasure.

'You're more lovely than ever,' she said.

'Oh, don't be so silly,' he laughed, squeezing her arm affectionately. 'You haven't got to go back till after dinner, have you?'

'I haven't got to go back till to-morrow. I've taken a couple of rooms at the Adelphi, so that we can have a real talk.'

'The Adelphi's a bit grand, isn't it?'

'Oh, well, you don't come back from America every day. Damn the expense.'

'Extravagant little thing, aren't you? I didn't know when we'd dock, so I told my people I'd wire when I was getting down to Cheltenham. I'll tell them I'll be coming along to-morrow.'

When they got to the hotel Michael came to Julia's room, at her suggestion, so that they could talk in peace and quiet. She sat on his knees, with her arm round his neck, her cheek against his.

'Oh, it's so good to be home again,' she sighed.

'You don't have to tell me that,' he said, not understanding that she referred to his arms and not to his arrival.

'D'you still like me?'

'Rather.'

She kissed him fondly.

'Oh, you don't know how I've missed you.'

'I was an awful flop in America,' he said. 'I didn't tell you in my letters, because I thought it would only worry you. They thought me rotten.'

'Michael,' she cried, as though she could not believe him.

'The fact is, I suppose, I'm too English. They don't want me another year. I didn't think they did, but just as a matter of form I asked them if they were going to exercise their option and they said no, not at any price.'

Julia was silent. She looked deeply concerned, but her heart was beating with exultation.

'I honestly don't care, you know. I didn't like America. It's a smack in the eye of course, it's no good denying that, but the only thing is to grin and bear it. If you only knew the people one has to deal with! Why, compared with some of them, Jimmie Langton's a great gentleman. Even if they had wanted me to stay I should have refused.'

Though he put a brave face on it, Julia felt that he was deeply mortified. He must have had to put up with a good deal of unpleasantness. She hated him to have been made unhappy, but, oh, she was so relieved.

'What are you going to do now?' she asked quietly.

'Well, I shall go home for a bit and think things over. Then I shall go to London and see if I can't get a part.'

She knew that it was no good suggesting that he should come back to Middlepool. Jimmie Langton would not have him.

'You wouldn't like to come with me, I suppose?'

Julia could hardly believe her ears.

'Me? Darling, you know I'd go anywhere in the world with you.'

'Your contract's up at the end of this season, and if you want to get anywhere you've got to make a stab at London soon. I saved every bob I could in America, they all called me a tight-wad but I just let them talk, I've brought back between twelve and fifteen hundred pounds.'

'Michael, how on earth can you have done that?'

'I didn't give much away, you know,' he smiled happily. 'Of course it's not enough to start management on, but it's enough to get married on, I mean we'd have something to fall back on if we didn't get parts right away or happened to be out of a job for a few months.'

It took Julia a second or two to understand what he meant.

'D'you mean to say, get married now?'

'Of course it's a risk, without anything in prospect, but one has to take a risk sometimes.'

44

Julia took his head in both her hands and pressed his lips with hers. Then she gave a sigh.

'Darling, you're wonderful and you're as beautiful as a Greek god, but you're the biggest damned fool I've ever known in my life.'

They went to a theatre that night and at supper drank champagne to celebrate their reunion and toast their future. When Michael accompanied her to her room she held up her face to his.

'D'you want me to say good-night to you in the passage? I'll just come in for a minute.'

'Better not, darling,' she said with quiet dignity.

She felt like a high-born damsel, with all the traditions of a great and ancient family to keep up; her purity was a pearl of great price; she also felt that she was making a wonderfully good impression: of course he was a great gentleman and 'damn it all' it behoved her to be a great lady. She was so pleased with her performance that when she had got into her room and somewhat noisily locked the door, she paraded up and down bowing right and left graciously to her obsequious retainers. She stretched out her lily white hand for the trembling old steward to kiss (as a baby he had often dandled her on his knee), and when he pressed it with his pallid lips she felt something fall upon it. A tear.

7

The first year of their marriage would have been stormy except for Michael's placidity. It needed the excitement of getting a part or a first night, the gaiety of a party where he had drunk several glasses of champagne, to turn his practical mind to thoughts of love. No flattery, no allurements, could tempt him when he had an engagement next day for which he had to keep his brain clear or a round of golf for which he needed a steady eye. Julia made him frantic scenes. She was jealous of his friends at the Green Room Club, jealous of the games that took him away from her, and jealous of the men's luncheons he went to under the pretext that he must cultivate people who might be useful to them. It infuriated her that when she worked herself up into a passion of tears he should sit there quite calmly, with his hands crossed and a good-humoured smile on his handsome face, as though she were merely making herself ridiculous.

'You don't think I'm running after any other woman, do you?' he asked.

'How do I know? It's quite obvious that you don't care two straws for me.'

'You know you're the only woman in the world for me.'

'My God!'

'I don't know what you want.'

'I want love. I thought I'd married the handsomest man in England and I've married a tailor's dummy.'

'Don't be so silly. I'm just the ordinary normal Englishman. I'm not an Italian organ-grinder.'

She swept up and down the room. They had a small flat at Buckingham Gate and there was not much space, but she did her best. She threw up her hands to heaven.

'I might be squint-eyed and hump-backed. I might be fifty. Am I so unattractive as all that? It's so humiliating to have to beg for love. Misery, misery.'

'That was a good movement, dear. As if you were throwing a cricket ball. Remember that.'

She gave him a look of scorn.

'That's all you can think of. My heart is breaking, and you can talk of a movement that I made quite accidentally.'

But he saw by the expression of her face that she was registering it in her memory, and he knew that when the occasion arose she would make effective use of it.

'After all love isn't everything. It's all very well at its proper time and in its proper place. We had a lot of fun

46

on our honeymoon, that's what a honeymoon's for, but now we've got to get down to work.'

They had been lucky. They had managed to get fairly good parts together in a play that had proved a success. Julia had one good acting scene in which she had brought down the house, and Michael's astonishing beauty had made a sensation. Michael with his gentlemanly push, with his breezy good-nature, had got them both a lot of publicity and their photographs appeared in the illustrated papers. They were asked to a number of parties and Michael, notwithstanding his thriftiness, did not hesitate to spend money on entertaining people who might be of service. Julia was impressed by his lavishness on these occasions. An actor-manager offered Julia the leading part in his next play, and though there was no part for Michael and she was anxious to refuse it, he would not let her. He said they could not afford to let sentiment stand in the way of business. He eventually got a part in a costume play.

They were both acting when the war broke out. To Julia's pride and anguish Michael enlisted at once, but with the help of his father, one of whose old brother officers was an important personage at the War Office, he very soon got a commission. When he went out to France Julia bitterly regretted the reproaches she had so often heaped upon him, and made up her mind that if he were killed she would commit suicide. She wanted to become a nurse so that she could go out to France too and at least be on the same soil as he, but he made her understand that patriotism demanded that she should go on acting, and she could not resist what might very well be his dying request. Michael thoroughly enjoyed the war. He was popular in the regimental mess, and the officers of the old army accepted him almost at once, even though he was an actor, as one of themselves. It was as though the family of soldiers from which he was born had set a seal on him so that he fell instinctively into the manner and way of thinking of the professional soldier. He had

47

tact and a pleasant manner, and he knew how to pull strings adroitly; it was inevitable that he should get on the staff of some general. He showed himself possessed of considerable organizing capacity and the last three years of the war he passed at G.H.Q. He ended it as a major, with the Military Cross and the Legion of Honour.

Meanwhile Julia had been playing a succession of important parts and was recognized as the best of the younger actresses. Throughout the war the theatre was very prosperous, and she profited by being seen in plays that had long runs. Salaries went up, and with Michael to advise her she was able to extort eighty pounds a week from reluctant managers. Michael came over to England on his leaves and Julia was divinely happy. Though he was in no more danger than if he had been sheep-farming in New Zealand, she acted as though the brief periods he spent with her were the last days the doomed man would ever enjoy on earth. She treated him as though he had just come from the horror of the trenches and was tender, considerate, and unexacting.

It was just before the end of the war that she fell out of love with him.

She was pregnant at the time. Michael had judged it imprudent to have a baby just then, but she was nearly thirty and thought that if they were going to have one at all they ought to delay no longer; she was so well established on the stage that she could afford not to appear for a few months, and with the possibility that Michael might be killed at any moment – it was true he said he was as safe as a house, he only said that to reassure her, and even generals were killed sometimes – if she was to go on living she must have a child by him. The baby was expected at the end of the year. She looked forward to Michael's next leave as she had never done before. She was feeling very well, but she had a great yearning to feel his arms around her, she felt a little lost, a little helpless, and she wanted his protective strength. He came, looking

48

wonderfully handsome in his well-cut uniform, with the red tabs and the crown on his shoulder-straps. He had filled out a good deal as the result of the hardships of G.H.Q. and his skin was tanned. With his close-cropped hair, breezy manner and military carriage he looked every inch a soldier. He was in great spirits, not only because he was home for a few days, but because the end of the war was in sight. He meant to get out of the army as quickly as possible. What was the good of having a bit of influence if you didn't use it? So many young men had left the stage, either from patriotism or because life was made intolerable for them by the patriotic who stayed at home, and finally owing to conscription, that leading parts had been in the hands either of people who were inapt for military service or those who had been so badly wounded that they had got their discharge. There was a wonderful opening, and Michael saw that if he were available quickly he could get his choice of parts. When he had recalled himself to the recollection of the public they could look about for a theatre, and with the reputation Julia had now acquired it would be safe to start in management.

They talked late into the night and then they went to bed. She cuddled up to him voluptuously and he put his arms round her. After three months of abstinence he was amorous.

'You're the most wonderful little wife,' he whispered.

He pressed his mouth on hers. She was filled on a sudden with a faint disgust. She had to resist an inclination to push him away. Before, to her passionate nostrils his body, his young beautiful body, had seemed to have a perfume of flowers and honey, and this had been one of the things that had most enchained her to him, but now in some strange way it had left him. She realized that he no longer smelt like a youth, he smelt like a man. She felt a little sick. She could not respond to his ardour, she was eager that he should get his desire satisfied quickly, turn over on his side, and go to sleep. For long she lay awake. She was dismayed. Her heart sank because she knew she had lost something that was infinitely precious to her, and pitying herself she was inclined to cry; but at the same time she was filled with a sense of triumph, it seemed a revenge that she enjoyed for the unhappiness he had caused her; she was free of the bondage in which her senses had held her to him and she exulted. Now she could deal with him on equal terms. She stretched her legs out in bed and sighed with relief.

'By God, it's grand to be one's own mistress.'

They had breakfast in their room, Julia in bed and Michael seated at a little table by her side. She looked at him while he read the paper. Was it possible that three months had made so much difference in him, or was it merely that for years she had still seen him with the eyes that had seen him when he came on the stage to rehearse at Middlepool in the glorious beauty of his youth and she had been stricken as with a mortal sickness? He was wonderfully handsome still, after all he was only thirty-six, but he was not a boy any more; with his close-cropped hair and weather-beaten skin, little lines beginning to mark the smoothness of his forehead and to show under his eyes, he was definitely a man. He had lost his coltish grace and his movements were set. Each difference was very small, but taken altogether they amounted, in her shrewd, calculating eyes, to all the difference in the world. He was a middle-aged man.

They still lived in the small flat that they had taken when first they came to London. Though Julia had been for some time earning a good income it had not seemed worth while to move while Michael was on active service, but now that a baby was coming the flat was obviously too small. Julia had found a house in Regent's Park that she liked very much. She wanted to be settled down in good time for her confinement.

The house faced the gardens. Above the drawing-room floor were two bedrooms and above these, two rooms that could be made into a day and a night nursery. Michael was pleased with everything; even the price seemed to him reasonable. Julia had, during the last four years, been earning so much more money than he that she had offered to furnish the house herself. They stood in one of the bedrooms.

'I can make do with a good deal of what we've got for my bedroom,' she said. 'I'll get you a nice suite at Maple's.'

'I wouldn't go to much expense,' he smiled. 'I don't suppose I shall use it much, you know.'

He liked to share a bed with her. Though not passionate he was affectionate, and he had an animal desire to feel her body against his. For long it had been her greatest comfort. The thought now filled her with irritation.

'Oh, I don't think there should be any more nonsense till after the baby's born. Until all that's over and done with I'm going to make you sleep by yourself.'

'I hadn't thought of that. If you think it's better for the kid . . .'

8

Michael got himself demobbed the moment the war was finished and stepped straight into a part. He returned to the stage a much better actor than he left it. The breeziness he had acquired in the army was effective. He was a well set-up, normal, high-spirited fellow, with a ready smile and a hearty laugh. He was well suited to drawing-room comedy. His light voice gave a peculiar effect to a flippant line, and though he never managed to make love convincingly he could carry off a chaffing love scene, making a proposal as if it were rather a joke, or a declaration as though he were laughing at himself, in a manner that the audience found engaging. He never attempted to play anyone but himself. He specialized in men about town, gentlemanly gamblers, guardsmen and young scamps with a good side to them. Managers liked him.

He worked hard and was amenable to direction. So long as he could get work he didn't mind much what sort of part it was. He stuck out for the salary he thought he was worth, but if he couldn't get it was prepared to take less rather than be idle.

He was making his plans carefully. During the winter that followed the end of the war there was an epidemic of influenza. His father and mother died. He inherited nearly four thousand pounds, and this with his own savings and Julia's brought up their joint capital to seven thousand. But the rent of theatres had gone up enormously, the salaries of actors and the wages of stagehands had increased, so that the expense of running a theatre was very much greater than it had been before the war. A sum that would then have been amply sufficient to start management on was now inadequate. The only thing was to find some rich man to go in with them so that a failure or two to begin with would not drive them from the field. It was said that you could always find a mug in the city to write a fat cheque for the production of a play, but when you came down to business you discovered that the main condition was that the leading part should be played by some pretty lady in whom he was interested. Years before, Michael and Julia had often joked about the rich old woman who would fall in love with him and set him up in management. He had long since learnt that no rich old woman was to be found to set up in management a young actor whose wife was an actress to whom he was perfectly faithful. In the end the money was found by a rich woman, and not an old one either, but who was interested not in him but in Julia.

Mrs de Vries was a widow. She was a short stout woman with a fine Jewish nose and fine Jewish eyes, a great deal of energy, a manner at once effusive and timid, and a somewhat virile air. She had a passion for the stage. When Julia and Michael had decided to try their luck in London Jimmie Langton, to whose rescue she had sometimes come when it looked as though he would be forced to close his repertory theatre, had written to her asking her to do what she could for them. She had seen Julia act in Middlepool. She gave parties so that the young actors might get to know managers, and asked them to stay at her grand house near Guildford where they enjoyed a luxury they had never dreamt of. She did not much like Michael. Julia accepted the flowers with which Dolly de Vries filled her flat and her dressing-room, she was properly delighted with the presents she gave her, bags, vanity cases, strings of beads in semi-precious stones, brooches; but appeared to be unconscious that Dolly's generosity was due to anything but admiration for her talent. When Michael went away to the war Dolly pressed her to come and live in her house in Montagu Square, but Julia, with protestations of extravagant gratitude, refused in such a way that Dolly, with a sigh and a tear, could only admire her the more. When Roger was born Julia asked her to be his godmother.

For some time Michael had been turning over in his mind the possibility that Dolly de Vries might put up the money they needed, but he was shrewd enough to know that while she might do it for Julia she would not do it for him. Julia refused to approach her.

'She's already been so kind to us I really couldn't ask her, and it would be so humiliating if she refused.'

'It's a good gamble, and even if she lost the money she wouldn't feel it. I'm quite sure you could get round her if you tried.'

Julia was pretty sure she could too. Michael was very simple-minded in some ways; she did not feel called upon to point out to him the obvious facts.

But he was not a man who let a thing drop when he had set his mind to it. They were going to Guildford to spend the week-end with Dolly, and were driving down after the Saturday night's performance in the new car that Julia had given Michael for his birthday. It was a warm beautiful night. Michael had bought options, though it wrung his heart to write the cheques, on three plays that they both liked, and he had heard of a theatre that they could get on reasonable terms. Everything was ready for the venture except the capital. He urged Julia to seize the opportunity that the week-end presented.

'Ask her yourself then,' said Julia impatiently. 'I tell you, I'm not going to.'

'She wouldn't do it for me. You can twist her round your little finger.'

'We know a thing or two about financing plays now. People finance plays for two reasons, either because they want notoriety, or because they're in love with someone. A lot of people talk about art, but you don't often find them paying out hard cash unless they're going to get something out of it for themselves.'

'Well, we'll give Dolly all the notoriety she wants.'

'That doesn't happen to be what she's after.'

'What do you mean?'

'Can't you guess?'

Light dawned on him, and he was so surprised that he slowed down. Was it possible that what Julia suspected was true? He had never even thought that Dolly liked him much, and as for supposing she was in love with him – why, the notion had never crossed his mind. Of course Julia had sharp eyes, not much got by her, but she was a jealous little thing, she was always thinking women were making a dead set at him. It was true that Dolly had given him a pair of cuff links at Christmas, but he thought that was only so that he shouldn't feel left out in the cold because she had given Julia a brooch that much have cost at least two hundred pounds. That might be only her cunning. Well, he could honestly say he'd never done a thing to make her think there was anything doing. Julia giggled.

'No, darling, it's not you she's in love with.'

It was disconcerting the way Julia knew what he was thinking. You couldn't hide a thing from that woman.

'Then why did you put the idea into my head? I wish

to goodness you'd express yourself so that a fellow can understand.'

Julia did.

'I never heard such nonsense,' he cried. 'What a filthy mind you've got, Julia!'

'Come off it, dear.'

'I don't believe there's a word of truth in it. After all I've got eyes in my head. Do you mean to say I shouldn't have noticed it?' He was more irritable than she had ever known him. 'And even if it were true I suppose you can take care of yourself. It's a chance in a thousand, and I think it would be madness not to take it.'

'Claudio and Isabella in "Measure for Measure." '

'That's a rotten thing to say, Julia. God damn it, I am a gentleman.'

'Nemo me impune lacessit.'

They drove the rest of the journey in stormy silence. Mrs de Vries was waiting up for them.

'I didn't want to go to bed till I'd seen you,' she said as she folded Julia in her arms and kissed her on both cheeks. She gave Michael a brisk handshake.

Julia spent a happy morning in bed reading the Sunday papers. She read first the theatrical news, then the gossip columns, after that the woman's pages, and finally cast an eye over the head-lines of the world's news. The book reviews she ignored; she could never understand why so much space was wasted on them. Michael, who had the room next hers, had come in to say good morning, and then gone out into the garden. Presently there was a timid little knock at her door and Dolly came in. Her great black eyes were shining. She sat on the bed and took Julia's hand.

'Darling, I've been talking to Michael. I'm going to put up the money to start you in management.'

Julia's heart gave a sudden beat.

'Oh, you mustn't. Michael shouldn't have asked you. I won't have it. You've been far, far too kind to us already.'

55

Dolly leant over and kissed Julia on the lips. Her voice was lower than usual and there was a little tremor in it.

'Oh, my love, don't you know there isn't anything in the world I wouldn't do for you? It'll be so wonderful; it'll bring us so close together and I shall be so proud of you.'

They heard Michael come whistling along the passage, and when he came into the room Dolly turned to him with her great eyes misty with tears.

'I've just told her.'

He was brimming over with excitement.

'What a grand woman!' He sat down on the other side of the bed and took Julia's disengaged hand. 'What d'you say, Julia?'

She gave him a little reflective look.

'*Vous l'avez voulu, Georges Dandin.*'

'What's that?'

'Molière.'

As soon as the deed of partnership had been signed and Michael had got his theatre booked for the autumn he engaged a publicity agent. Paragraphs were sent to the papers announcing the new venture and Michael and the publicity agent prepared interviews for him and Julia to give to the Press. Photographs of them, singly and together, with and without Roger, appeared in the weeklies. The domestic note was worked for all it was worth. They could not quite make up their minds which of the three plays they had it would be best to start with. Then one afternoon when Julia was sitting in her bedroom reading a novel, Michael came in with a manuscript in his hand.

'Look here, I want you to read this play at once. It's just come in from an agent. I think it's a knockout. Only we've got to give an answer right away.'

Julia put down her novel.

'I'll read it now.'

'I shall be downstairs. Let me know when you've

56

finished and I'll come up and talk it over with you. It's got a wonderful part for you.'

Julia read quickly, skimming over the scenes in which she was not concerned, but the principal woman's part, the part of course she would play, with concentration. When she had turned the last page she rang the bell and asked her maid (who was also her dresser) to tell Michael she was ready for him.

'Well, what d'you think?'

'The play's all right. I don't see how it can fail to be a success.'

He caught something doubtful in her tone.

'What's wrong then? The part's wonderful. I mean, it's the sort of thing that you can do better than anyone in the world. There's a lot of comedy and all the emotion you want.'

'It's a wonderful part, I know that; it's the man's part.'

'Well, that's a damned good part too.'

'I know; but he's fifty, and if you make him younger you take all the point out of the play. You don't want to take the part of a middle-aged man.'

'But I wasn't thinking of playing that. There's only one man for that. Monte Vernon. And we can get him. I'll play George.'

'But that's a tiny part. You can't play that.'

'Why not?'

'But I thought the point of going into management was that we should both play leads.'

'Oh, I don't care a hang about that. As long as we can find plays with star parts for you I don't matter. Perhaps in the next play there'll be a good part for me too.'

Julia leant back in her chair, and the ready tears filled her eyes and ran down her cheeks.

'Oh, what a beast I am.'

He smiled, and his smile was as charming as ever. He came over to her and kneeling by her side put his arms round her.

'Lor Lumme, what's the matter with the old lady now?'

57

When she looked at him now she wondered what there was in him that had ever aroused in her such a frenzy of passion. The thought of having sexual relations with him nauseated her. Fortunately he found himself very comfortable in the bedroom she had furnished for him. He was not a man to whom sex was important, and he was relieved when he discovered that Julia no longer made any demands on him. He thought with satisfaction that the birth of the baby had calmed her down, he was bound to say that he had thought it might, and he was only sorry they had not had one before. When he had two or three times, more out of amiability than out of desire, suggested that they should resume marital relations and she had made excuses, either that she was tired, not very well, or had two performances next day, to say nothing of a fitting in the morning, he accepted the situation with equanimity. Julia was much easier to get on with, she never made scenes any more, and he was happier than he had ever been before. It was a damned satisfactory marriage he had made, and when he looked at other people's marriages he couldn't help seeing he was one of the lucky ones. Julia was a damned good sort and clever, as clever as a bagful of monkeys; you could talk to her about anything in the world. The best companion a chap ever had, my boy. He didn't mind saying this, he'd rather spend a day alone with her than play a round of golf.

Julia was surprised to discover in herself a strange feeling of pity for him because she no longer loved him. She was a kindly woman, and she realized that it would be a bitter blow to his pride if he ever had an inkling how little he meant to her. She continued to flatter him. She noticed that for long now he had come to listen complacently to her praise of his exquisite nose and beautiful eyes. She got a little private amusement by seeing how much he could swallow. She laid it on with a trowel. But now she looked more often at his straight thin-lipped mouth. It grew meaner as he grew older, and by the time he was an old man it would be no more than a cold hard line. His thrift, which in the early days had seemed an amusing, rather touching trait, now revolted her. When people were in trouble, and on the stage they too often are, they got sympathy and kind friendly words from Michael, but very little cash. He looked upon himself as devilish generous when he parted with a guinea, and a five-pound note was to him the extreme of lavishness. He had soon discovered that Julia ran the house extravagantly, and insisting that he wanted to save her trouble took the matter in his own hands. After that nothing was wasted. Every penny was accounted for. Julia wondered why servants stayed with them. They did because Michael was so nice to them. With his hearty, jolly, affable manner he made them anxious to please him, and the cook shared his satisfaction when she had found a butcher from whom they could get meat a penny a pound cheaper than elsewhere. Julia could not but laugh when she thought how strangely his passion for economy contrasted with the devil-may-care, extravagant creatures he portrayed so well on the stage. She had often thought that he was incapable of a generous impulse; and now, as though it were the most natural thing in the world, he was prepared to stand aside so that she might have her chance. She was too deeply moved to speak. She reproached herself bitterly for all the unkind things she had for so long been thinking of him.

9

They put on the play, and it was a success. After that they continued to produce plays year after year. Because Michael ran the theatre with the method and thrift with which he ran his home they lost little over the failures, which of course they sometimes had, and made every possible penny out of their successes. Michael flattered himself that there was not a management in London where less money was spent on the productions. He exercised great ingenuity in disguising old sets so that they looked new, and by ringing the changes on the furniture that he gradually collected in the store-room saved the expense of hiring. They gained the reputation of being an enterprising management because Michael in order not to pay the high royalties of well-known authors was always willing to give an unknown one a trial. He sought out actors who had never been given a chance and whose salaries were small. He thus made some very profitable discoveries.

When they had been in management for three years they were sufficiently well established for Michael to be able to borrow from the bank enough money to buy the lease of a theatre that had just been built. After much discussion they decided to call it the Siddons Theatre. They opened with a failure and this was succeeded by another. Julia was frightened and discouraged. She thought that the theatre was unlucky and that the public were getting sick of her. It was then that Michael showed himself at his best. He was unperturbed.

'In this business you have to take the rough with the smooth. You're the best actress in England. There are only three people who bring money into the theatre regardless of the play, and you're one of them. We've had a couple of duds. The next play's bound to be all right and then we shall get back all we've lost and a packet into the bargain.'

As soon as Michael had felt himself safe he had tried to buy Dolly de Vries out, but she would not listen to his persuasion and was indifferent to his coldness. For once his cunning found its match. Dolly saw no reason to sell out an investment that seemed sound, and her half share in the partnership kept her in close touch with Julia. But now with great courage he made another effort to get rid of her. Dolly indignantly refused to desert them when they were in difficulties, and he gave it up as a bad job. He consoled himself by thinking that Dolly might leave Roger, her godson, a great deal of money. She had no one belonging to her but nephews in South Africa, and you could not look at her without suspecting that she had high blood pressure. Meanwhile it was convenient to have the house near Guildford to go to whenever they wished. It saved the expense of having a country house of their own. The third play was a winner, and Michael did not hesitate to point out how right he had been. He spoke as though he was directly responsible for its success. Julia could almost have wished that it had failed like the others in order to take him down a peg or two. For his conceit was outrageous. Of course you had to admit that he had a sort of cleverness, shrewdness rather, but he was not nearly so clever as he thought himself. There was nothing in which he did not think that he knew better than anybody else.

As time went on he began to act less frequently. He found himself much more interested in management.

'I want to run my theatre in as businesslike a way as a city office,' he said.

And he felt that he could more profitably spend his evenings, when Julia was acting, by going to outlying theatres and trying to find talent. He kept a little book in which he made a note for every actor who seemed to show promise. Then he had taken to directing. It had always grizzled him that directors should ask so much money for rehearsing a play, and of late some of them had even insisted on a percentage on the gross. At last an occasion came when the two directors Julia liked best were engaged and the only other one she trusted was acting and thus could not give them all his time.

'I've got a good mind to have a shot at it myself,' said Michael.

Julia was doubtful. He had no fantasy and his ideas were commonplace. She was not sure that he would have authority over the cast. But the only available director demanded a fee that they both thought exorbitant and there was nothing left but to let Michael try. He made a much better job of it than Julia expected. He was

61

thorough; he worked hard. Julia, strangely enough, felt he was getting more out of her than any other director had done. He knew what she was capable of, and, familiar with her every inflection, every glance of her wonderful eyes, every graceful movement of her body, he was able to give her suggestions out of which she managed to build up the best performance of her career. With the cast he was at once conciliatory and exacting. When tempers were frayed his good humour, his real kindliness, smoothed things over. After that there was no question but that he should continue to direct their plays. Authors liked him because, being unimaginative, he was forced to let the plays speak for themselves and often not being quite sure what they meant he was obliged to listen to them.

Julia was now a rich woman. She could not but admit that Michael was as careful of her money as of his own. He watched her investments and was as pleased when he could sell stocks at a profit on her account as if he had made the money for himself. He put her down for a very large salary, and was proud to be able to say that she was the most highly-paid actress in London, but when he himself acted he never put himself down for a higher salary than he thought the part was worth. When he directed a play he put down on the expense account the fee that a director of the second rank would have received. They shared the expenses of the house and the cost of Roger's education. Roger had been entered for Eton within a week of his birth. It was impossible to deny that Michael was scrupulously fair and honest. When Julia realized how much richer she was than he she wanted to pay all these expenses herself.

'There's no reason why you should,' said Michael. 'As long as I can pay my whack I'll pay it. You earn more than I do because you're worth more. I put you down for a good salary because you draw it.'

No one could do other than admire the self-abnegation with which he sacrificed himself for her sake. Any ambition he may have had for himself he had abandoned in order to foster her career. Even Dolly, who did not like him, acknowledged his unselfishness. A sort of modesty had always prevented Julia from discussing him with Dolly, but Dolly, with her shrewdness, had long seen how intensely Michael exasperated his wife, and now and then took the trouble to point out how useful he was to her. Everybody praised him. A perfect husband. It seemed to her that none but she knew what it was like to live with a man who was such a monster of vanity. His complacency when he had beaten an opponent at golf or got the better of someone in a business deal was infuriating. He gloried in his artfulness. He was a bore, a crashing bore. He liked to tell Julia everything he did and every scheme that passed through his head; it had been charming when merely to have him with her was a delight, but for years she had found his prosiness intolerable. He could describe nothing without circumstantial detail. Nor was he only vain of his business acumen; with advancing years he had become outrageously vain of his person. As a youth he had taken his beauty for granted: now he began to pay more attention to it and spared no pains to keep what was left of it. It became an obsession. He devoted anxious care to his figure. He never ate a fattening thing and never forgot his exercises. He consulted hair specialists when he thought his hair was thinning, and Julia was convinced that had it been possible to get the operation done secretly he would have had his face lifted. He had got into the way of sitting with his chin slightly thrust out so that the wrinkles in his neck should not show and he held himself with an arched back to keep his belly from sagging. He could not pass a mirror without looking into it. He hankered for compliments and beamed with delight when he had managed to extract one. They were food and drink to him. Julia laughed bitterly when she remembered that it was she who had accustomed him to them. For years she had told him how beautiful he was and now he could not live without flattery. It was the only chink in

63

his armour. An actress out of a job had only to tell him to his face that he was too handsome to be true for him to think that she might do for a part he had in mind. For years, so far as Julia knew, Michael had not bothered with women, but when he reached the middle forties he began to have little flirtations. Julia suspected that nothing much came of them. He was prudent, and all he wanted was admiration. She had heard that when women became pressing he used her as a pretext to get rid of them. Either he couldn't risk doing anything to hurt her, or she was jealous or suspicious and it seemed better that the friendship should cease.

'God knows what they see in him,' Julia exclaimed to the empty room.

She took up half a dozen of his later photographs at random and looked at them carefully one by one. She shrugged her shoulders.

'Well, I suppose I can't blame them. I fell in love with him too. Of course he was better-looking in those days.'

It made Julia a little sad to think how much she had loved him. Because her love had died she felt that life had cheated her. She sighed.

'And my back's aching,' she said.

10

There was a knock at the door.

'Come in,' said Julia.

Evie entered.

'Aren't you going to bed to-day, Miss Lambert?' She saw Julia sitting on the floor surrounded by masses of photographs. 'Whatever are you doing?'

'Dreaming.' She took up two of the photographs. 'Look here upon this picture, and on this.'

One was of Michael as Mercutio in all the radiant beauty of his youth and the other of Michael in the last part he had played, in a white topper and a morning coat, with a pair of field-glasses slung over his shoulder. He looked unbelievably self-satisfied.

Evie sniffed.

'Oh, well, it's no good crying over spilt milk.'

'I've been thinking of the past and I'm as blue as the devil.'

'I don't wonder. When you start thinking of the past it means you ain't got no future, don't it?'

'You shut your trap, you old cow,' said Julia, who could be very vulgar when she chose.

'Come on now, or you'll be fit for nothing to-night. I'll clear up all this mess.'

Evie was Julia's dresser and maid. She had come to her first at Middlepool and had accompanied her to London. She was a cockney, a thin, raddled, angular woman, with red hair which was always untidy and looked as if it much needed washing; two of her front teeth were missing but, notwithstanding Julia's offer, repeated for years, to provide her with new ones she would not have them replaced.

'For the little I eat I've got all the teeth I want. It'd only fidget me to 'ave a lot of elephant's tusks in me mouth.'

Michael had long wanted Julia at least to get a maid whose appearance was more suitable to their position, and he had tried to persuade Evie that the work was too much for her, but Evie would not hear of it.

'You can say what you like, Mr Gosselyn, but no one's going to maid Miss Lambert as long as I've got me 'ealth and strength.'

'We're all getting on, you know, Evie. We're not so young as we were.'

Evie drew her forefinger across the base of her nostrils and sniffed.

'As long as Miss Lambert's young enough to play women of twenty-five, I'm young enough to dress 'er. And maid 'er.' Evie gave him a sharp look. 'An' what d'you want to pay two lots of wages for, when you can get the work done for one?'

65

Michael chuckled in his good-humoured way.

'There's something in that, Evie dear.'

She bustled Julia upstairs. When she had no matinée Julia went to bed for a couple of hours in the afternoon and then had a light massage. She undressed now and slipped between the sheets.

'Damn, my hot water bottle's nearly stone cold.'

She looked at the clock on the chimney-piece. It was no wonder. It must have been there an hour. She had no notion that she had stayed so long in Michael's room, looking at those photographs and idly thinking of the past.

'Forty-six. Forty-six. Forty-six. I shall retire when I'm sixty. At fifty-eight South Africa and Australia. Michael says we can clean up there. Twenty thousand pounds. I can play all my old parts. Of course even at sixty I could play women of forty-five. But what about parts? Those bloody dramatists.'

Trying to remember any plays in which there was a first-rate part for a woman of five-and-forty she fell asleep. She slept soundly till Evie came to awake her because the masseuse was there. Evie brought her the evening paper, and Julia, stripped, while the masseuse rubbed her long slim legs and her belly, putting on her spectacles, read the same theatrical intelligence she had read that morning, the gossip column and the woman's page. Presently Michael came in and sat on her bed. He often came at that hour to have a little chat with her.

'Well, what was his name?' asked Julia.

'Whose name?'

'The boy who came to lunch?'

'I haven't a notion. I drove him back to the theatre. I never gave him another thought.'

Miss Phillips, the masseuse, liked Michael. You knew where you were with him. He always said the same things and you knew exactly what to answer. No side to him. And terribly good-looking. My word.

'Well, Miss Phillips, fat coming off nicely?'

66

'Oh, Mr Gosselyn, there's not an ounce of fat on Miss Lambert. I think it's wonderful the way she keeps her figure.'

'Pity I can't have you to massage me, Miss Phillips. You might be able to do something about mine.'

'How you talk, Mr Gosselyn. Why, you've got the figure of a boy of twenty. I don't know how you do it, upon my word I don't.'

'Plain living and high thinking, Miss Phillips.'

Julia was paying no attention to what they said, but Miss Phillips's reply reached her.

'Of course there's nothing like massage, I always say that, but you've got to be careful of your diet. That there's no doubt about at all.'

'Diet!' she thought. 'When I'm sixty I shall let myself go. I shall eat all the bread and butter I like. I'll have hot rolls for breakfast, I'll have potatoes for lunch and potatoes for dinner. And beer. God, how I like beer. Pea soup and tomato soup; treacle pudding and cherry tart. Cream, cream, cream. And so help me God, I'll never eat spinach again as long as I live.'

When the massage was finished Evie brought her a cup of tea, a slice of ham from which the fat had been cut, and some dry toast. Julia got up, dressed, and went down with Michael to the theatre. She liked to be there an hour before the curtain rang up. Michael went on to dine at his club. Evie had preceded her in a cab and when she got into her dressing-room everything was ready for her. She undressed once more and put on a dressing-gown. As she sat down at her dressing-table to make up she noticed some fresh flowers in a vase.

'Hulloa, who sent them? Mrs de Vries?'

Dolly always sent her a huge basket on her first nights, and on the hundredth night, and the two hundredth if there was one, and in between, whenever she ordered flowers for her own house, had some sent to Julia.

'No, miss.'

'Lord Charles?'

Lord Charles Tamerley was the oldest and the most constant of Julia's admirers, and when he passed a florist's he was very apt to drop in and order some roses for her.

'Here's the card,' said Evie.

Julia looked at it. Mr Thomas Fennell. Tavistock Square.

'What a place to live. Who the hell d'you suppose he is, Evie?'

'Some feller knocked all of a heap by your fatal beauty, I expect.'

'They must have cost all of a pound. Tavistock Square doesn't look very prosperous to me. For all you know he may have gone without his dinner for a week to buy them.'

'I don't think.'

Julia plastered her face with grease paint.

'You're so damned unromantic, Evie. Just because I'm not a chorus girl you can't understand why anyone should send me flowers. And God knows, I've got better legs than most of them.'

'You and your legs,' said Evie.

'Well, I don't mind telling you I think it's a bit of all right having an unknown young man sending me flowers at my time of life. I mean it just shows you.'

'If he saw you now 'e wouldn't, not if I know anything about men.'

'Go to hell,' said Julia.

But when she was made up to her satisfaction, and Evie had put on her stockings and her shoes, having a few minutes still to spare she sat down at her desk and in her straggling bold hand wrote to Mr Thomas Fennell a gushing note of thanks for his beautiful flowers. She was naturally polite and it was, besides, a principle with her to answer all fan letters. That was how she kept in touch with her public. Having addressed the envelope she threw the card in the wastepaper basket and was ready to slip into the first act dress. The call-boy came round knocking at the dressing-room doors.

'Beginners, please.'

Those words, though heaven only knew how often she had heard them, still gave her a thrill. They braced her like a tonic. Life acquired significance. She was about to step from the world of make-believe into the world of reality.

II

Next day Julia had luncheon with Charles Tamerley. His father, the Marquess of Dennorant, had married an heiress and he had inherited a considerable fortune. Julia often went to the luncheon parties he was fond of giving at his house in Hill Street. At the bottom of her heart she had a profound contempt for the great ladies and the noble lords she met there, because she was a working woman and an artist, but she knew the connection was useful. It enabled them to have first nights at the Siddons which the papers described as brilliant, and when she was photographed at week-end parties among a number of aristocratic persons she knew that it was good publicity. There were one or two leading ladies, younger than she, who did not like her any better because she called at least two duchesses by their first names. This caused her no regret. Julia was not a brilliant conversationalist, but her eyes were so bright, her manner so intelligent, that once she had learnt the language of society she passed for a very amusing woman. She had a great gift of mimicry, which ordinarily she kept in check thinking it was bad for her acting, but in these circles she turned it to good account and by means of it acquired the reputation of a wit. She was pleased that they liked her, these smart, idle women, but she laughed at them up her sleeve because they were dazzled by her glamour. She wondered what they would think if they really knew how unromantic the life of a successful actress was, the hard work it entailed, the constant care one had to take of oneself and the regular, monotonous habits which were essential. But she good-naturedly offered them advice on make-up and let them copy her clothes. She was always beautifully dressed. Even Michael, fondly thinking she got her clothes for nothing, did not know how much she really spent on them.

Morally she had the best of both worlds. Everyone knew that her marriage with Michael was exemplary. She was a pattern of conjugal fidelity. At the same time many people in that particular set were convinced that she was Charles Tamerley's mistress. It was an affair that was supposed to have been going on so long that it had acquired respectability, and tolerant hostesses when they were asked to the same house for a week-end gave them adjoining rooms. This belief had been started by Lady Charles, from whom Charles Tamerley had been long separated, and in point of fact there was not a word of truth in it. The only foundation for it was that Charles had been madly in love with her for twenty years, and it was certainly on Julia's account that the Tamerleys, who had never got on very well, agreed to separate. It was indeed Lady Charles who had first brought Julia and Charles together. They happened, all three, to be lunching at Dolly de Vries' when Julia, a young actress, had made her first great success in London. It was a large party and she was being made much of. Lady Charles, a woman of over thirty then, who had the reputation of being a beauty, though except for her eyes she had not a good feature, but by a sort of brazen audacity managed to produce an effective appearance, leant across the table with a gracious smile.

'Oh, Miss Lambert, I think I used to know your father in Jersey. He was a doctor, wasn't he? He used to come to our house quite often.'

Julia felt a slight sickness in the pit of her stomach; she remembered now who Lady Charles was before she married, and she saw the trap that was being set for her. She gave a rippling laugh.

70

'Not at all,' she answered. 'He was a vet. He used to go to your house to deliver the bitches. The house was full of them.'

Lady Charles for a moment did not quite know what to say.

'My mother was very fond of dogs,' she answered.

Julia was glad that Michael was not there. Poor lamb, he would have been terribly mortified. He always referred to her father as Dr Lambert, pronouncing it as though it were a French name, and when soon after the war he died and her mother went to live with her widowed sister at St. Malo he began to speak of her as Madame de Lambert. At the beginning of her career Julia had been somewhat sensitive on the point, but when once she was established as a great actress she changed her mind. She was inclined, especially among the great, to insist on the fact that her father had been a vet. She could not quite have explained why, but she felt that by so doing she put them in their place.

But Charles Tamerley knew that his wife had deliberately tried to humiliate the young woman, and angered, went out of his way to be nice to her. He asked her if he might be allowed to call and brought her some beautiful flowers.

He was then a man of nearly forty, with a small head on an elegant body not very good-looking, but of distinguished appearance. He looked very well-bred, which indeed he was, and he had exquisite manners. He was an amateur of the arts. He bought modern pictures and collected old furniture. He was a lover of music and exceedingly well read. At first it amused him to go to the tiny flat off the Buckingham Palace Road in which these two young actors lived. He saw that they were poor and it excited him to get into touch with what he fondly thought was Bohemia. He came several times and he thought it quite an adventure when they asked him to have a luncheon with them which was cooked and served by a scarecrow of a woman whom they called Evie. This was life. He did not pay much attention to Michael who seemed to him, notwithstanding his too obvious beauty, a somewhat ordinary young man, but he was taken by Julia. She had a warmth, a force of character, and a bubbling vitality which were outside his experience. He went to see her act several times and compared her performance with his recollections of the great foreign actresses. It seemed to him that she had in her something quite individual. Her magnetism was incontestable. It gave him quite a thrill to realize on a sudden that she had genius.

'Another Siddons perhaps. A greater Ellen Terry.'

In those days Julia did not think it necessary to go to bed in the afternoons, she was as strong as a horse and never tired, so he used often to take her for walks in the Park. She felt that he wanted her to be a child of nature. That suited her very well. It was no effort for her to be ingenuous, frank and girlishly delighted with everything. He took her to the National Gallery, and the Tate, and the British Museum, and she really enjoyed it almost as much as she said. He liked to impart information and she was glad to receive it. She had a retentive memory and learnt a great deal from him. If later she was able to talk about Proust and Cézanne with the best of them, so that you were surprised and pleased to find so much culture in an actress, it was to him she owed it. She knew that he had fallen in love with her some time before he knew it himself. She found it rather comic. From her standpoint he was a middle-aged man, and she thought of him as a nice old thing. She was madly in love with Michael. When Charles realized that he loved her his manner changed a little, he seemed struck with shyness and when they were together was often silent.

'Poor lamb,' she said to herself, 'he's such a hell of a gentleman he doesn't know what to do about it.'

But she had already prepared her course of conduct for the declaration which she felt he would sooner or later bring himself to make. One thing she was going to make quite clear to him. She wasn't going to let him think that

72

because he was a lord and she was an actress he had only to beckon and she would hop into bed with him. If he tried that sort of thing she'd play the outraged heroine on him, with the outflung arm and the index extended in the same line, as Jane Taitbout had taught her to make the gesture, pointed at the door. On the other hand if he was shattered and tongue-tied, she'd be all tremulous herself, sobs in the voice and all that, and she'd say it had never dawned on her that he felt like that about her, and no, no, it would break Michael's heart. They'd have a good cry together and then everything would be all right. With his beautiful manners she could count upon him not making a nuisance of himself when she had once got it into his head that there was nothing doing.

But when it happened it did not turn out in the least as she had expected. Charles Tamerley and Julia had been for a walk in St. James's Park, they had looked at the pelicans, and the scene suggesting it, they had discussed the possibility of her playing Millamant on a Sunday evening. They went back to Julia's flat to have a cup of tea. They shared a crumpet. Then Charles got up to go. He took a miniature out of his pocket and gave it to her.

'It's a portrait of Clairon. She was an eighteenth-century actress and she had many of your gifts.'

Julia looked at the pretty, clever face, with the powdered hair, and wondered whether the stones that framed the little picture were diamonds or only paste.

'Oh, Charles, how can you! You are sweet.'

'I thought you might like it. It's by way of being a parting present.'

'Are you going away?'

She was surprised, for he had said nothing about it. He looked at her with a faint smile.

'No. But I'm not going to see you any more.'

'Why?'

'I think you know just as well as I do.'

Then Julia did a disgraceful thing. She sat down and for a minute looked silently at the miniature. Timing it

73

perfectly, she raised her eyes till they met Charles's. She could cry almost at will, it was one of her most telling accomplishments, and now without a sound, without a sob, the tears poured down her cheeks. With her mouth slightly open, with the look in her eyes of a child that has been deeply hurt and does not know why, the effect was unbearably pathetic. His face was crossed by a twinge of agony. When he spoke his voice was hoarse with emotion.

'You're in love with Michael, aren't you?'

She gave a little nod. She tightened her lips as though she were trying to control herself, but the tears rolled down her cheeks.

'There's no chance for me at all?' He waited for some answer from her, but she gave none, she raised her hand to her mouth and seemed to bite a nail, and still she stared at him with those streaming eyes. 'Don't you know what torture it is to go on seeing you? D'you want me to go on seeing you?'

Again she gave a little nod.

'Clara's making me scenes about you. She's found out I'm in love with you. It's only common sense that we shouldn't see one another any more.'

This time Julia slightly shook her head. She gave a sob. She leant back in the chair and turned her head aside. Her whole body seemed to express the hopelessness of her grief. Flesh and blood couldn't stand it. Charles stepped forward and sinking to his knees took that broken woebegone body in his arms.

'For God's sake don't look so unhappy. I can't bear it. Oh, Julia, Julia, I love you so much, I can't make you so miserable. I'll accept anything. I'll make no demands on you.'

She turned her tear-stained face to him ('God, what a sight I must look now') and gave him her lips. He kissed her tenderly. It was the first time he had ever kissed her.

'I don't want to lose you,' she muttered huskily.

'Darling, darling!'

'It'll be just as it was before?'

'Just.'

She gave a deep sigh of contentment and for a minute or two rested in his arms. When he went away she got up and looked in the glass.

'You rotten bitch,' she said to herself.

But she giggled as though she were not in the least ashamed and then went into the bathroom to wash her face and eyes. She felt wonderfully exhilarated. She heard Michael come in and called out to him.

'Michael, look at that miniature Charles has just given me. It's on the chimney-piece. Are those diamonds or paste?'

Julia was somewhat nervous when Lady Charles left her husband. She threatened to bring proceedings for divorce, and Julia did not at all like the idea of appearing as intervenor. For two or three weeks she was very jittery. She decided to say nothing to Michael till it was necessary, and she was glad she had not, for in due course it appeared that the threats had been made only to extract more substantial alimony from the innocent husband. Julia managed Charles with wonderful skill. It was understood between them that her great love for Michael made any close relation between them out of the question, but so far as the rest was concerned he was everything to her, her friend, her adviser, her confidant, the man she could rely on in any emergency or go to for comfort in any disappointment. It was a little more difficult when Charles, with his fine sensitiveness, saw that she was no longer in love with Michael. Then Julia had to exercise a great deal of tact. It was not that she had any scruples about being his mistress; if he had been an actor who loved her so much and had loved her so long she would not have minded popping into bed with him out of sheer good nature; but she just did not fancy him. She was very fond of him, but he was so elegant, so well-bred, so cultured, she could not think of him as a lover. It would be like going to bed with an objet d'art. And his love of art filled her with a faint derision; after all she was a creator, when all was said and done he was only the public. He wished her to elope with him. They would buy a villa at Sorrento on the bay of Naples, with a large garden, and they would have a schooner so that they could spend long days on the beautiful wine-coloured sea. Love and beauty and art; the world well lost.

'The damned fool,' she thought. 'As if I'd give up my career to bury myself in some hole in Italy!'

She persuaded him that she had a duty to Michael, and then there was the baby; she couldn't let him grow up with the burden on his young life that his mother was a bad woman. Orange trees or no orange trees, she would never have a moment's peace in that beautiful Italian villa if she was tortured by the thought of Michael's unhappiness and her baby being looked after by strangers. One couldn't only think of oneself, could one? One had to think of others too. She was very sweet and womanly. She sometimes asked Charles why he did not arrange a divorce with his wife and marry some nice woman. She could not bear the thought of his wasting his life over her. He told her that she was the only woman he had ever loved and that he must go on loving her till the end.

'It seems so sad,' said Julia.

All the same she kept her eyes open, and if she noticed that any woman had predatory intentions on Charles she took care to queer her pitch. She did not hesitate if the danger seemed to warrant it to show herself extremely jealous. It had been long agreed, with all the delicacy that might be expected from his good-breeding and Julia's good heart, in no definite words, but with guarded hints and remote allusiveness, that if anything happened to Michael, Lady Charles should somehow or other be disposed of and they would then marry. But Michael had perfect health.

On this occasion Julia had much enjoyed lunching at Hill Street. The party had been very grand. Julia had never encouraged Charles to entertain any of the actors or authors he sometimes came across, and she was the only person there who had ever had to earn a living. She had sat between an old, fat, bald and loquacious Cabinet Minister who took a great deal of trouble to entertain her, and a young Duke of Westreys who looked like a stable-boy and who flattered himself that he knew French slang better than a Frenchman. When he discovered that Julia spoke French he insisted on conversing with her in that language. After luncheon she was persuaded to recite a tirade from 'Phèdre' as it was done at the Comédie Française and the same tirade as an English student at the Royal Academy of Dramatic Art would deliver it. She made the company laugh very much and came away from the party flushed with success. It was a fine bright day and she made up her mind to walk from Hill Street to Stanhope Place. A good many people recognized her as she threaded her way through the crowd in Oxford Street, and though she looked straight ahead of her she was conscious of their glances.

'What a hell of a nuisance it is that one can't go anywhere without people staring at one.'

She slackened her pace a little. It certainly was a beautiful day.

She let herself into her house with a latch-key and as she got in heard the telephone ringing. Without thinking she took up the receiver.

'Yes?'

She generally disguised her voice when she answered, but for once forgot to.

'Miss Lambert?'

'I don't know if Miss Lambert's in. Who is it please?' she asked, assuming quickly a cockney accent.

The monosyllable had betrayed her. A chuckle travelled over the wire.

'I only wanted to thank you for writing to me. You know, you needn't have troubled. It was so nice of you to ask me to lunch, I thought I'd like to send you a few flowers.'

77

The sound of his voice and the words told her who it was. It was the blushing young man whose name she did not know. Even now, though she had looked at his card, she could not remember it. The only thing that had struck her was that he lived in Tavistock Square.

'It was very sweet of you,' she answered, in her own voice.

'I suppose you wouldn't come to tea with me one day, would you?'

The nerve of it! She wouldn't go to tea with a duchess; he was treating her like a chorus girl. It was rather funny when you came to think of it.

'I don't know why not.'

'Will you really?' his voice sounded eager. He had a pleasant voice. 'When?'

She did not feel at all like going to bed that afternoon. 'To-day.'

'OK. I'll get away from the office. Half-past four? 138, Tavistock Square.'

It was nice of him to have suggested that. He might so easily have mentioned some fashionable place where people would stare at her. It proved that he didn't just want to be seen with her.

She took a taxi to Tavistock Square. She was pleased with herself. She was doing a good action. It would be wonderful for him in after years to be able to tell his wife and children that Julia Lambert had been to tea with him when he was just a little insignificant clerk in an accountant's office. And she had been so simple and so natural. No one to hear her prattling away would have guessed that she was the greatest actress in England. And if they didn't believe him he'd have her photograph to prove it, signed yours sincerely. He'd laugh and say that of course if he hadn't been such a kid he'd never have had the cheek to ask her.

When she arrived at the house and had paid off the taxi she suddenly remembered that she did not know his name and when the maid answered the door would not know whom to ask for. But on looking for the bell she noticed that there were eight of them, four rows of two, and by the side of each was a card or a name written in ink on a piece of paper. It was an old house that had been divided up into flats. She began looking, rather hopelessly, at the names wondering whether one of them would recall something, when the door opened and he stood before her.

'I saw you drive up and I ran down. I'm afraid I'm on the third floor. I hope you don't mind.'

'Of course not.'

She climbed the uncarpeted stairs. She was a trifle out of breath when she came to the third landing. He had skipped up eagerly, like a young goat, she thought, and she had not liked to suggest that she would prefer to go more leisurely. The room into which he led her was fairly large, but dingily furnished. On the table was a plate of cakes and two cups, a sugar basin and a milk-jug. The crockery was of the cheapest sort.

'Take a pew,' he said. 'The water's just on the boil. I'll only be a minute. I've got a gas-ring in the bathroom.'

He left her and she looked about.

'Poor lamb, he must be as poor as a church mouse.'

The room reminded her very much of some of the lodgings she had lived in when she was first on the stage. She noticed the pathetic attempts he had made to conceal the fact that it was a bedroom as well as a sitting-room. The divan against the wall was evidently his bed at night. The years slipped away from her in fancy and she felt strangely young again. What fun they had had in rooms very like that and how they had enjoyed the fantastic meals they had had, things in paper bags and eggs and bacon fried on the gas-ring! He came in with the tea in a brown pot. She ate a square sponge-cake with pink icing on it. That was a thing she had not done for years. The Ceylon tea, very strong, with milk and sugar in it, took her back to days she thought she had forgotten. She saw herself as a young, obscure, struggling actress. It was rather delicious. It needed a gesture, but she could only think of one: she took off her hat and gave her head a shake.

They talked. He seemed shy, much shyer than he had seemed over the telephone; well, that was not to be wondered at, now she was there he must be rather overcome, and she set herself to put him at his ease. He told her that his parents lived at Highgate, his father was a solicitor, and he had lived there too, but he wanted to be his own master and now in the last year of his articles he had broken away and taken this tiny flat. He was working for his final examination. They talked of the theatre. He had seen her in every play she had acted in since he was twelve years old. He told her that once when he was fourteen he had stood outside the stage door after a matinée and when she came out had asked her to sign her name in his autograph-book. He was sweet with his blue eyes and pale brown hair. It was a pity he plastered it down like that. He had a white skin and rather a high colour; she wondered if he was consumptive. Although his clothes were cheap he wore them well, she liked that, and he looked incredibly clean.

She asked him why he had chosen Tavistock Square. It was central, he explained, and he liked the trees. It was quite nice when you looked out of the window. She got up to look, that would be a good way to make a move, then she would put on her hat and say goodbye to him.

'Yes, it is rather charming, isn't it. It's so London; it gives one a sort of jolly feeling.'

She turned to him, standing by her side, as she said this. He put his arm round her waist and kissed her full on the lips. No woman was ever more surprised in her life. She was so taken aback that she never thought of doing anything. His lips were soft and there was a perfume of youth about him which was really rather delightful. But what he was doing was preposterous. He was forcing her lips apart with the tip of his tongue and now he had both arms round her. She did not feel angry, she did not feel inclined to laugh, she did not know what she felt. And now she had a notion that he was gently drawing her along, his lips still pressing hers, she felt quite distinctly the glow of his body, it was as though there was a furnace inside him, it was really remarkable; and then she found herself laid on the divan and he was beside her, kissing her mouth and her neck and her cheeks and her eyes. Julia felt a strange pang in her heart. She took his head in her hands and kissed his lips.

A few minutes later she was standing at the chimney-piece, in front of the looking-glass, making herself tidy.

'Look at my hair.'

He handed her a comb and she ran it through. Then she put on her hat. He was standing just behind her, and over her shoulder she saw his face with those eager blue eyes and a faint smile in them.

'And I thought you were such a shy young man,' she said to his reflection.

He chuckled.

'When am I going to see you again?'

'Do you want to see me again?'

'Rather.'

She thought rapidly. It was too absurd, of course she had no intention of seeing him again, it was stupid of her to have let him behave like that, but it was just as well to temporize. He might be tiresome if she told him that the incident would have no sequel.

'I'll ring up one of these days.'

'Swear.'

'On my honour.'

'Don't be too long.'

He insisted on coming downstairs with her and putting her into a cab. She had wanted to go down alone, so that she could have a look at the cards attached to the bells on the lintel.

'Damn it all, I ought at least to know his name.'

But he gave her no chance. When the taxi drove off she sank into one corner of it and gurgled with laughter.

'Raped, my dear. Practically raped. At my time of life. And without so much as a by your leave. Treated me like a tart. Eighteenth-century comedy, that's what it is. I might have been a waiting-maid. In a hoop, with those funny puffy things – what the devil are they called? – that they wore to emphasize their hips, an apron and a scarf round me neck.' Then with vague memories of Farquhar and Goldsmith she invented the dialogue. 'La, sir, 'tis shame to take advantage of a poor country girl. What would Mrs Abigail, her ladyship's woman, say an she knew her ladyship's brother had ravished me of the most precious treasure a young woman in my station of life can possess, videlicet her innocence. Fie, o fie, sir.'

When Julia got home the masseuse was already waiting for her. Miss Phillips and Evie were having a chat.

'Wherever 'ave you been, Miss Lambert?' said Evie. 'An' what about your rest, I should like to know.'

'Damn my rest.'

Julia tore off her clothes, and flung them with ample gestures all over the room. Then, stark naked, she skipped on to the bed, stood up on it for a moment, like Venus rising from the waves, and then throwing herself down stretched herself out.

'What's the idea?' said Evie.

'I feel good.'

'Well, if I behaved like that people'd say I'd been drinkin'.'

Miss Phillips began to massage her feet. She rubbed gently, to rest and not to tire her.

'When you came in just now, like a whirlwind,' she said, 'I thought you looked twenty years younger. Your eyes were shining something wonderful.'

'Oh, keep that for Mr Gosselyn, Miss Phillips.' And then as an afterthought, 'I feel like a two-year-old.'

And it was the same at the theatre later on. Archie Dexter, who was her leading man, came into her dressing-room to speak about something. She had just finished making-up. He was startled.

'Hulloa, Julia, what's the matter with you to-night? Gosh, you look swell. Why, you don't look a day more than twenty-five.'

'With a son of sixteen it's no good pretending I'm so terribly young any more. I'm forty and I don't care who knows it.'

'What have you done to your eyes? I've never seen them shine like that before.'

She felt in tremendous form. They had been playing the play, it was called 'The Powder Puff,' for a good many weeks, but to-night Julia played it as though it were the first time. Her performance was brilliant. She got laughs that she had never got before. She always had magnetism, but on this occasion it seemed to flow over the house in a great radiance. Michael happened to be watching the last two acts from the corner of a box and at the end he came into her dressing-room.

'D'you know the prompter says we played nine minutes longer to-night, they laughed so much.'

'Seven curtain calls. I thought the public were going on all night.'

'Well, you've only got to blame yourself, darling. There's no one in the world who could have given the performance you gave to-night.'

'To tell you the truth I was enjoying myself. Christ, I'm hungry. What have we got for supper?'

'Tripe and onions.'

'Oh, how divine!' She flung her arms round his neck and kissed him. 'I adore tripe and onions. Oh, Michael, Michael, if you love me, if you've got any spark of tenderness in that hard heart of yours, let me have a bottle of beer.'

'Julia.'

'Just this once. It's not often I ask you to do anything for me.'

'Oh well, after the performance you gave to-night I suppose I can't say no, but by God, I'll see that Miss Phillips pitches into you to-morrow.'

12

When Julia got to bed and slipped her feet down to the comfort of her hot-water bottle, she took a happy look at her room, rose-pink and Nattier-blue, with the gold cherubs of her dressing-table, and sighed with satisfaction. She thought how very Madame de Pompadour it was. She put out the light but she did not feel at all sleepy. She would have liked really to go to Quag's and dance, but not to dance with Michael, to dance with Louis XV or Ludwig of Bavaria or Alfred de Musset. Clairon and the Bal de l'Opéra. She remembered the miniature Charles had once given her. That was how she felt tonight. Such an adventure had not happened to her for ages. The last time was eight years before. That was an episode that she ought to have been thoroughly ashamed of; goodness, how scared she'd been afterwards, but she had in point of fact never been able to think of it since without a chuckle.

That had been an accident too. She had been acting for a long time without a rest and she badly needed one. The play she was in was ceasing to attract and they were about to start rehearsing a new one when Michael got the chance of letting the theatre to a French company for six weeks. It seemed a good opportunity for Julia to get away. Dolly had rented a house at Cannes for the season and Julia could stay with her. It was just before Easter when she started off and the trains south were so crowded that she had not been able to get a sleeper, but at a travel agency they had said that it would be quite all right and there would be one waiting for her at the station in Paris. To her consternation she found when they got to Paris that nothing seemed to be known about her, and the chef de train told her that every sleeper was engaged. The only chance was that someone should not turn up at the last moment. She did not like the idea of sitting up all night in the corner of a first-class carriage, and went in to dinner with a perturbed mind. She was given a table for two, and soon a man came and sat down opposite her. She paid no attention to him. Presently the chef de train came along and told her that he was very sorry, but he could do nothing for her. She made a useless scene. When the official had gone, the man at her table addressed her. Though he spoke fluent, idiomatic French, she recognized by his accent that he was not a Frenchman. She told him in answer to his polite enquiry the whole story and gave him her opinion of the travel agency, the railway company, and the general inefficiency of the human race. He was very sympathetic. He told her that after dinner he would go along the train and see for himself if something could not be arranged. One never knew what one of the conductors could not manage for a tip.

'I'm simply tired out,' she said. 'I'd willingly give five hundred francs for a sleeper.'

The conversation thus started, he told her that he was an attaché at the Spanish Embassy in Paris and was going down to Cannes for Easter. Though she had been talking to him for a quarter of an hour she had not troubled to notice what he was like. She observed now that he had a beard, a black curly beard and a black curly moustache, but the beard grew rather oddly on his face; there were two bare patches under the corners of his mouth. It gave him a curious look. With his black hair, drooping eyelids and rather long nose, he reminded her of someone she had seen. Suddenly she remembered, and it was such a surprise that she blurted out:

'D'you know, I couldn't think who you reminded me of. You're strangely like Titian's portrait of Francis I in the Louvre.'

'With his little pig's eyes?'

'No, not them, yours are large, I think it's the beard chiefly.'

She glanced at the skin under his eyes; it was faintly violet and unwrinkled. Notwithstanding the ageing beard he was quite a young man; he could not have been more than thirty. She wondered if he was a Spanish Grandee. He was not very well dressed, but then foreigners often weren't, his clothes might have cost a lot even if they were badly cut, and his tie, though rather loud, she recognised as a Charvet. When they came to the coffee he asked her whether he might offer her a liqueur.

'That's very kind of you. Perhaps it'll make me sleep better.'

He offered her a cigarette. His cigarette-case was silver, that put her off a little, but when he closed it she saw that in the corner was a small crown in gold. He must be a count or something. It was rather chic, having a silver cigarette-case with a gold crown on it. Pity he had to wear those modern clothes! If he'd been dressed like Francis I he would really look very distinguished. She set herself to be as gracious as she knew how.

'I think I should tell you,' he said presently, 'that I know who you are. And may I add that I have a great admiration for you?'

She gave him a lingering look of her splendid eyes.

'You've seen me act?'

'Yes, I was in London last month.'

'An interesting little play, wasn't it?'

'Only because you made it so.'

When the man came round to collect the money she had to insist on paying her own bill. The Spaniard accompanied her to the carriage and then said he would go along the train to see if he could find a sleeper for her. He came back in a quarter of an hour with a conductor and told her that he had got her a compartment and if she would give the conductor her things he would take her to it. She was delighted. He threw down his hat on the seat she vacated and she followed him along the corridor. When they reached the compartment he told the conduc-

tor to take the portmanteau and the dispatch-case that
were in the rack to the carriage madame had just left.

'But it's not your own compartment you're giving up
to me?' cried Julia.

'It's the only one on the train.'

'Oh, but I won't hear of it.'

'Allez,' the Spaniard said to the conductor.

'No, no.'

The conductor, on a nod from the stranger, took the
luggage away.

'I don't matter. I can sleep anywhere, but I shouldn't
sleep a wink if I thought that such a great artist was
obliged to spend the night in a stuffy carriage with three
other people.'

Julia continued to protest, but not too much. It was
terribly sweet of him. She didn't know how to thank him.
He would not even let her pay for the sleeper. He begged
her, almost with tears in his eyes, to let him have the great
privilege of making her that trifling present. She had with
her only a dressing-bag, in which were her face creams,
her night-dress and her toilet things, and this he put on
the table for her. All he asked was that he might be
allowed to sit with her and smoke a cigarette or two till
she wanted to go to bed. She could hardly refuse him
that. The bed was already made up and they sat down on
it. In a few minutes the conductor came back with a
bottle of champagne and a couple of glasses. It was an
odd little adventure and Julia was enjoying it. It was
wonderfully polite of him, all that, ah, those foreigners,
they knew how to treat a great actress. Of course that
was the sort of thing that happened to Bernhardt every
day. And Siddons, when she went into a drawing-room
everyone stood up as though she were royalty. He compli-
mented her on her beautiful French. Born in Jersey and
educated in France? Ah, that explained it. But why hadn't
she chosen to act in French rather than in English? She
would have as great a reputation as Duse if she had. She
reminded him of Duse, the same magnificent eyes and

the pale skin, and in her acting the same emotion and the wonderful naturalness.

They half finished the bottle of champagne and Julia realized that it was very late.

'I really think I ought to go to bed now.'

'I'll leave you.'

He got up and kissed her hand. When he was gone Julia bolted the door and undressed. Putting out all the lights except the one just behind her head she began to read. Presently there was a knock at the door.

'Yes?'

'I'm sorry to disturb you. I left my toothbrush in the lavabo. May I get it?'

'I'm in bed.'

'I can't go to sleep unless I brush my teeth.'

'Oh well, he's clean anyway.'

With a little shrug of her shoulders Julia slipped her hand to the door and drew back the bolt. It would be stupid in the circumstances to be prudish. He came in, went into the lavatory and in a moment came out, brandishing a toothbrush. She had noticed it when she brushed her own teeth, but thought it belonged to the person who had the compartment next door. At that period adjoining compartments shared a lavatory. The Spaniard seemed to catch sight of the bottle.

'I'm so thirsty, do you mind if I have a glass of champagne?'

Julia was silent for a fraction of a second. It was his champagne and his compartment. Oh, well, in for a penny, in for a pound.

'Of course not.'

He poured himself out a glass, lit a cigarette and sat down on the edge of her bed. She moved a little to give him more room. He accepted the situation as perfectly natural.

'You couldn't possibly have slept in that carriage,' he said. 'There's a man there who's a heavy breather. I'd almost rather he snored. If he snored one could wake him.'

'I'm so sorry.'

'Oh, it doesn't matter. If the worst comes to the worst I'll curl up in the corridor outside your door.'

'He can hardly expect me to ask him to come and sleep in here,' Julia said to herself. 'I'm beginning to think this was all a put-up job. Nothing doing, my lad.' And then aloud: 'Romantic, of course, but uncomfortable.'

'You're a terribly attractive woman.'

She was just as glad that her nightdress was pretty and that she had put no cream on her face. She had in point of fact not troubled to take off her make-up. Her lips were brightly scarlet, and with the reading light behind her she well knew that she did not look her worst. But she answered ironically.

'If you think that because you've given up your compartment to me I'm going to let you sleep with me, you're mistaken.'

'Just as you say, of course. But why not?'

'I'm not that sort of terribly attractive woman.'

'What sort of woman are you then?'

'A faithful wife and a devoted mother.'

He gave a little sigh.

'Very well. Then I'll say good night to you.'

He crushed the stub of his cigarette on the ashtray and took her hand and kissed it. He slowly ran his lips up her arm. It gave Julia a funny little sensation. The beard slightly tickled her skin. Then he leant over and kissed her lips. His beard had a somewhat musty smell, which she found peculiar; she was not sure if it revolted or thrilled her. It was odd when she came to think of it, she had never been kissed by a man with a beard before. It seemed strangely indecent. He snapped out the light.

He did not leave her till a chink of light through the drawn blind warned them that day had broken. Julia was shattered morally and physically.

'I shall look a perfect wreck when we get to Cannes.'

And what a risk to take! He might have murdered her or stolen her pearl necklace. She went hot and cold all over as she pictured to herself the danger she had incurred. He was going to Cannes too. Supposing he claimed acquaintance with her there, how on earth was she going to explain him to her friends? She felt sure Dolly wouldn't like him. He might try to blackmail her. And what should she do if he wanted to repeat the experience? He was passionate, there was no doubt about that, he had asked her where she was staying, and though she had not told him, he could certainly find out if he tried; in a place like Cannes, it would be almost impossible not to run across him. He might pester her. If he loved her as much as he said it was inconceivable that he should let her alone, and foreigners were so unreliable, he might make frightful scenes. The only comfort was that he was only staying over Easter, she would pretend she was tired and tell Dolly that she preferred to stay quietly at the villa.

'How could I have been such a fool?' she cried angrily.

Dolly would be there to meet her at the station, and if he was tactless enough to come up and say good-bye to her she would tell Dolly that he had given up his compartment to her. There was no harm in that. It was always best to tell as much of the truth as you could. But there was quite a crowd of passengers getting out at Cannes, and Julia got out of the station and into Dolly's car without catching a glimpse of him.

'I've arranged nothing for to-day,' said Dolly. 'I thought you'd be tired and I wanted to have you all to myself just for twenty-four hours.'

Julia gave her arm an affectionate squeeze.

'That'll be too wonderful. We'll just sit about the villa and grease our faces and have a good old gossip.'

But next day Dolly had arranged that they should go out to luncheon, and they were to meet their hosts at one of the bars on the Croisette to have cocktails. It was a beautiful day, clear, warm and sunny. When they got out of the car Dolly stopped to give the chauffeur instructions about fetching them and Julia waited for her. Suddenly her heart gave a great jump, for there was the Spaniard walking towards her, with a woman on one side of him clinging to his arm and on the other a little girl whose hand he held. She had not time to turn away. At that moment Dolly joined her to walk across the pavement. The Spaniard came, gave her a glance in which there was no sign of recognition, he was in animated conversation with the woman on his arm, and walked on. In a flash Julia understood that he was just as little anxious to see her as she was to see him. The woman and the child were obviously his wife and daughter whom he had come down to Cannes to spend Easter with. What a relief! Now she could enjoy herself without fear. But as she accompanied Dolly to the bar, Julia thought how disgusting men were. You simply couldn't trust them for a minute. It was really disgraceful that a man with a charming wife and such a sweet little girl should be willing to pick up a woman in the train. You would think they'd have some sense of decency.

But as time passed Julia's indignation was mitigated, and she had often thought of the adventure since with a good deal of pleasure. After all it had been fun. Sometimes she allowed her reveries to run away with her and she went over in her fancy the incidents of that singular night. He had been a most agreeable lover. It would be something to look back on when she was an old woman. It was the beard that had made such an impression on her, the odd feeling of it on her face and that slightly musty smell which was repulsive and yet strangely exciting. For years she looked out for men with beards, and she had a feeling that if one of them made proposals to her she simply wouldn't be able to resist him. But few men wore beards any more, luckily for her because the sight made her go a little weak at the knees, and none of those that did ever made any advance to her. She would have liked to know who the Spaniard was. She saw him a day or two later playing chemin de fer at the Casino and asked two or three people if they knew him. Nobody did, and he remained in her recollection, and in her bones, without a name. It was an odd coincidence that she didn't know the name either of the young man who had that afternoon behaved in so unexpected a manner. It struck her as rather comic.

'If I only knew beforehand that they were going to take liberties with me I'd at least ask for their cards.'

With this thought she fell happily asleep.

13

Some days passed, and one morning, while Julia was lying in bed reading a play, they rang through from the basement to ask if she would speak to Mr Fennell. The name meant nothing to her and she was about to refuse when it occurred to her that it might be the young man of her adventure. Her curiosity induced her to tell them to connect him. She recognized his voice.

'You promised to ring me up,' he said. 'I got tired of waiting, so I've rung you up instead.'

'I've been terribly busy the last few days.'

'When am I going to see you?'

'As soon as I have a moment to spare.'

'What about this afternoon?'

'I've got a matinée to-day.'

'Come to tea after the matinée.'

She smiled. ('No, young feller-me-lad, you don't catch me a second time like that.')

'I can't possibly,' she answered. 'I always stay in my dressing-room and rest till the evening performance.'

'Can't I come and see you while you're resting?'

She hesitated for an instant. Perhaps the best thing would be to let him come; with Evie popping in and out and Miss Phillips due at seven, there would be no chance of any nonsense, and it would be a good opportunity to tell him, amiably, because he was really a sweet little thing, but firmly, that the incident of the other afternoon was to have no sequel. With a few well-chosen words she would explain to him that it was quite unreasonable and that he must oblige her by erasing the episode from his memory.

'All right. Come at half-past five and I'll give you a cup of tea.'

There was no part of her busy life that she enjoyed more than those three hours that she spent in her dressing-room between the afternoon and the evening perform-ances. The other members of the cast had gone away; and Evie was there to attend to her wants and the door-keeper to guard her privacy. Her dressing-room was like the cabin of a ship. The world seemed a long way off, and she relished her seclusion. She felt an enchanting freedom. She dozed a little, she read a little, or lying on the comfort-able sofa she let her thoughts wander. She reflected on the part she was playing and the favourite parts she had played in the past. She thought of Roger her son. Pleasant reveries sauntered through her mind like lovers wander-ing in a green wood. She was fond of French poetry, and sometimes she repeated to herself verses of Verlaine.

Punctually at half-past five Evie brought her in a card. 'Mr Thomas Fennell,' she read.

'Send him in and bring some tea.'

She had decided how she was going to treat him. She would be amiable, but distant. She would take a friendly interest in his work and ask him about his examination. Then she would talk to him about Roger. Roger was seventeen now and in a year would be going to Cam-bridge. She would insinuate the fact that she was old enough to be his mother. She would act as if there had never been anything between them and he would go away, never to see her again except across the footlights, half convinced that the whole thing had been a figment of his fancy. But when she saw him, so slight, with his hectic flush and his blue eyes, so charmingly boyish, she

93

felt a sudden pang. Evie closed the door behind him. She was lying on the sofa and she stretched out her arm to give him her hand, the gracious smile of Madame Récamier on her lips, but he flung himself on his knees and passionately kissed her mouth. She could not help herself, she put her arms round his neck, and kissed him as passionately.

('Oh, my good resolutions. My God, I can't have fallen in love with him.')

'For goodness' sake, sit down. Evie's coming in with the tea.'

'Tell her not to disturb us.'

'What do you mean?' But what he meant was obvious. Her heart began to beat quickly. 'It's ridiculous. I can't. Michael might come in.'

'I want you.'

'What d'you suppose Evie would think? It'd be idiotic to take such a risk. No, no, no.'

There was a knock at the door and Evie came in with the tea. Julia gave her instructions to put the table by the side of her sofa and a chair for the young man on the other side of the table. She kept Evie with unnecessary conversation. She felt him looking at her. His eyes moved quickly, following her gestures and the expression of her face; she avoided them, but she felt their anxiety and the eagerness of his desire. She was troubled. It seemed to her that her voice did not sound quite natural.

('What the devil's the matter with me? God, I can hardly breathe.')

When Evie reached the door the boy made a gesture that was so instinctive that her sensitiveness rather than her sight caught it. She could not but look at him. His face had gone quite pale.

'Oh, Evie,' she said. 'This gentleman wants to talk to me about a play. See that no one disturbs me. I'll ring when I want you.'

'Very good, miss.'

Evie went out and closed the door.

('I'm a fool. I'm a bloody fool.')

But he had moved the table, and he was on his knees, and she was in his arms.

She sent him away a little before Miss Phillips was due, and when he was going rang for Evie.

'Play any good?' asked Evie.

'What play?'

'The play 'e was talkin' to you about.'

'He's clever. Of course he's young.'

Evie was looking down at the dressing-table. Julia liked everything always to be in the same place, and if a pot of grease or her eyeblack was not exactly where it should be made a scene.

'Where's your comb?'

He had used it to comb his hair and had carelessly placed it on the tea-table. When Evie caught sight of it she stared at it for a moment reflectively.

'How on earth did it get there?' cried Julia lightly.

'I was just wondering.'

It gave Julia a nasty turn. Of course it was madness to do that sort of thing in the dressing-room. Why, there wasn't even a key in the lock. Evie kept it. All the same the risk had given it a spice. It was fun to think that she could be so crazy. At all events they'd made a date now. Tom, she'd asked him what they called him at home and he said Thomas, she really couldn't call him that. Tom wanted to take her to supper somewhere so that they could dance, and it happened that Michael was going up to Cambridge for a night to rehearse a series of one-act plays written by undergraduates. They would be able to spend hours together.

'You can get back with the milk,' he'd said.

'And what about my performance next day?'

'We can't bother about that.'

She had refused to let him fetch her at the theatre, and when she got to the restaurant they had chosen he was waiting for her in the lobby. His face lit up as he saw her.

'It was getting so late, I was afraid you weren't coming.'

'I'm sorry, some tiresome people came round after the play and I couldn't get rid of them.'

But it wasn't true. She had been as excited all the evening as a girl going to her first ball. She could not help thinking how absurd she was. But when she had taken off her theatrical make-up and made up again for supper she could not satisfy herself. She put blue on her eyelids and took it off again, she rouged her cheeks, rubbed them clean and tried another colour.

'What are you trying to do?' said Evie.

'I'm trying to look twenty, you fool.'

'If you try much longer you'll look your age.'

She had never seen him in evening clothes before. He shone like a new pin. Though he was of no more than average height his slimness made him look tall. She was a trifle touched to see that for all his airs of the man of the world he was shy with the head-waiter when it came to ordering supper. They danced and he did not dance very well, but she found his slight awkwardness rather charming. People recognized her, and she was conscious that he enjoyed the reflected glory of their glances. A pair of young things who had been dancing came up to their table to say how do you do to her. When they had left he asked:

'Wasn't that Lord and Lady Dennorant?'

'Yes. I've known George since he was at Eton.'

He followed them with his eyes.

'She was Lady Cecily Laweston, wasn't she?'

'I've forgotten. Was she?'

It seemed a matter of no interest to her. A few minutes later another couple passed them.

'Look, there's Lady Lepard.'

'Who's she?'

'Don't you remember, they had a big party at their place in Cheshire a few weeks ago and the Prince of Wales was there. It was in the *Bystander*.'

Oh, that was how he got all his information. Poor sweet. He read about grand people in the papers and now and then, at a restaurant or a theatre, saw them in the flesh. Of course it was a thrill for him. Romance. If he only knew how dull they were really! This innocent passion for the persons whose photographs appear in the illustrated papers made him seem incredibly naïve, and she looked at him with tender eyes.

'Have you ever taken an actress out to supper before?'
He blushed scarlet.
'Never.'

She hated to let him pay the bill, she had an inkling that it was costing pretty well his week's salary, but she knew it would hurt his pride if she offered to pay it herself. She asked casually what the time was and instinctively he looked at his wrist.

'I forgot to put on my watch.'
She gave him a searching look.
'Have you pawned it?'
He reddened again.
'No. I dressed in rather a hurry to-night.'

She only had to look at his tie to know that he had done no such thing. He was lying to her. She knew that he had pawned his watch in order to take her out to supper. A lump came into her throat. She could have taken him in her arms then and there and kissed his blue eyes. She adored him.

'Let's go,' she said.
They drove back to his bed-sitting room in Tavistock Square.

14

Next day Julia went to Cartier's and bought a watch to send to Tom Fennell instead of the one he had pawned, and two or three weeks later, discovering that it was his birthday, she sent him a gold cigarette-case.

'D'you know, that's the one thing I've wanted all my life.'

She wondered if there were tears in his eyes. He kissed her passionately.

Then, on one excuse and another, she sent him pearl studs and sleeve-links and waistcoat buttons. It thrilled her to make him presents.

'It's so awful that I can't give you anything in return,' he said.

'Give me the watch you pawned to stand me a supper.'

It was a little gold watch that could not have cost more than ten pounds, but it amused her to wear it now and then.

It was not till after that night when they had first supped together that Julia confessed to herself that she had fallen in love with Tom. It came to her as a shock. But she was exhilarated.

'I who thought I could never be in love again. Of course it can't last. But why shouldn't I get what fun out of it I can?'

She decided that he must come again to Stanhope Place. It was not long before an opportunity presented itself.

'You know that young accountant of yours,' she said to Michael. 'Tom Fennell's his name. I met him out at supper the other night and I've asked him to dinner next Sunday. We want an extra man.'

'Oh, d'you think he'll fit in?'

It was rather a grand party. It was on that account she had asked him. She thought it would please him to meet some of the people he had known only from their pictures. She had realized already that he was a bit of a snob. Well, that was all to the good; she could give him all the smart people he wanted. For Julia was shrewd, and she knew very well that Tom was not in love with her. To have an affair with her flattered his vanity. He was a highly-sexed young man and enjoyed sexual exercise. From hints, from stories that she had dragged out of him, she discovered that since he was seventeen he had had a great many women. He loved the act rather than the person. He looked upon it as the greatest lark in the

98

world. And she could understand why he had so much success. There was something appealing in his slightness, his body was just skin and bone, that was why his clothes sat on him so well, and something charming in his clean freshness. His shyness and his effrontery combined to make him irresistible. It was strangely flattering for a woman to be treated as a little bit of fluff that you just tumbled on to a bed.

'What he's got, of course, is sex appeal.'

She knew that his good looks were due to his youth. He would grow wizened as he grew older, dried up and haggard; that charming flush on his cheeks would turn into a purple glow and his delicate skin would go lined and sallow; but the feeling that what she loved in him would endure so short a time increased her tenderness. She felt a strange compassion for him. He had the high spirits of youth, and she lapped them up as a kitten laps up milk. But he was not amusing. Though he laughed when Julia said a funny thing he never said one himself. She did not mind. She found his dullness restful. She never felt so light-hearted as in his company, and she could be brilliant enough for two.

People kept on telling Julia that she was looking ten years younger and that she had never acted better. She knew it was true and she knew the reason. But it behoved her to walk warily. She must keep her head. Charles Tamerley always said that what an actress needed was not intelligence, but sensibility, and he might be right; perhaps she wasn't clever, but her feelings were alert and she trusted them. They told her now that she must never tell Tom that she loved him. She was careful to make it plain to him that she laid no claims on him and that he was free to do whatever he liked. She took up the attitude that the whole thing was a bit of nonsense to which neither of them must attach importance. But she left nothing undone to bind him to her. He liked parties and she took him to parties. She got Dolly and Charles Tamerley to ask him to luncheon. He was fond of dancing and she got him cards for balls. For his sake she would go to them herself for an hour, and she was conscious of the satisfaction he got out of seeing how much fuss people made of her. She knew that he was dazzled by the great, and she introduced him to eminent persons. Fortunately Michael took a fancy to him. Michael liked to talk, and Tom was a good listener. He was clever at his business. One day Michael said to her:

'Smart fellow, Tom. He knows a lot about income-tax. I believe he's shown me a way of saving two or three hundred pounds on my next return.'

Michael, looking for new talent, often took him to the play in the evenings, either in London or the suburbs; they would fetch Julia after the performance, and the three of them supped together. Now and then Michael asked Tom to play golf with him on Sundays and then if there was no party would bring him home to dinner.

'Nice to have a young fellow like that around,' he said. 'It keeps one from growing rusty.'

Tom was very pleasant about the house. He would play backgammon with Michael, or patience with Julia, and when they turned on the gramophone he was always there to change the records.

'He'll be a nice friend for Roger,' said Michael. 'Tom's got his head screwed on his shoulders the right way, and he's a lot older than Roger. He ought to have a good influence on him. Why don't you ask him to come and spend his holiday with us?'

('Lucky I'm a good actress.') But it wanted an effort to keep the joy out of her voice and to prevent her face from showing the exultation that made her heart beat so violently. 'That's not a bad idea,' she answered. 'I'll ask him if you like.'

Their play was running through August, and Michael had taken a house at Taplow so that they could spend the height of the summer there. Julia was to come up for her performances and Michael when business needed it, but she would have the day in the country and Sundays.

Tom had a fortnight's holiday; he accepted the invitation with alacrity.

But one day Julia noticed that he was unusually silent. He looked pale and his buoyant spirits had deserted him. She knew that something was wrong, but he would not tell her what it was; he would only say that he was worried to death. At last she forced him to confess that he had got into debt and was being dunned by tradesmen. The life into which she had led him had made him spend more money than he could afford, and ashamed of his cheap clothes at the grand parties to which she took him, he had gone to an expensive tailor and ordered himself new suits. He had backed a horse hoping to make enough money to get square and the horse was beaten. To Julia it was a very small sum that he owed, a hundred and twenty-five pounds, and she found it absurd that anyone should allow a trifle like that to upset him. She said at once that she would give it to him.

'Oh, I couldn't. I couldn't take money from a woman.'

He went scarlet; the mere thought of it made him ashamed. Julia used all her arts of cajolery. She reasoned, she pretended to be affronted, she even cried a little, and at last as a great favour he consented to borrow the money from her. Next day she sent him a letter in which were bank notes to the value of two hundred pounds. He rang her up and told her that she had sent far more than he wanted.

'Oh, I know people always lie about their debts,' she said with a laugh. 'I'm sure you owe more than you said.

'I promise you I don't. You're the last person I'd lie to.'

'Then keep the rest for anything that turns up. I hate seeing you pay the bill when we go out to supper. And taxis and all that sort of thing.'

'No, really. It's so humiliating.'

'What nonsense! You know I've got more money than I know what do do with. Can you grudge me the happiness it gives me to get you out of a hole?'

'It's awfully kind of you. You don't know what a relief it is. I don't know how to thank you.'

But his voice was troubled. Poor lamb, he was so conventional. But it was true, it gave her a thrill she had never known before to give him money; it excited in her a surprising passion. And she had another scheme in her head which during the fortnight Tom was to spend at Taplow she thought she could easily work. Tom's bed-sitting room in Tavistock Square had at first seemed to her charming in its sordidness, and the humble furniture had touched her heart. But time had robbed it of these moving characteristics. Once or twice she had met people on the stairs and thought they stared at her strangely. There was a slatternly housekeeper who made Tom's room and cooked his breakfast, and Julia had a feeling that she knew what was going on and was spying on her. Once the locked door had been tried while Julia was in the room, and when she went out the housekeeper was dusting the banisters. She gave Julia a sour look. Julia hated the smell of stale food that hung about the stairs and with her quick eyes she soon discovered that Tom's room was none too clean. The dingy curtains, the worn carpet, the shoddy furniture; it all rather disgusted her. Now it happened that a little while before, Michael, always on the look out for a good investment, had bought a block of garages near Stanhope Place. By letting off those he did not want he found that he could get their own for nothing. There were a number of rooms over. He divided them into two small flats, one for their chauffeur and one which he proposed to let. This was still vacant and Julia suggested to Tom that he should take it. It would be wonderful. She could slip along and see him for an hour when he got back from the office; sometimes she could drop in after the theatre and no one would be any the wiser. They would be free there. She talked to him of the fun they would have furnishing it; she was sure they had lots of things in their house that they did not want, and by storing them he would be doing them a kindness. The rest they would buy together. He was tempted by the idea of having a flat of his own, but it was out of the question; the rent, though small, was beyond his means. Julia knew that. She knew also that if she offered to pay it herself he would indignantly refuse. But she had a notion that during that idle, luxurious fortnight by the river she would be able to overcome his scruples. She saw how much the idea tempted him, and she had little doubt that she could devise some means to persuade him that by falling in with her proposal he was really doing her a service.

'People don't want reasons to do what they'd like to,' she reflected. 'They want excuses.'

Julia looked forward to Tom's visit to Taplow with excitement. It would be lovely to go on the river with him in the morning and in the afternoon sit about the garden with him. With Roger in the house she was determined that there should be no nonsense between her and Tom; decency forbad. But it would be heaven to spend nearly all day with him. When she had matinées he could amuse himself with Roger.

But things did not turn out at all as she expected. It had never occurred to her that Roger and Tom would take a great fancy to one another. There were five years between them and she thought, or would have if she had thought about it at all, that Tom would look upon Roger as a hobbledehoy, quite nice of course, but whom you treated as such, who fetched and carried for you and whom you told to go and play when you did not want to be bothered with him. Roger was seventeen. He was a nice-looking boy, with reddish hair and blue eyes, but that was the best you could say of him. He had neither his mother's vivacity and changing expression nor his father's beauty of feature. Julia was somewhat disappointed in him. As a child when she had been so constantly photographed with him he was lovely. He was rather stolid now and he had a serious look. Really when you came to examine him his only good features were his teeth and his hair. Julia was very fond of him, but she could not but find him a trifle dull. When she was alone with him the time hung somewhat heavily on her hands. She exhibited a lively interest in the things she supposed must interest him, cricket and such like, but he did not seem to have much to say about them. She was afraid he was not very intelligent.

'Of course he's young,' she said hopefully. 'Perhaps he'll improve as he grows older.'

From the time that he first went to his preparatory school she had seen little of him. During the holidays she was always acting at night and he went out with his father or with a boy friend, and on Sundays he and his father played golf together. If she happened to be lunching out it often happened that she did not see him for two or three days together except for a few minutes in the morning when he came to her room. It was a pity he could not always have remained a sweetly pretty little boy who could play in her room without disturbing her and be photographed, smiling into the camera, with his arm round her neck. She went down to see him at Eton occasionally and had tea with him. It flattered her that there were several photographs of her in his room. She was conscious that when she went to Eton it created quite a little excitement, and Mr Brackenbridge, in whose house he was, made a point of being very polite to her. When the half ended Michael and Julia had already moved to Taplow and Roger came straight there. Julia kissed him emotionally. He was not so much excited at getting home as she had expected him to be. He was rather casual. He seemed suddenly to have grown very sophisticated.

He told Julia at once that he desired to leave Eton at Christmas, he thought he had got everything out of it that he could, and he wanted to go to Vienna for a few months and learn German before going up to Cambridge. Michael had wished him to go into the army, but this he had set his face against. He did not yet know what he wanted to be. Both Julia and Michael had from the first been obsessed by the fear that he would go on the stage, but for this apparently he had no inclination.

'Anyhow he wouldn't be any good,' said Julia.

He led his own life. He went out on the river and lay about the garden reading. On his seventeenth birthday Julia had given him a very smart roadster, and in this he careered about the country at breakneck speeds.

'There's one comfort,' said Julia. 'He's no bother. He seems quite capable of amusing himself.'

On Sundays they had a good many people down for the day, actors and actresses, an occasional writer, and a sprinkling of some of their grander friends. Julia found these parties very amusing and she knew that people liked to come to them. On the first Sunday after Roger's arrival there was a great mob. Roger was very polite to the guests. He did his duty as part host like a man of the world. But it seemed to Julia that he held himself in some curious way aloof, as though he were playing a part in which he had not lost himself, and she had an uneasy feeling that he was not accepting all these people, but coolly judging them. She had an impression that he took none of them very seriously.

Tom had arranged to come on the following Saturday and she drove him down after the theatre. It was a moonlit night and at that hour the roads were empty. The drive was enchanting. Julia would have liked it to go on for ever. She nestled against him and every now and then in the darkness he kissed her.

'Are you happy?' she asked.

'Absolutely.'

Michael and Roger had gone to bed, but supper was waiting for them in the dining-room. The silent house gave them the feeling of being there without leave. They might have been a couple of wanderers who had strolled out of the night into a strange house and found a copious repast laid out for them. It was romantic. It had a little the air of a tale in the *Arabian Nights*. Julia showed him his room, which was next door to Roger's, and then went to bed. She did not wake till late next morning. It was a lovely day. So that she might have Tom all to herself she had not asked anybody down. When she was dressed they would go on the river together. She had her breakfast and her bath. She put on a little white frock that suited the sunny riverside and her, and a large-brimmed red straw hat whose colour threw a warm glow on her face. She was very little made-up. She looked at herself in the glass and smiled with satisfaction. She really looked very pretty and young. She strolled down into the garden. There was a lawn that stretched down to the river, and here she saw Michael surrounded by the Sunday papers. He was alone.

'I thought you'd gone to play golf.'

'No, the boys have gone. I thought they'd have more fun if I let them go alone.' He smiled in his friendly way. 'They're a bit too active for me. They were bathing at eight o'clock this morning, and as soon as they'd swallowed their breakfast they bolted off in Roger's car.'

'I'm glad they've made friends.'

Julia meant it. She was slightly disappointed that she would not be able to go on the river with Tom, but she was anxious that Roger should like him, she had a feeling that Roger did not like people indiscriminately; and after all she had the next fortnight to be with Tom.

'They make me feel damned middle-aged, I don't mind telling you that,' Michael remarked.

'What nonsense. You're much more beautiful than either of them, and well you know it, my pet.'

Michael thrust out his jaw a little and pulled in his belly.

The boys did not come back till luncheon was nearly ready.

'Sorry we're so late,' said Roger. 'There was a filthy crowd and we had to wait on nearly every tee. We halved the match.'

They were hungry and thirsty, excited and pleased with themselves.

'It's grand having no one here to-day,' said Roger. 'I was

afraid you'd got a whole gang coming and we'd have to behave like little gentlemen.'

'I thought a rest would be rather nice,' said Julia.

Roger gave her a glance.

'It'll do you good, mummy. You're looking awfully fagged.'

('Blast his eyes. No, I mustn't show I mind. Thank God, I can act.')

She laughed gaily.

'I had a sleepless night wondering what on earth we were going to do about your spots.'

'I know, aren't they sickening? Tom says he used to have them too.'

Julia looked at Tom. In his tennis shirt open at the neck, with his hair ruffled, his face already caught by the sun, he looked incredibly young. He really looked no older than Roger.

'Anyhow, his nose is going to peel,' Roger went on with a chuckle. 'He'll look a sight then.'

Julia felt slightly uneasy. It seemed to her that Tom had shed the years so that he was become not only in age Roger's contemporary. They talked a great deal of nonsense. They ate enormously and drank tankards of beer. Michael, eating and drinking as sparingly as usual, watched them with amusement. He was enjoying their youth and their high spirits. He reminded Julia of an old dog lying in the sun and gently beating his tail on the ground as he looked at a pair of puppies gambolling about him. They had coffee on the lawn. Julia found it very pleasant to sit there in the shade, looking at the river. Tom was slim and graceful in his long white trousers. She had never seen him smoke a pipe before. She found it strangely touching. But Roger mocked him.

'Do you smoke it because it makes you feel manly or because you like it?'

'Shut up,' said Tom.

'Finished your coffee?'

'Yes.'

'Come on then, let's go on the river.'

Tom gave her a doubtful look. Roger saw it.

'Oh, it's all right, you needn't bother about my respected parents, they've got the Sunday papers. Mummy's just given me a racing punt.'

('I must keep my temper. I must keep my temper. Why was I such a fool as to give him a racing punt?')

'All right,' she said, with an indulgent smile, 'go on the river, but don't fall in.'

'It won't hurt us if we do. We'll be back for tea. Is the court marked out, daddy? We're going to play tennis after tea.'

'I daresay your father can get hold of somebody and you can have a four.'

'Oh, don't bother. Singles are better fun really and one gets more exercise.' Then to Tom. 'I'll race you to the boathouse.'

Tom leapt to his feet and dashed off with Roger in quick pursuit. Michael took up one of the papers and looked for his spectacles.

'They've clicked all right, haven't they?'

'Apparently.'

'I was afraid Roger would be rather bored alone here with us. It'll be fine for him to have someone to play around with.'

'Don't you think Roger's rather inconsiderate?'

'You mean about the tennis? Oh, my dear, I don't really care if I play or not. It's only natural that those two boys should want to play together. From their point of view I'm an old man, and they think I'll spoil their game. After all the great thing is that they should have a good time.'

Julia had a pang of remorse. Michael was prosy, near with his money, self-complacent, but how extraordinarily kind he was and how unselfish! He was devoid of envy. It gave him a real satisfaction, so long as it did not cost money, to make other people happy. She read his mind like an open book. It was true that he never had any but a commonplace thought; on the other hand he never had a shameful one. It was exasperating that with so much to make him worthy of her affection, she should be so excruciatingly bored by him.

'I think you're a much better man that I am a woman, my sweet,' she said.

He gave her his good, friendly smile and slightly shook his head.

'No, dear, I had a wonderful profile, but you've got genius.'

Julia giggled. There was a certain fun to be got out of a man who never knew what you were talking about. But what did they mean when they said an actress had genius? Julia had often asked herself what it was that had placed her at last head and shoulders above her contemporaries. She had had detractors. At one time people had compared her unfavourably with some actress or other who at the moment enjoyed the public favour, but now no one disputed her supremacy. It was true that she had not the world-wide notoriety of the film-stars; she had tried her luck on the pictures, but had achieved no success; her face on the stage so mobile and expressive for some reason lost on the screen, and after one trial she had with Michael's approval refused to accept any of the offers that were from time to time made her. She had got a good deal of useful publicity out of her dignified attitude. But Julia did not envy the film-stars; they came and went; she stayed. When it was possible she went to see the performance of actresses who played leading parts on the London stage. She was generous in her praise of them and her praise was sincere. Sometimes she honestly thought them so very good that she could not understand why people made so much fuss over her. She was much too intelligent not to know in what estimation the public held her, but she was modest about herself. It always surprised her when people raved over something she had done that came to her so naturally that she had never thought it possible to do anything else. The critics admired her variety. They praised especially her capacity for insinuating herself into a part. She was not aware that she deliberately observed people, but when she came to study a new part vague recollections surged up in her from she knew not where, and she found that she knew things about the character she was to represent that she had had no inkling of. It helped her to think of someone she knew or even someone she had seen in the street or at a party; she combined with this recollection her own personality, and thus built up a character founded on fact but enriched with her experience, her knowledge of technique and her amazing magnetism. People thought that she only acted during the two or three hours she was on the stage; they did not know that the character she was playing dwelt in the back of her mind all day long, when she was talking to others with all the appearance of attention, or in whatever business she was engaged. It often seemed to her that she was two persons, the actress, the popular favourite, the best-dressed woman in London, and that was a shadow; and the woman she was playing at night, and that was the substance.

'Damned if I know what genius is,' she said to herself. 'But I know this, I'd give all I have to be eighteen.'

But she knew that wasn't true. If she were given the chance to go back again would she take it? No. Not really. It was not the popularity, the celebrity if you like, that she cared for, nor the hold she had over audiences, the real love they bore her, it was certainly not the money this had brought her; it was the power she felt in herself, her mastery over the medium, that thrilled her. She could step into a part, not a very good one perhaps, with silly words to say, and by her personality, by the dexterity which she had at her fingertips, infuse it with life. There was no one who could do what she could with a part. Sometimes she felt like God.

'And besides,' she chuckled, 'Tom wouldn't be born.'

After all it was very natural that he should like to play about with Roger. They belonged to the same generation. It was the first day of his holiday, she must let him enjoy himself; there was a whole fortnight more. He would soon get sick of being all the time with a boy of seventeen. Roger was sweet, but he was dull; she wasn't going to let maternal affection blind her to that. She must be very careful not to show that she was in the least put out. From the beginning she had made up her mind that she would never make any claim on Tom; it would be fatal if he felt that he owed something to her.

'Michael, why don't you let that flat in the mews to Tom? Now that he's passed his exam and is a chartered accountant he can't go on living in a bed-sitting room.'

'That's not a bad idea. I'll suggest it to him.'

'It would save an agent's fees. We could help him to furnish it. We've got a lot of stuff stored away. We might just as well let him use it as have it moulder away in the attics.'

Tom and Roger came back to eat an enormous tea and then played tennis till the light failed. After dinner they played dominoes. Julia gave a beautiful performance of a still young mother fondly watching her son and his boy friend. She went to bed early. Presently they too went upstairs. Their rooms were just over hers. She heard Roger go into Tom's room. They began talking, her windows and theirs were open, and she heard their voices in animated conversation. She wondered with exasperation what they found to say to one another. She had never found either of them very talkative. After a while Michael's voice interrupted them.

'Now then, you kids, you go to bed. You can go on talking to-morrow.'

She heard them laugh.

'All right, daddy,' cried Roger.

'A pair of damned chatterboxes, that's what you are.'

She heard Roger's voice again.

'Well, good-night, old boy.'

And Tom's hearty answer: 'So long, old man.'

'Idiots!' she said to herself crossly.

Next morning while she was having her breakfast Michael came into Julia's room.

'The boys have gone off to play golf at Huntercombe. They want to play a couple of rounds and they asked if they need come back to lunch. I told them that was quite all right.'

'I don't know that I particularly like the idea of Tom treating the house as if it was a hotel.'

'Oh, my dear, they're only a couple of kids. Let them have all the fun they can get, I say.'

She would not see Tom at all that day, for she had to start for London between five and six in order to get to the theatre in good time. It was all very well for Michael to be so damned good-natured about it. She was hurt. She felt a little inclined to cry. He must be entirely indifferent to her, it was Tom she was thinking of now; and she had made up her mind that to-day was going to be quite different from the day before. She had awakened determined to be tolerant and to take things as they came, but she hadn't been prepared for a smack in the face like this.

'Have the papers come yet?' she asked sulkily.

She drove up to town with rage in her heart.

The following day was not much better. The boys did not go off to play golf, but they played tennis. Their incessant activity profoundly irritated Julia. Tom in shorts, with his bare legs, and a cricket shirt, really did not look more than sixteen. Bathing as they did three or four times a day he could not get his hair to stay down, and the moment it was dry it spread over his head in unruly curls. It made him look younger than ever, but oh, so charming. Julia's heart was wrung. And it seemed to her that his demeanour had strangely changed; in the constant companionship of Roger he had shed the young man about town who was so careful of his dress, so particular about wearing the right thing, and was become again a sloppy little schoolboy. He never gave a hint, no glance even betrayed, that he was her lover; he treated her as if she were no more than Roger's mother. In every remark he made, in his mischievousness, in his polite little ways, he made her feel that she belonged to an older generation. His behaviour had nothing of the chivalrous courtesy a young man might show to a fascinating woman; it was the tolerant kindness he might display to a maiden aunt.

Julia was irritated that Tom should docilely follow the lead of a boy so much younger than himself. It indicated lack of character. But she did not blame him; she blamed Roger. Roger's selfishness revolted her. It was all very well to say he was young. His indifference to anyone's pleasure but his own showed a vile disposition. He was tactless and inconsiderate. He acted as though the house, the servants, his father and mother were there for his particular convenience. She would often have been rather sharp with him, but that she did not dare before Tom assume the rôle of the correcting mother. And when you reproved Roger he had a maddening way of looking deeply hurt, like a stricken hind, which made you feel that you had been unkind and unjust. She could look like that too, it was an expression of the eyes that he had inherited from her; she had used it over and over again on the stage with moving effect, and she knew it need not mean very much, but when she saw it in his it shattered her. The mere thought of it now made her feel tenderly towards him. And that sudden change of feeling showed her the truth; she was jealous of Roger, madly jealous. The realization gave her something of a shock; she did not know whether to laugh or to be ashamed. She reflected a moment.

'Well, I'll cook his goose all right.'

She was not going to let the following Sunday pass like the last. Thank God, Tom was a snob. 'A woman attracts men by her charm and holds them by their vices,' she murmured and wondered whether she had invented the aphorism or remembered it from some play she had once acted in.

She gave instructions for some telephoning to be done.

She got the Dennorants to come for the week-end. Charles Tamerley was staying at Henley and accepted an invitation to come over for Sunday and bring his host, Sir Mayhew Bryanston, who was Chancellor of the Exchequer. To amuse him and the Dennorants, because she knew that the upper classes do not want to meet one another in what they think is Bohemia, but artists of one sort or another, she asked Archie Dexter, her leading man, and his pretty wife who acted under her maiden name of Grace Hardwill.She felt pretty sure that with a marquess and marchioness to hover round and a Cabinet Minister to be impressed by, Tom would not go off to play golf with Roger or spend the afternoon in a punt. In such a party Roger would sink into his proper place of a schoolboy that no one took any notice of, and Tom would see how brilliant she could be when she took the trouble. In the anticipation of her triumph she managed to bear the intervening days with fortitude. She saw little of Roger and Tom. On her matinée days she did not see them at all. If they were not playing some game they were careering about the country in Roger's car.

Julia drove the Dennorants down after the play. Roger had gone to bed, but Michael and Tom were waiting up to have supper with them. It was a very good supper. The servants had gone to bed too and they helped themselves. Julia noticed the shy eagerness with which Tom saw that the Dennorants had everything they wanted, and his alacrity to jump up if he could be of service. His civility was somewhat officious. The Dennorants were an unassuming young couple to whom it had never occurred that their rank could impress anyone, and George Dennorant was a little embarrassed when Tom took away his dirty plate and handed him a dish to help himself to the next course.

'No golf for Roger to-morrow, I think,' said Julia to herself.

They stayed up talking and laughing till three in the morning, and when Tom said good night to her his eyes were shining; but whether from love or champagne she did not know. He pressed her hand.

'What a lovely party,' he said.

It was late when Julia, dressed in organdie, looking her best, came down into the garden. She saw Roger in a long chair with a book.

'Reading?' she said, lifting her really beautiful eye-brows. 'Why aren't you playing golf?'

Roger looked a trifle sulky.

'Tom said it was too hot.'

'Oh?' she smiled charmingly. 'I was afraid you thought you ought to stay and entertain my guests. There are going to be so many people, we could easily have managed without you. Where are the others?'

'I don't know. Tom's making chichi with Cecily Denn-orant.'

'She's very pretty, you know.'

'It looks to me as though it's going to be a crashing bore to-day.'

'I hope Tom won't find it so,' she said, as though she were seriously concerned.

Roger remained silent.

The day passed exactly as she had hoped. It was true that she saw little of Tom, but Roger saw less. Tom made a great hit with the Dennorants; he explained to them how they could get out of paying as much income-tax as they did. He listened respectfully to the Chancellor while he discoursed on the stage and to Archie Dexter while he gave his views on the political situation. Julia was at the top of her form. Archie Dexter had a quick wit, a fund of stage stories and a wonderful gift for telling them; between the two of them they kept the table during lunch-eon laughing uproariously; and after tea, when the tennis players were tired of playing tennis, Julia was persuaded (not much against her will) to do her imitations of Gladys Cooper, Constance Collier and Gertie Lawrence. But Julia did not forget that Charles Tamerley was her devoted, unrewarded lover, and she took care to have a little stroll alone with him in the gloaming. With him she sought to be neither gay nor brilliant, she was tender and wistful. Her heart ached, notwithstanding the scintillating performance she had given during the day; and it was with almost complete sincerity that with sighs, sad looks and broken sentences, she made him understand that her life was hollow and despite the long continued success of her career she could not but feel that she had missed something. Sometimes she thought of the villa at Sorrento on the bay of Naples. A beautiful dream. Happiness might have been hers for the asking, perhaps; she had been a fool; after all what were the triumphs of the stage but illusion? *Pagliacci*. People never realized how true that was; *Vesti la giubba* and all that sort of thing. She was desperately lonely. Of course there was no need to tell Charles that her heart ached not for lost opportunities, but because a young man seemed to prefer playing golf with her son to making love to her.

But then Julia and Archie Dexter got together. After dinner when they were all sitting in the drawing-room, without warning, starting with a few words of natural conversation they burst, as though they were lovers, into a jealous quarrel. For a moment the rest did not realize it was a joke till their mutual accusations became so outrageous and indecent that they were consumed with laughter. Then they played an extempore scene of an intoxicated gentleman picking up a French tart in Jermyn Street. After that, with intense seriousness, while their little audience shook with laughter, they did Mrs Alving in 'Ghosts' trying to seduce Pastor Manders. They finished with a performance that they had given often enough before at theatrical parties to enable them to do it with effect. This was a Chekov play in English, but in moments of passion breaking into something that sounded exactly like Russian. Julia exercised all her great gift for tragedy, but underlined it with a farcical emphasis, so that the effect was incredibly funny. She put into her performance the real anguish of her heart, and with her lively sense of the ridiculous made a mock of it. The audience rolled about in their chairs; they held their sides; they groaned in an agony of laughter. Perhaps Julia had never acted before. She was acting for Tom and for him alone.

'I've seen Bernhardt and Réjane,' said the Chancellor; 'I've seen Duse and Ellen Terry and Mrs Kendal. *Nunc Dimittis.*'

Julia, radiant, sank back into a chair and swallowed at a draught a glass of champagne.

'If I haven't cooked Roger's goose I'll eat my hat,' she thought.

But for all that the two lads had gone off to play golf when she came downstairs next morning. Michael had taken the Dennorants up to town. Julia was tired. She found it an effort to be bright and chatty when Tom and Roger came in to lunch. In the afternoon the three of them went on the river, but Julia had the feeling that they took her, not because they much wanted to, but because they could not help it. She stifled a sigh when she reflected how much she had looked forward to Tom's holiday. Now she was counting the days that must pass till it ended. She drew a deep breath of relief when she got into the car to go to London. She was not angry with Tom, but deeply hurt; she was exasperated with herself because she had so lost control over her feelings. But when she got into the theatre she felt that she shook off the obsession of him like a bad dream from which one awoke; there, in her dressing-rom, she regained possession of herself and the affairs of the common round of daily life faded to insignificance. Nothing really mattered when she had within her grasp this possibility of freedom.

Thus the week went by. Michael, Roger and Tom enjoyed themselves. They bathed, they played tennis, they played golf, they lounged about on the river. There were only four days more. There were only three days more.

('I can stick it out now. It'll be different when we're

back in London again. I mustn't show how miserable I am. I must pretend it's all right.')

'A snip having this spell of fine weather,' said Michael. 'Tom's been a success, hasn't he? Pity he can't stay another week.'

'Yes, a terrible pity.'

'I think he's a nice friend for Roger to have. A thoroughly normal, clean-minded English boy.'

'Oh, thoroughly.' ('Bloody fool, bloody fool.')

'To see the way they eat is a fair treat.'

'Yes, they seem to have enjoyed their food.' ('My God, I wish it could have choked them.')

Tom was to go up to town by an early train on Monday morning. The Dexters, who had a house at Bourne End, had asked them all to lunch on Sunday. They were to go down in the launch. Now that Tom's holiday was nearly over Julia was glad that she had never by so much as a lifted eyebrow betrayed her irritation. She was certain that he had no notion how deeply he had wounded her. After all she must be tolerant, he was only a boy, and if you must cross your t's, she was old enough to be his mother. It was a bore that she had a thing about him, but there it was, she couldn't help it; she had told herself from the beginning that she must never let him feel that she had any claims on him. No one was coming to dinner on Sunday. She would have liked to have Tom to herself on his last evening; that was impossible, but at all events they could go for a stroll by themselves in the garden.

'I wonder if he's noticed that he hasn't kissed me since he came here?'

They might go out in the punt. It would be heavenly to lie in his arms for a few minutes; it would make up for everything.

The Dexters' party was theatrical. Grace Hardwill, Archie's wife, played in musical comedy, and there was a bevy of pretty girls who danced in the piece in which she was then appearing. Julia acted with great naturalness the part of a leading lady who put on no frills. She was charming to the young ladies, with their waved platinum hair, who earned three pounds a week in the chorus. A good many of the guests had brought Kodaks and she submitted with affability to being photographed. She applauded enthusiastically when Grace Hardwill sang her famous song to the accompaniment of the composer. She laughed as heartily as anyone when the comic woman did an imitation of her in one of her best-known parts. It was all very gay, rather rowdy, and agreeably light-hearted. Julia enjoyed herself, but when it was seven o'clock was not sorry to go. She was thanking her hosts effusively for the pleasant party when Roger came up to her.

'I say, mum, there's a whole crowd going on to Maidenhead to dine and dance, and they want Tom and me to go too. You don't mind, do you?'

The blood rushed to her cheeks. She could not help answering rather sharply.

'How are you to get back?'

'Oh, that'll be all right. We'll get someone to drop us.'

She looked at him helplessly. She could not think what to say.

'It's going to be a tremendous lark. Tom's crazy to go.'

Her heart sank. It was with the greatest difficulty that she managed not to make a scene. But she controlled herself.

'All right, darling. But don't be too late. Remember that Tom's got to rise with the lark.'

Tom had come up and heard the last words.

'You're sure you don't mind?' he asked.

'Of course not. I hope you'll have a grand time.'

She smiled brightly at him, but her eyes were steely with hatred.

'I'm just as glad those two kids have gone off,' said Michael when they got into the launch. 'We haven't had an evening to ourselves for ever so long.'

She clenched her hands in order to prevent herself from telling him to hold his silly tongue. She was in a black rage. This was the last straw. Tom had neglected her for a fortnight, he had not even treated her with civility, and she had been angelic. There wasn't a woman in the world who would have shown such patience. Any other woman would have told him that if he couldn't behave with common decency he'd better get out. Selfish, stupid and common, that's what he was. She almost wished he wasn't going to-morrow so that she could have the pleasure of turning him out bag and baggage. And to dare to treat her like that, a two-penny half-penny little man in the city; poets, cabinet ministers, peers of the realm would be only to glad to break the most important engagements to have the chance of dining with her, and he threw her over to go and dance with a pack of peroxide blondes who couldn't act for nuts. That showed what a fool he was. You would have thought he'd have some gratitude. Why, the very clothes he had on she'd paid for. That cigarette-case he was so proud of, hadn't she given him that? And the ring he wore. My God, she'd get even with him. Yes, and she knew how she could do it. She knew where he was most sensitive and how she could most cruelly wound him. That would get him on the raw. She felt a faint sensation of relief as she turned the scheme over in her mind. She was impatient to carry out her part of it at once, and they had no sooner got home than she went up to her room. She got four single pounds out of her bag and a ten-shilling note. She wrote a brief letter.

DEAR TOM,

I'm enclosing the money for your tips as I shan't see you in the morning. Give three pounds to the butler, a pound to the maid who's been valeting you, and ten shillings to the chauffeur.

JULIA.

She sent for Evie and gave instructions that the letter should be given to Tom by the maid who awoke him. When she went down to dinner she felt much better. She carried on an animated conversation with Michael while they dined and afterwards they played six pack bezique. If she had racked her brains for a week she couldn't have thought of anything that would humiliate Tom more bitterly.

But when she went to bed she could not sleep. She was waiting for Roger and Tom to come home. A notion came to her that made her restless. Perhaps Tom would realize that he had behaved rottenly, if he gave it a moment's thought he must see how unhappy he was making her; it might be that he would be sorry and when he came in, after he had said good night to Roger, he would creep down to her room. If he did that she would forgive everything. The letter was probably in the butler's pantry; she could easily slip down and get it back. At last a car drove up. She turned on her light to look at the time. It was three. She heard the two young men go upstairs and to their respective rooms. She waited. She put on the light by her bedside so that when he opened the door he should be able to see. She would pretend she was sleeping and then as he crept forward on tiptoe slowly open her eyes and smile at him. She waited. In the silent night she heard him get into bed and switch off the light. She stared straight in front of her for a minute, then with a shrug of the shoulders opened a drawer by her bedside and from a little bottle took a couple of sleeping-tablets.

'If I don't sleep I shall go mad.'

15

Julia did not wake till after eleven. Among her letters was one that had not come by post. She recognized Tom's neat, commercial hand and tore it open. It contained nothing but the four pounds and the ten-shilling note. She felt slightly sick. She did not quite know what she had expected him to reply to her condescending letter and the humiliating present. It had not occurred to her that he would return it. She was troubled, she had wanted to hurt his feelings, but she had a fear now that she had gone too far.

'Anyhow I hope he tipped the servants,' she muttered to reassure herself. She shrugged her shoulders. 'He'll come round. It won't hurt him to discover that I'm not all milk and honey.'

But she remained thoughtful throughout the day. When she got to the theatre a parcel was waiting for her. As soon as she looked at the address she knew what it contained. Evie asked if she should open it.

'No.'

But the moment she was alone she opened it herself. There were the cuff-links and the waistcoat buttons, the pearl studs, the wrist-watch and the cigarette-case of which Tom was so proud. Not a word of explanation. Her heart sank and she noticed that she was trembling.

'What a damned fool I was! Why didn't I keep my temper?'

Her heart now beat painfully. She couldn't go on the stage with that anguish gnawing at her vitals, she would give a frightful performance; at whatever cost she must speak to him. There was a telephone in his house and an extension to his room. She rang him. Fortunately he was in.

'Tom.'

'Yes?'

He had paused for a moment before answering and his voice was peevish.

'What does this mean? Why have you sent me all those things?

'Did you get the notes this morning?'

'Yes. I couldn't make head or tail of it. Have I offended you?'

'Oh no,' he answered. 'I like being treated like a kept boy. I like having it thrown in my face that even my tips have to be given me. I thought it rather strange that you didn't send me the money for a third-class ticket back to London.'

Although Julia was in a pitiable state of anxiety, so that she could hardly get the words out of her mouth, she almost smiled at his fatuous irony. He was a silly little thing.

'But you can't imagine that I wanted to hurt your feelings. You surely know me well enough to know that's the last thing I should do.'

'That only makes it worse.' ('Damn and curse,' thought Julia.) 'I ought never to have let you make me those presents. I should never have let you lend me money.'

'I don't know what you mean. It's all some horrible misunderstanding. Come and fetch me after the play and we'll have it out. I know I can explain.'

'I'm going to dinner with my people and I shall sleep at home.'

'To-morrow then.'

'I'm engaged to-morrow.'

'I must see you, Tom. We've been too much to one another to part like this. You can't condemn me unheard. It's so unjust to punish me for no fault of mine.'

'I think it's much better that we shouldn't meet again.'

Julia was growing desperate.

'But I love you, Tom. I love you. Let me see you once more and then, if you're still angry with me, we'll call it a day.'

There was a long pause before he answered.

'All right. I'll come after the matinée on Wednesday.'

'Don't think unkindly of me, Tom.'

She put down the receiver. At all events he was coming. She wrapped up again the things he had returned to her, and hid them away where she was pretty sure Evie would not see them. She undressed, put on her old pink dressing-gown and began to make-up. She was out of humour: this was the first time she had ever told him that she loved him. It vexed her that she had been forced to humiliate herself by begging him to come and see her. Till then it had always been he who sought her company. She was not pleased to think that the situation between them now was openly reversed.

Julia gave a very poor performance at the matinée on Wednesday. The heat wave had affected business and the house was apathetic. Julia was indifferent. With that sickness of apprehension gnawing at her heart she could not care how the play went. ('What the hell do they want to come to the theatre for on a day like this anyway?') She was glad when it was over.

'I'm expecting Mr. Fennell,' she told Evie. 'While he's here I don't want to be disturbed.'

Evie did not answer. Julia gave her a glance and saw that she was looking grim.

('To hell with her. What do I care what she thinks!')

He ought to have been there by now. It was after five. He was bound to come; after all, he'd promised, hadn't he? She put on a dressing-gown, not the one she made up in, but a man's dressing-gown, in plum-coloured silk. Evie took an interminable time to put things straight.

'For God's sake don't fuss, Evie. Leave me alone.'

Evie did not speak. She went on methodically arranging the various objects on the dressing-table exactly as Julia always wanted them.

'Why the devil don't you answer when I speak to you?'

Evie turned round and looked at her. She thoughtfully rubbed her finger along her nostrils.

'Great actress you may be . . .'

'Get the hell out of here.'

After taking off her stage make-up Julia had done nothing to her face except put the very faintest shading of blue under her eyes. She had a smooth, pale skin and without rouge on her cheeks or red on her lips she looked wan. The man's dressing-gown gave an effect at once helpless, fragile and gallant. Her heart was beating painfully and she was very anxious, but looking at herself in the glass she murmured: Mimi in the last act of *Bohème*. Almost without meaning to she coughed once or twice consumptively. She turned off the bright lights on her dressing-table and lay down on the sofa. Presently there was a knock at the door and Evie announced Mr. Fennell. Julia held out a white, thin hand.

'I'm lying down. I'm afraid I'm not very well. Find yourself a chair. It's nice of you to come.'

'I'm sorry. What's the matter?'

'Oh, nothing.' She forced a smile to her ashy lips. 'I haven't been sleeping very well the last two or three nights.'

She turned her beautiful eyes on him and for a while gazed at him in silence. His expression was sullen, but she had a notion that he was frightened.

'I'm waiting for you to tell me what you've got against me,' she said at last in a low voice.

It trembled a little, she noticed, but quite naturally. ('Christ, I believe I'm frightened too.')

'There's no object in going back to that. The only thing I wanted to say to you was this: I'm afraid I can't pay you the two hundred pounds I owe you right away, I simply haven't got it, but I'll pay you by degrees. I hate having to ask you to give me time, but I can't help myself.'

She sat up on the sofa and put both her hands to her breaking heart.

'I don't understand. I've lain awake for two whole nights turning it all over in my mind. I thought I should go mad. I've been trying to understand. I can't. I can't.'

('What play did I say that in?')

'Oh yes, you can, you understand perfectly. You were angry with me and you wanted to get back on me. And you did. You got back on me all right. You couldn't have shown your contempt for me more clearly.'

'But why should I want to get back on you? Why should I be angry with you?'

'Because I went to Maidenhead with Roger to that party and you wanted me to come home.'

'But I told you to go. I said I hoped you'd have a good time.'

'I know you did, but your eyes were blazing with

125

passion. I didn't want to go, but Roger was keen on it. I told him I thought we ought to come back and dine with you and Michael, but he said you'd be glad to have us off your hands, and I didn't like to make a song and dance about it. And when I saw you were in a rage it was too late to get out of it.'

'I wasn't in a rage. I can't think how you got such an idea in your head. It was so natural that you should want to go to the party. You can't think I'm such a beast as to grudge you a little fun in your fortnight's holiday. My poor lamb, my only fear was that you would be bored. I so wanted you to have a good time.'

'Then why did you send me that money and write me that letter? It was so insulting.'

Julia's voice faltered. Her jaw began to tremble and the loss of control over her muscles was strangely moving. Tom looked away uneasily.

'I couldn't bear to think of you having to throw away your good money on tips. I know that you're not terribly rich and I knew you'd spent a lot on green fees. I hate women who go about with young men and let them pay for everything. It's so inconsiderate. I treated you just as I'd have treated Roger. I never thought it would hurt your feelings.'

'Will you swear that?'

'Of course I will. My God, is it possible that after all these months you don't know me better than that? If what you think were true, what a mean cruel, despicable woman I should be, what a cad, what a heartless, vulgar beast! Is that what you think I am?'

A poser.

'Anyhow it doesn't matter. I ought never to have accepted valuable presents from you and allowed you to lend me money. It's put me in a rotten position. Why I thought you despised me is that I can't help feeling that you've got a right to. The fact is I can't afford to run around with people who are so much richer than I am. I was a fool to think I could. It's been fun and I've had a grand time, but now I'm through. I'm not going to see you any more.'

She gave a deep sigh.

'You don't care two hoots for me. That's what that means.'

'That's not fair.'

'You're everything in the world to me. You know that. I'm so lonely and your friendship meant a great deal to me. I'm surrounded by hangers-on and parasites and I knew you were disinterested. I felt I could rely on you. I so loved being with you. You were the only person in the world with whom I could be entirely myself. Don't you know what a pleasure it was to me to help you a little? It wasn't for your sake I made you little presents, it was for my own; it made me so happy to see you using the things I'd given you. If you'd cared for me at all they wouldn't have humiliated you, you'd have been touched to owe me something.'

She turned her eyes on him once more. She could always cry easily, and she was really so miserable now that she did not have to make even a small effort. He had never seen her cry before. She could cry, without sobbing, her wonderful dark eyes wide open, with a face that was almost rigid. Great heavy tears ran down it. And her quietness, the immobility of the tragic body, were terribly moving. She hadn't cried like that since she cried in 'The Stricken Heart.' Christ, how that play had shattered her. She was not looking at Tom, she was looking straight in front of her; she was really distracted with grief, but, what was it? another self within her knew what she was doing, a self that shared in her unhappiness and yet watched its expression. She felt him go white. She felt a sudden anguish wring his heartstrings, she felt that his flesh and blood could not support the intolerable pain of hers.

'Julia.'

His voice was broken. She slowly turned her liquid eyes on him. It was not a woman crying that he saw, it was all the woe of human kind, it was the immeasurable, the inconsolable grief that is the lot of man. He threw himself down on his knees and took her in his arms. He was shattered.

'Dearest, dearest.'

For a minute she did not move. It was as if she did not know that he was there. He kissed her streaming eyes and with his mouth sought hers. She gave it to him as though she were powerless, as though, scarcely conscious of what was befalling her, she had no will left. With a scarcely perceptible movement she pressed her body to his and gradually her arms found their way round his neck. She lay in his arms, not exactly inert, but as though all the strength, all the vitality, had gone out of her. In his mouth he tasted the saltness of her tears. At last, exhausted, clinging to him with soft arms she sank back on the sofa. His lips clung to hers.

You would never have thought had you seen her a quarter of an hour later, so quietly gay, flushed a little, that so short a while before she had passed through such a tempest of weeping. They each had a whisky and soda and a cigarette and looked at one another with fond eyes.

'He's a sweet little thing,' she thought.

It occurred to her that she would give him a treat.

'The Duke and Duchess of Rickaby are coming to the play to-night and we're going to have supper at the Savoy. I suppose you wouldn't come, would you? I want a man badly to make a fourth.'

'If you'd like me to, of course I will.'

The heightened colour on his cheeks told her how excited he was to meet such distinguished persons. She did not tell him that the Rickabys would go anywhere for a free meal. Tom took back the presents that he had returned to her rather shyly, but he took them. When he had gone she sat down at the dressing-table and had a good look at herself.

'How lucky I am that I can cry without my eyelids

swelling,' she said. She massaged them a little. 'All the same, what mugs men are.'

She was happy. Everything would be all right now. She had got him back. But somewhere, at the back of her mind or in the bottom of her heart, was a feeling of ever so slight contempt for Tom because he was such a simple fool.

16

Their quarrel, destroying in some strange way the barrier between them, brought them closer together. Tom offered less resistance than she had expected when she mooted once more the question of the flat. It looked as though, after their reconciliation, having taken back her presents and consented to forget the loan, he had put aside his moral scruples. They had a lot of fun furnishing it. The chauffeur's wife kept it clean for him and cooked his breakfast. Julia had a key and would sometimes let herself in and sit by herself in the little sitting-room till he came back from his office. They supped together two or three times a week and danced, then drove back to the flat in a taxi. Julia enjoyed a happy autumn. The play they put on was a success. She felt alert and young. Roger was coming home at Christmas, but only for a fortnight, and was then going to Vienna. Julia expected him to monopolize Tom and she was determined not to mind. Youth naturally appealed to youth and she told herself that there was no reason for her to feel anxious if for a few days the two of them were so wrapped up in one another that Tom had no thought for her. She held him now. He was proud to be her lover, it gave him confidence in himself, and he was pleased to be on familiar terms with a large number of more or less distinguished persons whom after all he only knew through her. He was anxious now to join a good club and Julia was preparing the ground. Charles had never refused her anything, and with tact she was certain that she could wheedle him into proposing Tom for one of those to which he belonged. It was a new and delicious sensation for Tom to have money to spend; she encouraged him to be extravagant; she had a notion that he would get used to living in a certain way and then would realize that he could not do without her.

'Of course it can't last,' she told herself, 'but when it comes to an end it will have been a wonderful experience for him. It'll really have made a man of him.'

But though she told herself that it could not last she did not see really why it shouldn't. As the years went by and he grew older there wouldn't be any particular difference between them. He would no longer be so very young in ten or fifteen years and she would be just the same age as she was now. They were very comfortable together. Men were creatures of habit; that gave women such a hold on them. she did not feel a day older than he, and she was convinced that the disparity in their ages had never even occurred to him. It was true that on this point she had once had a moment's disquietude. She was lying on his bed. He was standing at the dressing-table, in his shirt sleeves, brushing his hair. She was stark naked and she lay in the position of a Venus by Titian that she remembered to have seen in a country house at which she had stayed. She felt that she made really a lovely picture, and in complete awareness of the charming sight she offered, held the pose. She was happy and satisfied.

'This is romance,' she thought, and a light, quick smile hovered over her lips.

He caught sight of her in the mirror, turned round and without a word, twitched the sheet over her. Though she smiled at him affectionately, it gave her quite a turn. Was he afraid that she would catch cold or was it that his English modesty was shocked at her nakedness? Or could it be that, his boyish lust satisfied, he was a trifle disgusted at the sight of her ageing body? When she got home she again took all her clothes off and examined herself in the looking-glass. She determined not to spare herself. She looked at her neck, there was no sign of age there, especially when she held her chin up; and her breasts were small and firm; they might have been a girl's. Her belly was flat, her hips were small, there was a very small roll of fat there, like a long sausage, but everyone had that, and anyhow Miss Phillips could have a go at it. No one could say that her legs weren't good, they were long and slim and comely; she passed her hands over her body, her skin was as soft as velvet and there wasn't a blemish on it. Of course there were a few wrinkles under her eyes, but you had to peer to see them; they said there was an operation now by which you could get rid of them, it might be worth while to inquire into that; it was lucky that her hair had retained its colour; however well hair was dyed, to dye hardened the face; hers remained a rich, deep brown. Her teeth were all right too.

'Prudishness, that's all it was.'

She had a moment's recollection of the Spaniard with the beard in the wagon-lit and she smiled roguishly at herself in the glass.

'No damned modesty about him.'

But all the same from that day on she took care to act up to Tom's standards of decency.

Julia's reputation was so good that she felt she need not hesitate to show herself with Tom in public places. It was a new experience for her to go to night-clubs, she enjoyed it, and though no one could have been better aware than she that she could go nowhere without being stared at, it never entered her head that such a change in her habits must excite comment. With twenty years of fidelity behind her, for of course she did not count the Spaniard, an accident that might happen to any woman, Julia was confident that no one would imagine for a moment that she was having an affair with a boy young enough to be her son. It never occurred to her that perhaps Tom was not always so discreet as he might have been. It never occurred to her that the look in her eyes when they danced together betrayed her. She looked upon her position as so privileged that it never occurred to her that people at last were beginning to gossip.

When this gossip reached the ears of Dolly de Vries she laughed. At Julia's request she had invited Tom to parties and once or twice had him down for a week-end in the country, but she had never paid any attention to him. He seemed a nice little thing, a useful escort for Julia when Michael was busy, but perfectly insignificant. He was one of those persons who everywhere pass unnoticed, and even after you had met him you could not remember what he was like. He was the extra man you invited to dinner to make an odd number even. Julia talked of him gaily as 'me boy friend' or as 'my young man'; she could hardly have been so cool about it, so open, if there were anything in it. Besides Dolly knew very well that the only two men there had ever been in Julia's life were Michael and Charles Tamerley. But it was funny of Julia, after taking so much care of herself for years, suddenly to start going to night clubs three or four times a week. Dolly had seen little of her of late and indeed had been somewhat piqued by her neglect. She had many friends in theatrical circles and she began to make enquiries. She did not at all like what she heard. She did not know what to think. One thing was evident, Julia couldn't know what was being said about her, and someone must tell her. Not she; she hadn't the courage. Even after all these years she was a little frightened of Julia. Julia was a very good-tempered woman, and though her language was often brusque it was hard to ruffle her; but there was something about her that prevented you from taking liberties with her; you had a feeling that if once you went too far you would regret it. But something must be done. Dolly turned the matter over in her mind for a fortnight, anxiously; she tried to put her own wounded feelings aside and look at it only from the point of view of Julia's career, and at last she came to the conclusion that Michael must speak to her. She had never liked Michael, but after all he was Julia's husband and it was her duty to tell him at least enough to make him put a stop to whatever was going on.

She rang Michael up and made an appointment with him at the theatre. Michael liked Dolly as little as she liked him, though for other reasons, and when he heard that she wanted to see him he swore. He was annoyed that he had never been able to induce her to sell out her shares in the management, and he resented whatever suggestions she made as an unwarrantable interference. But when she was shown into his office he greeted her with cordiality. He kissed her on both cheeks.

'Sit down and make yourself comfy. Come to see that the old firm's still raking in dividends for you?'

Dolly de Vries was now a woman of sixty. She was very fat, and her face, with its large nose and heavy red lips, seemed larger than life. There was a slightly masculine touch in her black satin dress, but she wore a double string of pearls round her neck, a diamond brooch at her waist and another in her hat. Her short hair was dyed a rich copper. Her lips and her fingernails were bright red. Her voice was loud and deep, but when she got excited the words were apt to tumble over one another and a slight cockney accent revealed itself.

'Michael, I'm upset about Julia.'

Michael, always the perfect gentleman, slightly raised his eyebrows and compressed his thin lips. He was not prepared to discuss his wife even with Dolly.

'I think she's doing a great deal too much. I don't know what's come over her. All these parties she's going to now. These night clubs and things. After all, she's not a young woman any more; she'll just wear herself out.'

'Oh, nonsense. She's as strong as a horse and she's in the best of health. She's looking younger than she has for years. You're not going to grudge her a bit of fun when her day's work is over. The part she's playing just now doesn't take it out of her; I'm very glad that she should want to go out and amuse herself. It only shows how much vitality she has.'

'She never cared for that sort of thing before. It seems so strange that she should suddenly take to dancing till two in the morning in the horrible atmosphere of those places.'

'It's the only exercise she gets. I can't expect her to put on shorts and come for a run with me in the park.'

'I think you ought to know that people are beginning to talk. It's doing her reputation a lot of harm.'

'What the devil d'you mean by that?'

'Well, it's absurd that at her age she should make herself so conspicuous with a young boy.'

He looked at her for a moment without understanding, and when he caught what she meant he laughed loud.

'Tom? Don't be such a fool, Dolly.'

'I'm not a fool. I know what I'm talking about. When anyone's as well known as Julia and she's always about with the same man naturally people talk.'

'But Tom's just as much my friend as hers. You know very well that I can't take Julia out dancing. I have to get up every morning at eight to get my exercise in before my day's work. Hang it all, I do know something about human nature after thirty years on the stage. Tom's a very good type of clean honest English boy and he's by way of being a gentleman. I daresay he admires Julia, boys of that age often think they're in love with women older than themselves, well, it won't do him any harm, it'll do him good; but to think Julia could possibly give him a thought – my poor Dolly, you make me laugh.'

'He's boring, he's dull, he's common and he's a snob.'

'Well, if you think he's all that doesn't it strike you as rather strange that Julia should be so wrapped up in him as you seem to think?'

'Only a woman knows what a woman can do.'

'That's not a bad line, Dolly. We shall have you writing a play next. Now let's get this straight. Can you look me in the face and tell me that you really think Julia is having an affair with Tom?'

She looked him in the face. Her eyes were anguished.

For though at first she had only laughed at what was being said about Julia she had not been able altogether to suppress the doubts that soon assailed her; she remembered a dozen little incidents that at the time had escaped her notice, but when considered in cold blood looked terribly suspicious. She had suffered such torture as she had never thought it possible to endure. Proof? She had no proof; she only had an intuition that she could not mistrust; she wanted to say yes, the impulse to do so was almost uncontrollable; she controlled it. She could not give Julia away. The fool might go and tell her and Julia would never speak to her again. He might have Julia watched and catch her out. No one could tell what might happen if she told the truth.

'No, I don't.'

Her eyes filled with tears and began to roll down her massive cheeks. Michael saw her misery. He thought her ridiculous, but he realized that she was suffering and in the kindness of his heart sought to console her.

'I was sure you didn't really. You know how fond Julia is of you, you mustn't be jealous, you know, if she has other friends.'

'God knows I don't grudge her anything,' she sobbed. 'She's been so different to me lately. She's been so cold. I've been such a loyal friend to her, Michael.'

'Yes, dear, I know you have.'

'Had I but served my God with half the zeal I served my King . . .'

'Oh, come now, it's not so bad as that. You know, I'm not the sort of chap to talk about his wife to other people. I always think that's such frightfully bad form. But you know, honestly you don't know the first thing about Julia. Sex doesn't mean a thing to her. When we were first married it was different, and I don't mind telling you after all these years that she made life a bit difficult for me. I don't say she was a nymphomaniac or anything like that, but she was inclined to be rather tiresome sometimes. Bed's all very well in its way, but there are other things

135

in life. But after Roger was born she changed completely. Having a baby settled her. All those instincts went into her acting. You've read Freud, Dolly; what does he call it when that happens?'

'Oh, Michael, what do I care about Freud?'

'Sublimation. That's it. I often think that's what's made her such a great actress. Acting's a whole time job and if you want to be really good you've got to give your whole self to it. I'm so impatient with the public who think actors and actresses lead a devil of a life. We haven't got the time for that sort of nonsense.'

What Michael was saying made her so angry that she recovered her self-control.

'But Michael, it may be that you and I know that there's nothing wrong in Julia's going about all the time with that miserable little pip-squeak. It's so bad for her reputation. After all, one of your great assets has been your exemplary married life. Everyone has looked up to you. The public has loved to think of you as such a devoted and united couple.'

'And so we are, damn it.'

Dolly was growing impatient.

'But I tell you people are talking. You can't be so stupid as not to see that they're bound to. I mean, if Julia had had one flagrant affair after another, nobody would take any notice, but after the life she's led for so many years suddenly to break out like this – naturally everybody starts chattering. It's so bad for business.'

Michael gave her a swift glance. He smiled a little.

'I see what you mean, Dolly. I daresay there's something in what you say and in the circumstances I feel that you have a perfect right to say it. You were awfully good to us when we started and I should hate to see you let down now. I'll tell you what, I'll buy you out.'

'Buy me out?'

Dolly straightened herself and her face, a moment ago rumpled and discomposed, hardened. She was seized with indignation. He went on suavely.

'I see your point. If Julia's gadding about all night it must tell on her performances. That's obvious. She's got a funny sort of public, a lot of old ladies come to our matinées because they think she's such a sweet good woman. I don't mind admitting that if she gets herself unpleasantly talked about it might have some effect on the takings. I know Julia well enough to know that she wouldn't put up with any interference with her liberty of action. I'm her husband and I've got to put up with it. But you're in a different position altogether. I shouldn't blame you if you wanted to get out while the going was good.'

Dolly was alert now. She was far from a fool and when it came to business was a match for Michael. She was angry, but her anger gave her self-control.

'I should have thought after all these years, Michael, that you knew me better than that. I thought it my duty to warn you, but I'm prepared to take the rough with the smooth. I'm not the woman to desert a sinking ship. I daresay I can afford to lose my money better than you can.'

It gave her a great deal of satisfaction to see the disappointment that was clearly expressed on Michael's face. She knew how much money meant to him and she had a hope that what she had said would rankle. He pulled himself together quickly.

'Well, think it over, Dolly.'

She gathered up her bag and they parted with mutual expressions of affection and good will.

'Silly old bitch,' he said when the door was closed behind her.

'Pompous old ass,' she hissed as she went down in the lift.

But when she got into her magnificent and very expensive car and drove back to Montagu Square she could not hold back the heavy, painful tears that filled her eyes. She felt old, lonely, unhappy, and desperately jealous.

17

Michael flattered himself on his sense of humour. On the Sunday evening that followed his conversation with Dolly he strolled into Julia's room while she was dressing. They were going to the pictures after an early dinner.

'Who's coming to-night besides Charles?' he asked her.

'I couldn't find another woman. I've asked Tom.'

'Good! I wanted to see him.'

He chuckled at the thought of the joke he had up his sleeve. Julia was looking forward to the evening. At the cinema she would arrange the seating so that Tom sat next to her and he would hold her hand while she chatted in undertones to Charles on the other side of her. Dear Charles, it was nice of him to have loved her so long and so devotedly; she would go out of her way to be very sweet to him. Charles and Tom arrived together. Tom was wearing his new dinner jacket for the first time and he and Julia exchanged a little private glance, of satisfaction on his part and of compliment on hers.

'Well, young feller,' said Michael heartily, rubbing his hands, 'do you know what I hear about you? I hear that you're compromising my wife.'

Tom gave him a startled look and went scarlet. The habit of flushing mortified him horribly, but he could not break himself of it.

'Oh my dear,' cried Julia gaily, 'how marvellous! I've been trying to get someone to compromise me all my life. Who told you, Michael?'

'A little bird,' he said archly.

'Well, Tom, if Michael divorces me you'll have to marry me, you know.'

Charles smiled with his gentle, rather melancholy eyes.

'What have you been doing, Tom?' he asked.

Charles was gravely, Michael boisterously, diverted by the young man's obvious embarrassment. Julia, though she seemed to share their amusement, was alert and watchful.

'Well, it appears that the young rip has been taking Julia to night clubs when she ought to have been in bed and asleep.'

Julia crowed with delight.

'Shall we deny it, Tom, or shall we brazen it out?'

'Well, I'll tell you what I said to the little bird,' Michael broke in. 'I said to her, as long as Julia doesn't want me to go to night clubs with her . . .'

Julia ceased to listen to what he said. Dolly, she thought, and oddly enough she described her to herself in exactly the words Michael had used a couple of days before. Dinner was announced and their bright talk turned to other things. But though Julia took part in it with gaiety, though she appeared to be giving her guests all her attention and even listened with a show of appreciation to one of Michael's theatrical stories that she had heard twenty times before, she was privately holding an animated conversation with Dolly. Dolly cowered before her while she told her exactly what she thought of her.

'You old cow,' she said to her. 'How dare you interfere with my private concerns? No, don't speak. Don't try to excuse yourself. I know exactly what you said to Michael. It was unpardonable. I thought you were a friend of mine. I thought I could rely on you. Well, that finishes it. I'll never speak to you again. Never. Never. D'you think I'm impressed by your rotten old money? Oh, it's no good saying you didn't mean it. Where would you be except for me, I should like to know. Any distinction you've got, the only importance you have in the world, is that you happen to know me. Who's made your parties go all these years? D'you think that people came to them to see you? They came to see me. Never again. Never.'

It was in point of fact a monologue rather than a conversation.

Later on, at the cinema, she sat next to Tom as she had intended and held his hand, but it seemed to her singularly unresponsive. Like a fish's fin. She suspected that he was thinking uncomfortably of what Michael had said. She wished that she had had an opportunity of a few words with him so that she might have told him not to worry. After all no one could have carried off the incident with more brilliance than she had. Aplomb; that was the word. She wondered what it was exactly that Dolly had told Michael. She had better find out. It would not do to ask Michael, that would look as though she attached importance to it; she must find out from Dolly herself. It would be much wiser not to have a row with her. Julia smiled as she thought of the scene she would have with Dolly. She would be sweetness itself, she would wheedle it all out of her, and never give her an inkling that she was angry. It was curious that it should send a cold shiver down her back to think that people were talking about her. After all if she couldn't do what she liked who could? Her private life was nobody's business. All the same one couldn't deny that it wouldn't be very nice if people were laughing at her. She wondered what Michael would do if he found out the truth. He couldn't very well divorce her and continue to manage for her. If he had any sense he'd shut his eyes. But Michael was funny in some ways; every now and then he would get up on his hind legs and start doing his colonel stuff. He was quite capable of saying all of a sudden that damn it all, he must behave like a gentleman. Men were such fools; there wasn't one of them who wouldn't cut off his nose to spite his face. Of course it wouldn't really matter very much to her. She could go and act in America for a year till the scandal had died down and then go into management with somebody else. But it would be a bore. And then there was Roger to consider; he'd feel it, poor lamb; he'd be humiliated, naturally; it was no good shutting one's eyes to the fact, at her age she'd look a perfect fool being divorced on account of a boy of three-and-twenty. Of course she wouldn't be such a fool as to marry Tom. Would Charles marry her? She turned and in the half-light looked at his distinguished profile. He had been madly in love with her for years; he was one of those chivalrous idiots that a woman could turn round her little finger; perhaps he wouldn't mind being co-respondent instead of Tom. That might be a very good way out. Lady Charles Tamerley. It sounded all right. Perhaps she *had* been a little imprudent. She had always been very careful when she went to Tom's flat, but it might be that one of the chauffeurs in the mews had seen her go in or come out and had thought things. That class of people had such filthy minds. As far as the night clubs were concerned, she'd have been only too glad to go with Tom to quiet little places where no one would see them, but he didn't like that. He loved a crowd, he wanted to see smart people, and be seen. He liked to show her off.

'Damn,' she said to herself. 'Damn, damn.'

Julia didn't enjoy her evening at the cinema as much as she had expected.

18

Next day Julia got Dolly on her private number.

'Darling, it seems ages since I've seen you. What have you been doing with yourself all this time?'

'Nothing very much.'

Dolly's voice sounded cold.

'Now listen, Roger's coming home to-morrow. You know he's leaving Eton for good. I'm sending the car for him early and I want you to come to lunch. Not a party; only you and me, Michael and Roger.'

'I'm lunching out to-morrow.'

In twenty years Dolly had never been engaged when Julia wanted her to do something with her. The voice at the other end of the telephone was hostile.

'Dolly, how can you be so unkind? Roger'll be terribly

disappointed. His first day at home; besides, I want to see you. I haven't seen you for ages and I miss you terribly. Can't you break your engagement, just for this once, darling, and we'll have a good old gossip after lunch, just you and me?'

No one could be more persuasive than Julia when she liked, no one could put more tenderness into her voice, nor a more irresistible appeal. There was a moment's pause and Julia knew that Dolly was struggling with her wounded feelings.

'All right, darling, I'll manage.'

'Darling.' But when she rang off Julia through clenched teeth muttered: 'The old cow.'

Dolly came. Roger listened politely while she told him that he had grown and with his grave smile answered her suitably when she said the sort of things she thought proper to a boy of his age. Julia was puzzled by him. Without talking much he listened, apparently with attention, to what the rest of them were saying, but she had an odd feeling that he was occupied with thoughts of his own. He seemed to observe them with a detached curiosity like that with which he might have observed animals in a zoo. It was faintly disquieting. When the opportunity presented itself she delivered the little bit of dialogue she had prepared for Dolly's benefit.

'Oh, Roger darling, you know your wretched father's busy to-night. I've got a couple of seats for the second house at the Palladium and Tom wants you to dine with him at the Café Royal.'

'Oh!' He paused for a second. 'All right.'

She turned to Dolly.

'It's so nice for Roger to have somebody like Tom to go about with. They're great friends, you know.'

Michael gave Dolly a glance. There was a twinkle in his eyes. He spoke.

'Tom's a very decent sort of boy. He won't let Roger get into any mischief.'

'I should have thought Roger would prefer to go about with his Eton friends,' said Dolly.

'Old cow,' thought Julia. 'Old cow.'

But when luncheon was over she asked her to come up to her room.

'I'll get into bed and you can talk to me while I'm resting. A good old girls' gossip, that's what I want.'

She put her arm affectionately round Dolly's vast waist and led her upstairs. For a while they spoke of indifferent things, clothes and servants, make-up and scandal; then Julia, leaning on her elbow, looked at Dolly with confiding eyes.

'Dolly, there's something I want to talk to you about. I want advice and you're the only person in the world whose advice I would take. I know I can trust you.'

'Of course, darling.'

'It appears that people are saying rather disagreeable things about me. Someone's been to Michael and told him that there's a lot of gossip about me and poor Tom Fennell.'

Though her eyes still wore the charming and appealing look that she knew Dolly found irresistible, she watched her closely for a start or for some change in her expression. She saw nothing.

'Who told Michael?'

'I don't know. He won't say. You know what he is when he starts being a perfect gentleman.'

She wondered if she only imagined that Dolly's features at this slightly relaxed.

'I want the truth, Dolly.'

'I'm so glad you've asked me, darling. You know how I hate to interfere in other people's business and if you hadn't brought the matter up yourself nothing would have induced me to mention it.'

'My dear, if I don't know that you're a loyal friend, who does?'

Dolly slipped off her shoes and settled down massively in her chair. Julia never took her eyes off her.

'You know how malicious people are. You've always led such a quiet, regular life. You've gone out so little, and then only with Michael or Charles Tamerley. He's different; of course everyone knows he's adored you for ages. It seems so funny that all of a sudden you should run around all over the place with a clerk in the firm that does your accounts.'

'He isn't exactly that. His father has bought him a share in the firm and he's a junior partner.'

'Yes, he gets four hundred a year.'

'How d'you know?' asked Julia quickly.

This time she was certain that Dolly was disconcerted.

'You persuaded me to go to his firm about my income tax. One of the head partners told me. It seems a little strange that on that he should be able to have a flat, dress the way he does and take people to night clubs.'

'For all I know his father may make him an allowance.'

'His father's a solicitor in the North of London. You know very well that if he's bought him a partnership he isn't making him an allowance as well.'

'Surely you don't imagine that I'm keeping him,' said Julia, with a ringing laugh.

'I don't imagine anything, darling. Other people do.'

Julia liked neither the words Dolly spoke nor the way she said them. But she gave no sign of her uneasiness.

'It's too absurd. He's Roger's friend much more than mine. Of course I've been about with him. I felt I was getting too set. I'm tired of just going to the theatre and taking care of myself. It's no life. After all if I don't enjoy myself a little now I never shall. I'm getting on, you know, Dolly, it's no good denying it. You know what Michael is; of course he's sweet, but he is a bore.'

'No more a bore than he's ever been,' said Dolly acidly.

'I should have thought I was the last person anyone would dream would have an affair with a boy twenty years younger than myself.'

'Twenty-five,' corrected Dolly. 'I should have thought so too. Unfortunately he's not very discreet.'

'What do you mean by that?'

'Well, he's told Avice Crichton that he'll get her a part in your next play.'

'Who the devil is Avice Crichton?'

'Oh, she's a young actress I know. She's as pretty as a picture.'

'He's only a silly kid. I suppose he thinks he can get round Michael. You know what Michael is with his little bits.'

'He says he can get you to do anything he wants. He says you just eat out of his hand.'

It was lucky for Julia that she was a good actress. For a second her heart stood still. How could he say a thing like that? The fool. The blasted fool. But recovering herself at once she laughed lightly.

'What nonsense! I don't believe a word of it.'

'He's a very commonplace, rather vulgar young man. It's not surprising if all the fuss you've made of him has turned his head.'

Julia, smiling good-naturedly, looked at her with ingenuous eyes.

'But, darling, *you* don't think he's my lover, do you?'

'If I don't, I'm the only person who doesn't.'

'And do you?'

For a minute Dolly did not answer. They looked at one another steadily, their hearts were black with hatred; but Julia still smiled.

'If you give me your solemn word of honour that he isn't, of course I'll believe you.'

Julia dropped her voice to a low, grave note. It had a true ring of sincerity.

'I've never told you a lie yet, Dolly, and I'm too old to begin now. I give you my solemn word of honour that Tom has never been anything more to me than just a friend.'

'You take a great weight off my mind.'

Julia knew that Dolly did not believe her and Dolly was aware that Julia knew it. She went on.

'But in that case, for your own sake, Julia dear, do be sensible. Don't go about with this young man any more. Drop him.'

'Oh, I couldn't do that. That would be an admission that people were right in what they thought. After all, my conscience is clear. I can afford to hold my head high. I should despise myself if I allowed my behaviour to be influenced by malicious gossip.'

Dolly slipped her feet back into he shoes and getting her lipstick out of her bag did her lips.

'Well, dear, you're old enough to know your own mind.'

They parted coldly.

But one or two of Dolly's remarks had been somewhat of a shock to Julia. They rankled. It was disconcerting that gossip had so nearly reached the truth. But did it matter? Plenty of women had lovers and who bothered? And an actress. No one expected an actress to be a pattern of propriety.

'It's my damned virtue. That's at the bottom of the trouble.'

She had acquired the reputation of a perfectly virtuous woman, whom the tongue of scandal could not touch, and now it looked as though her reputation was a prison that she had built round herself. But there was worse. What had Tom meant by saying that she ate out of his hand? That deeply affronted her. Silly little fool. How dare he? She didn't know what to do about it either. She would have liked to tax him with it. What was the good? He would deny it. The only thing was to say nothing; it had all gone too far now, she must accept everything. It was no good not facing the truth, he didn't love her, he was her lover because it gratified his self-esteem, because it brought him various things he cared for and because in his own eyes at least it gave him a sort of position.

'If I had any sense I'd chuck him.' She gave an angry laugh. 'It's easy to say that. I love him.'

The strange thing was that when she looked into her heart it was not Julia Lambert the woman who resented the affront, she didn't care for herself, it was the affront to Julia Lambert the actress that stung her. She had often felt that her talent, genius the critics called it, but that was a very grand word, her gift, if you like, was not really herself, not even part of her, but something outside that used her, Julia Lambert the woman, in order to express itself. It was a strange, immaterial personality that seemed to descend upon her and it did things through her that she did not know she was capable of doing. She was an ordinary, prettyish, ageing woman. Her gift had neither age nor form. It was a spirit that played on her body as the violinist plays on his violin. It was the slight to that that galled her.

She tried to sleep. She was so accustomed to sleeping in the afternoon that she could always drop off the moment she composed herself, but on this occasion she turned restlessly from side to side and sleep would not come. At last she looked at the clock. Tom often got back from his office soon after five. She yearned for him; in his arms was peace, when she was with him nothing else mattered. She dialled his number.

'Hulloa? Yes. Who is it?'

She held the receiver to her ear, panic-stricken. It was Roger's voice. She hung up.

19

Nor did Julia sleep well that night. She was awake when she heard Roger come in, and turning on her light she saw that it was four. She frowned. He came clattering down the stone stairs next morning just when she was beginning to think of getting up.

'Can I come in, mummy?'

'Come in.'

He was still in his pyjamas and dressing-gown. She smiled at him because he looked so fresh and young.

'You were very late last night.'

'No, not very. I was in by one.'

'Liar. I looked at my clock. It was four.'

'All right. It was four then,' he agreed cheerfully.

'What on earth were you doing?'

'We went on to some place after the show and had supper. We danced.'

'Who with?'

'A couple of girls we picked up. Tom knew them before.'

'What were their names?'

'One was called Jill and one was called Joan. I don't know what their other names were. Joan's on the stage. She asked me if I couldn't get her an understudy in your next play.'

At all events neither of them was Avice Crichton. That name had been in her thoughts ever since Dolly had mentioned it.

'But those places aren't open till four.'

'No, we went back to Tom's flat. Tom made me promise I wouldn't tell you. He said you'd be furious.'

'Oh, my dear, it takes a great deal more than that to make me furious. I promise you I won't say a word.'

'If anyone's to blame I am. I went to see Tom yesterday afternoon and we arranged it then. All this stuff about love that one hears about in plays and reads in novels. I'm nearly eighteen. I thought I ought to see for myself what it was all about.'

Julia sat up in bed and looked at Roger with wide, enquiring eyes.

'Roger, what *do* you mean?'

He was composed and serious.

'Tom said he knew a couple of girls who were all right. He's had them both himself. They live together and so we phoned and asked them to meet us after the show. He told them I was a virgin and they'd better toss up for me. When we got back to the flat he took Jill into the bedroom and left me the sitting-room and Joan.'

For the moment she did not think of Tom, she was so disturbed at what Roger was saying.

'I don't think it's so much really. I don't see it's anything to make all that fuss about.'

She could not speak. The tears filled her eyes and ran quickly down her face.

'Mummy, what's the matter? Why are you crying?'

'But you're a little boy.'

He came over to her and sitting on the side of her bed took her in his arms.

'Darling, don't cry. I wouldn't have told you if I'd thought it was going to upset you. After all, it had to happen sooner or later.'

'But so soon. So soon. It makes me feel so old.'

'Not you, darling. Age cannot wither her, nor custom stale her infinite variety.'

She giggled through her tears.

'You fool, Roger, d'you think Cleopatra would have liked what that silly old donkey said of her? You might have waited a little longer.'

'It's just as well I didn't. I know all about it now. To tell you the truth I think it's rather disgusting.'

She sighed deeply. It was a comfort to feel him holding her so tenderly. But she felt terribly sorry for herself.

'You're angry with me, darling?' he asked.

'Angry? No. But if it had to come I wish it hadn't been quite so matter of fact. You talk as though it had just been a rather curious experiment.'

'I suppose it was in a way.'

She gave him a little smile.

'And you really think that was love?'

'Well, it's what most people mean by it, isn't it?'

'No, they don't, they mean pain and anguish, shame, ecstasy, heaven and hell; they mean the sense of living more intensely, and unutterable boredom; they mean freedom and slavery; they mean peace and unrest.'

Something in the stillness with which he listened to her made her give him a glance through her eyelashes.

149

There was a curious expression in his eyes. She did not know what it meant. It was as though he were gravely listening to a sound that came from a long way off.

'It doesn't sound as though it were much fun,' he murmured.

She took his smooth face in her hands and kissed his lips.

'I'm a fool, aren't I? You see, I still see you as a little baby boy that I'm holding in my arms.'

A twinkle shone in his eyes.

'What are you grinning at, you ape?'

'It made a damned good photograph, didn't it?'

She could not but laugh.

'You pig. You filthy pig.'

'I say, about the understudy, is there any chance for Joan?'

'Tell her to come and see me one day.'

But when Roger left her she sighed. She was depressed. She felt very lonely. Her life had always been so full and so exciting that she had never had the time to busy herself much with Roger. She got in a state, of course, when he had whooping-cough or measles, but he was for the most part in robust health, and then he occupied a pleasant place in the background of her consciousness. But she had always felt that he was there to be attended to when she was inclined and she had often thought it would be nice when he was old enough really to share her interests. It came to her as a shock now to realize that, without ever having really possessed him, she had lost him. Her lips tightened when she thought of the girl who had taken him from her.

'An understudy. My foot.'

Her pain absorbed her so that she could not feel the grief she might have felt from her discovery of Tom's perfidy. She had always known in her bones that he was unfaithful to her. At his age, with his wanton temperament, with herself tied down by her performances at the theatre, by all manner of engagements which her position forced upon her, it was plain that he had ample opportunity to gratify his inclinations. She had shut her eyes. All she asked was that she should not know. This was the first time that an actual fact had been thrust upon her notice.

'I must just put up with it,' she sighed. Thoughts wandered through her mind. 'It's like lying and not knowing you're lying, that's what's fatal; I suppose it's better to be a fool and know it than a fool and not know it.'

20

Tom went to Eastbourne with his family for Christmas. Julia had two performances on Boxing Day, so the Gosselyns stayed in town; they went to a large party at the Savoy that Dolly de Vries gave to see the New Year in; and a few days later Roger set off for Vienna. While he was in London Julia saw little of Tom. She did not ask Roger what they did when they tore about the town together, she did not want to know, she steeled herself not to think and distracted her mind by going to as many parties as she could. And there was always her acting; when once she got into the theatre her anguish, her humiliation, her jealousy were allayed. It gave her a sense of triumphant power to find, as it were in her pot of grease paint, another personality that could be touched by no human griefs. With that refuge always at hand she could support anything.

On the day that Roger left, Tom rang her up from his office.

'Are you doing anything to-night? What about going out on the binge?'

'No, I'm busy.'

It was not true, but the words slipped out of her mouth independent of her will.

'Oh, are you? Well, what about to-morrow?'

If he had expressed disappointment, if he had asked her

to cut the date he supposed she had, she might have had strength to break with him then and there. His casualness defeated her.

'To-morrow's all right.'

'O.K. I'll fetch you at the theatre after the show. Bye-bye.'

Julia was ready and waiting when he was shown into her dressing-room. She was strangely nervous. His face lit up when he saw her, and when Evie went out of the room for a moment he caught her in his arms and warmly kissed her on the lips.

'I feel all the better for that,' he laughed.

You would never have thought to look at him, so young, fresh and ingenuous, in such high spirits, that he was capable of giving her so much pain. You would never have thought that he was so deceitful. It was quite plain that he had not noticed that for more than a fortnight he had hardly seen her.

('Oh, God, if I could only tell him to go to hell.')

But she looked at him with a gay smile in her lovely eyes.

'Where are we going?'

'I've got a table at Quag's. They've got a new turn there, an American conjurer, who's grand.'

She talked with vivacity all through supper. She told him about the various parties she had been to, and the theatrical functions she had not been able to get out of, so that it seemed only on account of her engagements that they had not met. It disconcerted her to perceive that he took it as perfectly natural. He was glad to see her, that was plain, he was interested in what she had been doing and in the people she had seen, but it was plain also that he had not missed her. To see what he would say she told him that she had had an offer to take the play in which she was acting to New York. She told him the terms that had been suggested.

'They're marvellous,' he said, his eyes glittering. 'What a snip! You can't lose and you may make a packet.'

'The only thing is, I don't much care for leaving London.'

'Why on earth not? I should have thought you'd jump at it. The play's had a good long run, for all you know it'll be pretty well through by Easter, and if you want to make a stab at America you couldn't have a better vehicle.'

'I don't see why it shouldn't run through the summer. Besides, I don't like strangers very much. I'm fond of my friends.'

'I think that's silly. Your friends'll get along without you all right. And you'll have a grand time in New York.'

Her gay laugh was very convincing.

'One would think you were terribly anxious to get rid of me.'

'Of course I should miss you like hell. But it would only be for a few months. If I had a chance like that I'd jump at it.'

But when they had finished supper and the commissionaire had called up a taxi for them he gave the address of the flat as if it were an understood thing that they should go back to it. In the taxi he put his arm round her waist and kissed her, and later, when she lay in his arms, in the little single bed, she felt that all the pain she had suffered during that last fortnight was not too great a price to pay for the happy peace that filled her heart.

Julia continued to go to the smart supper places and to night clubs with Tom. If people wanted to think he was her lover, let them; she was past caring. But it happened more than once that he was engaged when she wanted him to go somewhere with her. It had spread around among Julia's grander friends that Tom was very clever at helping one with one's income-tax returns. The Dennorants had asked him down to the country for a week-end, and here he had met a number of persons who were glad to take advantage of his technical knowledge. He began to get invitations from people whom Julia did not know. Acquaintances would mention him to her.

'You know Tom Fennell, don't you? He's very clever, isn't he? I hear he's saved the Gillians hundreds of pounds on their income-tax.'

Julia was none too pleased. It was through her that he had got asked to parties that he wanted to go to. It began to look as if in this respect he could do without her. He was pleasant and unassuming, very well-dressed now, and with a fresh, clean look that was engaging; he was able to save people money; Julia knew the world which he was so anxious to get into well enough to realize that he would soon establish himself in it. She had no very high opinion of the morals of the women he would meet there and she could name more than one person of title who would be glad to snap him up. Julia's comfort was that they were all as mean as cat's meat. Dolly had said he was only earning four hundred a year; he certainly couldn't live in those circles on that.

Julia had with decision turned down the American offer before ever she mentioned it to Tom; their play was playing to very good business. But one of those inexplicable slumps that occasionally affect the theatre now swept over London and the takings suddenly dropped. It looked as though they would not be able to carry on long after Easter. They had a new play on which they set great hopes. It was called 'Nowadays,' and the intention had been to produce it early in the autumn. It had a great part for Julia and the advantage of one that well suited Michael. It was the sort of play that might easily run a year. Michael did not much like the idea of producing it in May, with the summer coming on, but there seemed no help for it and he began looking about for a cast.

One afternoon, during the interval at a matinée, Evie brought a note in to Julia. She was surprised to see Roger's handwriting.

Dear Mother,

    This is to introduce to you Miss Joan Denver who I talked to you about. She's awfully keen on getting in the Siddons Theatre and would be quite satisfied with an understudy however small.

Your affectionate son,

ROGER.

Julia smiled at the formal way in which he wrote; she was tickled because he was so grown up as to try to get jobs for his girl friends. Then she suddenly remembered who Joan Denver was. Joan and Jill. She was the girl who had seduced poor Roger. Her face went grim. But she was curious to see her.

'Is George there?' George was the doorkeeper. Evie nodded and opened the door.

'George.'

He came in.

'Is the lady who brought this letter here now?'

'Yes, miss.'

'Tell her I'll see her after the play.'

She wore in the last act an evening dress with a train; it was a very grand dress and showed her beautiful figure to advantage. She wore diamonds in her dark hair and diamond bracelets on her arms. She looked, as indeed the part required, majestic. She received Joan Denver the moment she had taken her last call. Julia could in the twinkling of an eye leap from her part into private life, but now without an effort she continued to play the imperious, aloof, stately and well-bred woman of the play.

'I've kept you waiting so long I thought I wouldn't keep you till I'd got changed.'

Her cordial smile was the smile of a queen; her graciousness kept you at a respectful distance. In a glance she had taken in the young girl who entered her dressing-room. She was young, with a pretty little face and a snub nose, a good deal made-up and not very well made-up.

'Her legs are too short,' thought Julia. 'Very second-rate.'

She had evidently put on her best clothes and the same glance had told Julia all about them.

155

('Shaftesbury Avenue. Off the rail.')

The poor thing was at the moment frightfully nervous. Julia made her sit down and offered her a cigarette.

'There are matches by your side.'

She saw her hands tremble when she tried to strike one. It broke and she rubbed a second three times against the box before she could get it to light.

('If Roger could only see her now! Cheap rouge, cheap lipstick, and scared out of her wits. Gay little thing, he thought she was.')

'Have you been on the stage long, Miss— I'm so sorry I've forgotten your name.'

'Joan Denver.' Her throat was dry and she could hardly speak. Her cigarette went out and she held it helplessly. She answered Julia's question. 'Two years.'

'How old are you?'

'Nineteen.'

('That's a lie. You're twenty-two if you're a day.') 'You know my son, don't you?'

'Yes.'

'He's just left Eton. He's gone to Vienna to learn German. Of course he's very young, but his father and I thought it would be good for him to spend a few months abroad before going up to Cambridge. And what parts have you played? Your cigarette's gone out. Won't you have another?'

'Oh, it's all right, thanks. I've been playing on tour. But I'm frightfully anxious to be in town.' Despair gave her courage and she uttered the speech she had evidently prepared. 'I've got the most tremendous admiration for you, Miss Lambert. I always say you're the greatest actress on the stage. I've learnt more from you than I did all the years I was at the R.A.D.A. My greatest ambition is to be in your theatre, Miss Lambert, and if you could see your way to giving me a little something, I know it would be the most wonderful chance a girl could have.'

'Will you take off your hat?'

156

Joan Denver took the cheap little hat off her head and with a quick gesture shook out her close-cropped curls.

'What pretty hair you have,' said Julia.

Still with that slightly imperious, but infinitely cordial smile, the smile that a queen in royal procession bestows on her subjects, Julia gazed at her. She did not speak. She remembered Jane Taitbout's maxim: Don't pause unless it's necessary, but then pause as long as you can. She could almost hear the girl's heart beating and she felt her shrinking in her ready-made clothes, shrinking in her skin.

'What made you think of asking my son to give you a letter to me?'

Joan grew red under her make-up and she swallowed before she answered.

'I met him at a friend's house and I told him how much I admired you and he said he thought perhaps you'd have something for me in your next play.'

'I'm just turning over the parts in my mind.'

'I wasn't thinking of a part. If I could have an under-study – I mean, that would give me a chance of attending rehearsals and studying your technique. That's an education in itself. Everyone agrees about that.'

('Silly little fool, trying to flatter me. As if I didn't know that. And why the hell should I educate her?') 'It's very sweet of you to put it like that. I'm only a very ordinary person really. The public is so kind, so very kind. You're a pretty little thing. And young. Youth is so beautiful. Our policy has always been to give the younger people a chance. After all we can't go on for ever, and we look upon it as a duty we owe the public to train up actors and actresses to take our place when the time comes.'

Julia said these words so simply, in her beautifully modulated voice, that Joan Denver's heart was warmed. She'd got round the old girl and the understudy was as good as hers. Tom Fennell had said that if she played her cards well with Roger it might easily lead to something.

'Oh, that won't be for a long while yet, Miss Lambert,' she said, her eyes, her pretty dark eyes glowing.

('You're right there, my girl, dead right. I bet I could play you off the stage when I was seventy.')

'I must think it over. I hardly know yet what understudies we shall want in our next play.'

'I hear there's some talk of Avice Crichton for the girl's part. I thought perhaps I could understudy her.'

Avice Crichton. No flicker of the eyes showed that the name meant anything to Julia.

'My husband has mentioned her, but nothing is settled yet. I don't know her at all. Is she clever?'

'I think so. I was at the Academy with her.'

'And pretty as a picture, they tell me.' Rising to her feet to show that the audience was at an end, Julia put off her royalty. She changed her tone and became on a sudden the jolly, good-natured actress who would do a good turn to anyone if she could. 'Well, dear, leave me your name and address and if there's anything doing I'll let you know.'

'You won't forget me, Miss Lambert?'

'No, dear, I promise you I won't. It's been so nice to see you. You have a very sweet personality. You'll find your way out, won't you? Good-bye.'

'A fat chance she's got of ever setting foot in this theatre,' said Julia to herself when she was gone. 'Dirty little bitch to seduce my son. Poor lamb. It's a shame, that's what it is; women like that oughtn't to be allowed.'

She looked at herself in the glass as she slipped out of her beautiful gown. Her eyes were hard and her lips had a sardonic curl. She addressed her reflection.

'And I may tell you this, old girl: there's one person who isn't going to play in 'Nowadays' and that's Miss Avice Crichton.'

21

But a week or so later Michael mentioned her.

'I say, have you ever heard of a girl called Avice Crichton?'

'Never.'

'I'm told she's rather good. A lady and all that sort of thing. Her father's in the army. I was wondering if she'd do for Honor.'

'How did you hear about her?'

'Through Tom. He knows her, he says she's clever. She's playing in a Sunday night show. Next Sunday, in point of fact. He says he thinks it might be worth while to go and have a look-see.'

'Well, why don't you?'

'I was going down to Sandwich to play golf. Would it bore you awfully to go? I expect the play's rotten, but you'd be able to tell if it was worth while letting her read the part. Tom'll go with you.'

Julia's heart was beating nineteen to the dozen.

'Of course I'll go.'

She phoned to Tom and asked him to come round and have a snack before they went to the theatre. He arrived before she was ready.

'Am I late or were you early?' she said, when she came into the drawing-room.

She saw that he had been waiting impatiently. He was nervous and eager.

'They're going to ring up sharp at eight,' he said. 'I hate getting to a play after it's begun.'

His agitation told her all she wanted to know. She lingered a little over the cocktails.

'What is the name of this actress we're going to see to-night?' she asked.

'Avice Crichton. I'm awfully anxious to know what you think about her. I think she's a find. She knows you're coming to-night. She's frightfully nervous, but I told her she needn't be. You know what these Sunday night plays are; scratch rehearsals and all that; I said you'd quite understand and you'd make allowances.'

All through dinner he kept looking at his watch. Julia acted the woman of the world. She talked of one thing and another and noticed that he listened with distraction. As soon as he could he brought the conversation back to Avice Crichton.

'Of course I haven't said anything to her about it, but I believe she'd be all right for Honor.' He had read 'Nowadays,' as he read, 'before they were produced, all Julia's plays. 'She looks the part all right, I'm sure of that. She's had a struggle and of course it would be a wonderful chance for her. She admires you tremendously and she's terribly anxious to get into a play with you.'

'That's understandable. It means the chance of a year's run and a lot of managers seeing her.'

'She's the right colour, she's very fair; she'd be a good contrast to you.'

'What with platinum and peroxide there's no lack of blondes on the stage.'

'But hers is natural.'

'Is it? I had a long letter from Roger this morning. He seems to be having quite a good time in Vienna.'

Tom's interest subsided. He looked at his watch. When the coffee came Julia said it was undrinkable. She said she must have some more made.

'Oh, Julia, it isn't worth while. We shall be awfully late.'

'I don't suppose it matters if we miss the first few minutes.'

His voice was anguished.

'I promised we wouldn't be late. She's got a very good scene almost at the beginning.'

'I'm sorry, but I can't go without my coffee.'

While they waited for it she maintained a bright flow of conversation. He scarcely answered. He looked anxiously at the door. And when the coffee came she drank it with maddening deliberation. By the time they got in the car he was in a state of cold fury and he stared silently in front of him with a sulky pout on his mouth. Julia was not dissatisfied with herself. They reached the theatre two minutes before the curtain rose and as Julia appeared there was burst of clapping from the audience. Julia, apologizing to the people she disturbed, threaded her way to her seat in the middle of the stalls. Her faint smile acknowledged the applause that greeted her beautifully-timed entrance, but her downcast eyes modestly disclaimed that it could have any connection with her.

The curtain went up and after a short scene two girls came in, one very pretty and young, the other much older and plain. In a minute Julia turned to Tom and whispered:

'Which is Avice Crichton, the young one or the old one?'

'The young one.'

'Oh, of course, you said she was fair, didn't you?'

She gave his face a glance. He had lost his sulky look; a happy smile played on his lips. Julia turned her attention to the stage. Avice Crichton was very pretty, no one could deny that, with lovely golden hair, fine blue eyes and a little straight nose; but it was a type that Julia did not care for.

'Insipid,' she said to herself. 'Chorus-girly.'

She watched her performance for a few minutes. She watched intently; then she leant back in her stall with a little sigh.

'She can't act for toffee,' she decided.

When the curtain fell Tom turned to her eagerly. He had completely got over his bad temper.

'What do you think of her?'

'She's as pretty as a picture.'

'I know that. But her acting. Don't you think she's good?'

'Yes, clever.'

'I wish you'd come round and tell her that yourself. It would buck her up tremendously.'

'I?'

He did not realize what he was asking her to do. It was unheard-of that she, Julia Lambert, should go behind and congratulate a small-part actress.

'I promised I'd take you round after the second act. Be a sport Julia. It'll please her so much.'

('The fool. The blasted fool. All right, I'll go through with it.') 'Of course if you think it'll mean anything to her, I'll come with pleasure.'

After the second act they went through the iron door and Tom led her to Avice Crichton's dressing-room. She was sharing it with the plain girl with whom she had made her first entrance. Tom effected the introductions. She held out a limp hand in a slightly affected manner.

'I'm so glad to meet you, Miss Lambert. Excuse the dressing-room, won't you? But it was no good trying to make it look nice just for one night.'

She was not in the least nervous. Indeed, she seemed self-assured.

('Hard as nails. And with an eye to the main chance. Doing the colonel's daughter on me.')

'It's awfully nice of you to come round. I'm afraid it's not much of a play, but when one's starting like I am one has to put up with what one can get. I was rather doubtful about it when they sent it me to read, but I took a fancy to the part.'

'You play it charmingly,' said Julia.

'It's awfully nice of you to say so. I wish we could have had a few more rehearsals. I particularly wanted to show *you* what I could do.'

'Well, you know, I've been connected with the profession a good many years. I always think, if one has talent one can't help showing it. Don't you?'

'I know what you mean. Of course I want a lot more experience, I know that, but it's only a chance I want

162

really. I know I can act. If I could only get a part that I could really get my teeth into.'

She waited a little in order to let Julia say that she had in her new play just the part that would suit her, but Julia continued to look at her smilingly. Julia was grimly amused to find herself treated like a curate's wife to whom the squire's lady was being very kind.

'Have you been on the stage long?' she said at last. 'It seems funny I should never have heard of you.'

'Well, I was in revue for a while, but I felt I was just wasting my time. I was out on tour all last season. I don't want to leave London again if I can help it.'

'The theatrical profession's terribly overcrowded,' said Julia.

'Oh, I know. It seems almost hopeless unless you've got influence or something. I hear you're putting a new play on soon.'

'Yes.'

Julia continued to smile with an almost intolerable sweetness.

'If there's a part for me in it, I'd most awfully like to play with you. I'm so sorry Mr Gosselyn couldn't come to-night.'

'I'll tell him about you.'

'D'you really think there's a chance for me?' Through her self-assurance, through the country-house manner she assumed in order to impress Julia, there pierced an anxious eagerness. 'If you'd put in a word for me it would help so much.'

Julia gave her a reflective look.

'I take my husband's advice more often than he takes mine,' she smiled.

When they left the dressing-room so that Avice Crichton might change for the third act, Julia caught the questioning glance she gave Tom as she said good-bye to him. Julia was conscious, though she saw no movement, that he slightly shook his head. Her sensibility at that moment was extraordinarily acute and she translated the mute dialogue into words.

'Coming to supper afterwards?'

'No, damn it, I can't, I've got to see her home.'

Julia listened to the third act grimly. That was in order since the play was serious. When it was over and a pale shattered author had made a halting speech, Tom asked her where she would like to go for supper.

'Let's go home and talk,' she said. 'If you're hungry I'm sure we can find you something to eat in the kitchen.'

'D'you mean to Stanhope Place?'

'Yes.'

'All right.'

She felt his relief that she did not want to go back to the flat. He was silent in the car and she knew that it irked him to have to come back with her. She guessed that someone was giving a supper party to which Avice Crichton was going and he wanted to be there. The house was dark and empty when they reached it. The servants were in bed. Julia suggested that they should go down to the basement and forage.

'I don't want anything to eat unless you do,' he said. 'I'll just have a whisky and soda and go to bed. I've got a very heavy day to-morrow at the office.'

'All right. Bring it up to the drawing-room. I'll go and turn on the lights.'

When he came up she was doing her face in front of a mirror and she continued till he had poured out the whisky and sat down. Then she turned round. He looked very young, and incredibly charming, in his beautiful clothes, sitting there in the big armchair, and all the bitterness she had felt that evening, all the devouring jealousy of the last few days, were dissipated on a sudden by the intensity of her passion. She sat down on the arm of his chair and caressingly passed her hand over his hair. He drew back with an angry gesture.

'Don't do that,' he said. 'I do hate having my hair mussed about.'

164

It was like a knife in her heart. He had never spoken to her in that tone before. But she laughed lightly and getting up took the whisky he had poured out for her and sat down in a chair opposite him. The movement he had made, the words he had spoken were instinctive and he was a trifle abashed. He avoided her glance and his face once more bore a sulky look. The moment was decisive. For a while they were silent. Julia's heart beat painfully, but at last she forced herself to speak.

'Tell me,' she said, smiling, 'have you been to bed with Avice Crichton?'

'Of course not,' he cried.

'Why not? She's pretty.'

'She's not that sort of girl. I respect her.'

Julia let none of her feelings appear on her face. Her manner was wonderfully casual; she might have been talking of the fall of empires or the death of kings.

'D'you know what I should have said? I should have said you were madly in love with her.' He still avoided her eyes. 'Are you engaged to her by any chance?'

'No.'

He looked at her now, but the eyes that met Julia's were hostile.

'Have you asked her to marry you?'

'How could I? A damned rotter like me.'

He spoke so passionately that Julia was astonished.

'What *are* you talking about?'

'Oh what's the good of beating about the bush? How could I ask a decent girl to marry me? I'm nothing but a kept boy and, God knows, you have good reason to know it.'

'Don't be so silly. What a fuss to make over a few little presents I've given you.'

'I oughtn't to have taken them. I knew all the time it was wrong. It all came so gradually that I didn't realize what was happening till I was in it up to my neck. I couldn't afford to lead the life you made me lead; I was absolutely up against it. I had to take money from you.'

'Why not? After all, I'm a very rich woman.'

'Damn your money.'

He was holding a glass in his hands and yielding to a sudden impulse, he flung it into the fireplace. It shattered.

'You needn't break up the happy home,' said Julia ironically.

'I'm sorry. I didn't mean to do that.' He sank back into his chair and turned his head away. 'I'm so ashamed of myself. It's not very nice to have lost one's self-respect.'

Julia hesitated. She did not quite know what to say.

'It seemed only natural to help you when you were in a hole. It was a pleasure to me.'

'I know, you were wonderfully tactful about it. You almost persuaded me that I was doing you a service when you paid my debts. You made it easy for me to behave like a cad.'

'I'm sorry you should feel like that about it.'

She spoke rather tartly. She was beginning to feel a trifle irritated.

'There's nothing for you to be sorry about. You wanted me and you bought me. If I was such a skunk as to let myself be bought that was no business of yours.'

'How long have you been feeling like this?'

'From the beginning.'

'That isn't true.'

She knew that what had awakened his conscience was the love that had seized him for a girl who he believed was pure. The poor fool! Didn't he know that Avice Crichton would go to bed with an assistant stage manager if she thought it would get her a part?

'If you're in love with Avice Crichton why don't you tell me so?' He looked at her miserably, but did not answer. 'Are you afraid it'll crab her chances of getting a part in the new play? You ought to know me well enough by now to know that I would never let sentiment interfere with business.'

He could hardly believe his ears.

'What do you mean by that?'

'I think she's rather a find. I'm going to tell Michael that I think she'll do very well.'

'Oh, Julia, you are a brick. I never knew what a wonderful woman you were.'

'You should have asked me and I'd have told you.'

He gave a sigh of relief.

'My dear, I'm so terribly fond of you.'

'I know, and I'm terribly fond of you. You're great fun to go about with and you're always so well turned out, you're a credit to any woman. I've liked going to bed with you and I've a sort of notion you've liked going to bed with me. But let's face it, I've never been in love with you any more than you've been in love with me. I knew it couldn't last. Sooner or later you were bound to fall in love and that would end it. And you have fallen in love, haven't you?'

'Yes.'

She was determined to make him say it, but when he did the pang it gave her was dreadful. Notwithstanding, she smiled good-humouredly.

'We've had some very jolly times together, but don't you think the moment has come to call it a day?'

She spoke so naturally, almost jestingly, that no one could have guessed that the pain at her heart seemed past bearing. She waited for her answer with sickening dread.

'I'm awfully sorry, Julia; I must regain my self-respect.' He looked at her with troubled eyes. 'You aren't angry with me?'

'Because you've transferred your volatile affections from me to Avice Crichton?' Her eyes danced with mischievous laughter. 'My dear, of course not. After all they stay in the profession.'

'I'm very grateful to you for all you've done for me. I don't want you to think I'm not.'

'Oh, my pet, don't talk such nonsense. I've done nothing for you.' She got up. 'Now you really must go. You've got a heavy day at the office to-morrow and I'm dog-tired.'

It was a load off his mind. But he wasn't quite happy for all that, he was puzzled by her tone, which was so friendly and yet at the same time faintly ironical; he felt a trifle let down. He went up to her to kiss her good-night. She hesitated for the fraction of a second, then with a friendly smile gave him first one cheek and then the other.

'You'll find your way out, won't you?' She put her hand to her mouth to hide an elaborate yawn. 'Oh, I'm so sleepy.'

The moment he had gone she turned out the lights and went to the window. She peered cautiously through the curtains. She heard him slam the front door and saw him come out. He looked right and left. She guessed at once that he was looking for a taxi. There was none in sight and he started to walk in the direction of the Park. She knew that he was going to join Avice Crichton at the supper party and tell her the glad news. Julia sank into a chair. She had acted, she had acted marvellously, and now she felt all in. Tears, tears that nobody could see, rolled down her cheeks. She was miserably unhappy. There was only one thing that enabled her to bear her wretchedness, and that was the icy contempt that she could not but feel for the silly boy who could prefer to her a small-part actress who didn't even begin to know how to act. It was grotesque. She couldn't use her hands; why, she didn't even know how to walk across the stage.

'If I had any sense of humour I'd just laugh my head off,' she cried. 'It's the most priceless joke I've ever heard.'

She wondered what Tom would do now. The rent of the flat would be falling due on quarter-day. A lot of the things in it belonged to her. He wouldn't much like going back to his bed-sitting-room in Tavistock Square. She thought of the friends he had made through her. He'd been clever with them. They found him useful and he'd keep them. But it wouldn't be so easy for him to take Avice about. She was a hard, mercenary little thing, Julia was sure of that, she wouldn't be much inclined to bother about him when his money flowed less freely. The fool to be taken in by her pretence of virtue! Julia knew the type. It was quite obvious, she was only using Tom to get a part at the Siddons and the moment she got it she would give him the air. Julia started when this notion crossed her mind. She had promised Tom that Avice should have the part in 'Nowadays' because it fell into the scene she was playing, but she had attached no importance to her promise. Michael was always there to put his foot down.

'By God, she shall have the part,' she said, out loud. She chuckled maliciously. 'Heaven knows, I'm a good-natured woman, but there are limits to everything.'

It would be a satisfaction to turn the tables on Tom and Avice Crichton. She sat on in the darkness grimly thinking how she would do it. But every now and then she started to cry again, for from the depths of her subconscious surged up recollections that were horribly painful. Recollections of Tom's slim, youthful body against hers, his warm nakedness and the peculiar feel of his lips, his smile, at once shy and roguish, and the smell of his curly hair.

'If I hadn't been a fool I'd have said nothing. I ought to know him by now. It's only an infatuation. He'd have got over it and then he'd have come hungrily back to me.'

Now she was nearly dead with fatigue. She got up and went to bed. She took a sleeping-draught.

22

But she woke early next morning, at six, and began to think of Tom. She repeated to herself all she had said to him and all he had said to her. She was harassed and unhappy. Her only consolation was that she had carried the rupture through with so careless a gaiety that he could not guess how miserable he had made her.

She spent a wretched day, unable to think of anything

169

else, and angry with herself because she could not put Tom out of her mind. It would not have been so bad if she could have confided her grief to a friend. She wanted someone to console her, someone to tell her that Tom was not worth troubling about and to assure her that he had treated her shamefully. As a rule she took her troubles to Charles or to Dolly. Of course Charles would give her all the sympathy she needed, but it would be a terrible blow to him, after all he had loved her to distraction for twenty years, and it would be cruel to tell him that she had given to a very ordinary young man what he would gladly have sacrificed ten years of his life for. She was his ideal and it would be heartless on her part to shatter it. It certainly did her good at that moment to be assured that Charles Tamerley, so distinguished, so cultured, so elegant, loved her with an imperishable devotion. Of course Dolly would be delighted if she confided in her. They had not seen much of one another lately, but Julia knew that she had only to call up and Dolly would come running. Even though she more than suspected the truth already she'd be shocked and jealous when Julia made a clean breast of it, but she'd be so thankful that everything was over, she'd forgive. It would be a comfort to both of them to tear Tom limb from limb. Of course it wouldn't be very nice to admit that Tom had chucked her, and Dolly was so shrewd, she would never get away with the lie that she had chucked him. She wanted to have a good cry with somebody, and there didn't seem to be any reason for it if she had made the break herself. It would be a score for Dolly, and however sympathetic she was it was asking too much of human nature to expect that she would be altogether sorry that Julia had been taken down a peg or two. Dolly had always worshipped her. She wasn't going to give her a peep at her feet of clay.

'It almost looks as if the only person I can go to is Michael,' she giggled. 'But I suppose it wouldn't do.'

She knew exactly what he would say.

'My dear girl, I'm really not the sort of feller you ought to come to with a story like that. Damn it all, you put me in a very awkward position. I flatter myself I'm pretty broad-minded, I may be an actor, but when all's said and done I am a gentleman, and well, I mean, I mean it's such damned bad form.'

Michael did not get home till the afternoon, and when he came into her room she was resting. He told her about his week-end and the result of his matches. He had played very well, some of his recoveries had been marvellous, and he described them in detail.

'By the way, what about that girl you saw last night, is she any good?'

'I really think she is, you know. She's very pretty. You're sure to fall for her.'

'Oh, my dear, at my time of life. Can she act?'

'She's inexperienced of course, but I think she's got it in her.'

'Oh well, I'd better have her up and give her the once over. How can I get hold of her?'

'Tom's got her address.'

'I'll phone him right away.'

He took off the receiver and dialled Tom's number. Tom was in and Michael wrote down the address on a pad.

The conversation went on.

'Oh, my dear old chap, I'm sorry to hear that. What rotten luck!'

'What's the matter?' asked Julia.

He motioned her to be quiet.

'Oh, well, I don't want to be hard on you. Don't you worry. I'm sure we can come to some arrangement that will be satisfactory to you.' He put his hand over the receiver and turned to Julia. 'Shall I ask him to dinner next Sunday?'

'If you like.'

'Julia says, will you come and dine on Sunday? Oh, I'm sorry. Well, so long, old man.'

He put down the receiver.

'He's got a date. Is the young ruffian having an affair with this girl?'

'He assures me not. He respects her. She's a colonel's daughter.'

'Oh, she's a lady.'

'I don't know that that follows,' said Julia acidly. 'What were you talking to him about?'

'He says they've cut his salary. Bad times. He wants to give up the flat.' Julia's heart gave a sudden sickening beat. 'I've told him not to worry. I'll let him stay there rent free till times improve.'

'I don't know why you should do that. After all, it was a purely business arrangement.'

'It seems rather tough luck on a young chap like that. And you know he's very useful to us; if we want an extra man we can always call upon him, and it's convenient having him round the corner when I want someone to play golf with me. It's only twenty-five pounds a quarter.'

'You're the last person I should expect to see indulge in indiscriminate generosity.'

'Oh, don't you be afraid, if I lose on the swings I'll get back on the roundabouts.'

The masseuse came in and put an end to the conversation. Julia was thankful that it would soon be time to go down to the theatre and so put an end for a while to the misery of that long day; when she got back she would take a sleeping-draught again and so get some hours of forgetfulness. She had a notion that in a few days the worst of her pain would be over; the important thing was to get through them as best she could. She must distract her mind. When she left for the theatre she told the butler to ring up Charles Tamerley and see if she could lunch with him at the Ritz next day.

He was extraordinarily nice at luncheon. His look, his manner bespoke the different world he lived in, and she felt a sudden abhorrence for the circle in which on Tom's account she had moved during the last year. He spoke of politics, of art, of books; and peace entered into her soul. Tom had been an obsession and she saw now that it had been hurtful; but she would escape from it. Her spirits rose. She did not want to be alone, she knew that even though she went home after luncheon she would not sleep, so she asked Charles if he would take her to the National Gallery. She could give him no greater pleasure; he liked to talk about pictures and he talked of them well. It took them back to the old days when she had made her first success in London and they used to spend so many afternoons together, walking in the park or sauntering through museums. The day after that she had a matinée and the next a luncheon-party, but when they separated they arranged to lunch again together on the Friday and go to the Tate.

A few days later Michael told her that he had engaged Avice Crichton.

'She has the looks for the part, there's no doubt about that, and she'll be a good contrast to you. I'm taking her acting on the strength of what you said.'

Next morning they rang through from the basement to say that Mr Fennell was on the telephone. It seemed to her that her heart stopped beating.

'Put him through.'

'Julia, I wanted to tell you, Michael has engaged Avice.'

'Yes, I know.'

'He told her he was engaging her on what you'd told him. You are a brick.'

Julia, her heart now beating nineteen to the dozen, made an effort to control her voice.

'Oh, don't talk such nonsense,' she answered gaily. 'I told you it would be all right.'

'I'm awfully glad it's fixed up. She's accepted the part on what I've told her about it. Ordinarily she won't take anything unless she's read the play.'

It was just as well he could not see Julia's face when she heard him say this. She would have liked to answer tartly that it was not their habit when they engaged small-

173

part actresses to let them read the play, but instead she said mildly.

'Well, I think she'll like it, don't you? It's quite a good part.'

'And you know, she'll play it for all it's worth. I believe she'll make a sensation.'

Julia took a long breath.

'It'll be wonderful, won't it. I mean, it may make her.'

'Yes, I've told her that. I say, when am I going to see you again?'

'I'll phone you, shall I? It's such a bore, I'm terribly full of engagements for the next few days.'

'You're not going to drop me just because . . .'

She gave a low, rather hoarse chuckle, that chuckle which so delighted audiences.

'Don't be so silly. Oh lord, there's my bath running. I must go and have it. Good-bye, my sweet.'

She put down the receiver. The sound of his voice! The pain in her heart was unendurable. Sitting up in her bed she rocked to and fro in an agony.

'What shall I do? What shall I do?'

She had thought she was getting over it, and now that brief, silly conversation had shown her that she loved him as much as ever. She wanted him. She missed him every minute of the day. She could not do without him.

'I shall never get over it,' she moaned.

Once again the theatre was her only refuge. By an ironic chance the great scene of the play in which she was then acting, the scene to which the play owed its success, showed the parting of two lovers. It was true that they parted from a sense of duty; and Julia, in the play, sacrificed her love, her hopes of happiness, all that she held dear, to an ideal of uprightness. It was a scene that had appealed to her from the beginning. She was wonderfully moving in it. She put into it now all the agony of her spirit; it was no longer the broken heart of a character that she portrayed but her own. In ordinary life she tried to stifle a passion that she knew very well was ridiculous,

174

a love that was unworthy of the woman she was, and she steeled herself to think as little as possible of the wretched boy who had wrought such havoc with her; but when she came to this scene she let herself go. She gave free rein to her anguish. She was hopeless with her own loss, and the love she poured out on the man who was playing opposite to her was the love she still felt, the passionate, devouring love, for Tom. The prospect of the empty life that confronted the woman of the play was the prospect of her own empty life. There was at least that solace, she felt she had never played so magnificently.

'My God, it's almost worth while to suffer so frightfully to give such a performance.'

She had never put more of herself into a part.

One night a week or two later when she came into her dressing-room at the end of the play, exhausted by all the emotion she had displayed, but triumphant after innumerable curtain calls, she found Michael sitting there.

'Hulloa? You haven't been in front, have you?'

'Yes.'

'But you were in front two or three days ago.'

'Yes, I've sat through the play for the last four nights.'

She started to undress. He got up from his chair and began to walk up and down. She gave him a glance and saw that he was frowning slightly.

'What's the matter?'

'That's what I want to know.'

She gave a start. The thought flashed through her mind that he had once more heard something about Tom.

'Why the devil isn't Evie here?' she asked.

'I told her to get out. I've got something to say to you, Julia. It's no good your flying in a temper. You've just got to listen.'

A cold shiver ran down her spine.

'Well, what is it?'

'I heard something was up and I thought I'd better see for myself. At first I thought it was just an accident.

That's why I didn't say anything till I was quite sure. What's wrong with you, Julia?'

'With me?'

'Yes. Why are you giving such a lousy performance?'

'Me?' That was the last thing she expected to hear him say. She faced him with blazing eyes. 'You damned fool, I've never acted better in my life.'

'Nonsense. You're acting like hell.'

Of course it was a relief that he was talking about her acting, but what he was saying was so ridiculous that, angry as she was, she had to laugh.

'You blasted idiot, you don't know what you're talking about. Why, what I don't know about acting isn't worth knowing. Everything you know about it I've taught you. If you're even a tolerable actor, it's due to me. After all, the proof of the pudding's in the eating. D'you know how many curtain calls I got to-night? The play's never gone better in all its run.'

'I know all about that. The public are a lot of jackasses. If you yell and scream and throw yourself about you'll always get a lot of damned fools to shout themselves silly. Just barn-storming, that's what you've been doing the last four nights. It was false from beginning to end.'

'False? But I felt every word of it.'

'I don't care what you felt, you weren't acting it. Your performance was a mess. You were exaggerating; you were over-acting; you didn't carry conviction for a moment. It was about as rotten a piece of ham acting as I've ever seen in my life.'

'You bloody swine, how dare you talk to me like that? It's you the ham.'

With her open hand she gave him a great swinging blow on the face. He smiled.

'You can hit me, you can swear at me, you can yell your head off, but the fact remains that your acting's gone all to hell. I'm not going to start rehearsing "Nowadays" with you acting like that.'

'Find someone who can act the part better than I can then.'

'Don't be silly, Julia. I may not be a very good actor myself, I never thought I was, but I know good acting from bad. And what's more there's nothing about *you* I don't know. I'm going to put up the notices on Saturday and then I want you to go abroad. We'll make "Nowadays" our autumn production.'

The quiet, decisive way in which he spoke calmed her. It was true that when it came to acting Michael knew everything there was to know about her.

'Is it true that I'm acting badly?'

'Rottenly.'

She thought it over. She knew exactly what had happened. She had let her emotion run away with her; she had been feeling, not acting. Again a cold shiver ran down her spine. This was serious. It was all very fine to have a broken heart, but if it was going to interfere with her acting . . . no, no, no. That was quite another pair of shoes. Her acting was more important than any love affair in the world.

'I'll try and pull myself together.'

'It's no good trying to force oneself. You're tired out. It's my fault, I ought to have insisted on your taking a holiday long ago. What you want is a good rest.'

'What about the theatre?'

'If I can't let it, I'll revive some play that I can play in. There's "Hearts are Trumps." You always hated your part in that.'

'Everyone says the season's going to be wonderful. You can't expect much of a revival with me out of the cast; you won't make a penny.'

'I don't care a hang about that. The only thing that matters is your health.'

'Oh, Christ, don't be so magnanimous,' she cried. 'I can't bear it.'

Suddenly she burst into a storm of weeping.

'Darling!'

177

He took her in his arms and sat her down on the sofa with himself beside her. She clung to him desperately.

'You're so good to me, Michael, and I hate myself. I'm a beast, I'm a slut, I'm just a bloody bitch. I'm rotten through and through.'

'All that may be,' he smiled, 'but the fact remains that you're a very great actress.'

'I don't know how you can have the patience you have with me. I've treated you foully. You've been too wonderful and I've sacrificed you heartlessly.'

'Now, dear, don't say a lot of things that you'll regret later. I shall only bring them up against you another time.'

His tenderness melted her and she reproached herself bitterly because for years she had found him so boring.

'Thank God, I've got you. What should I do without you?'

'You haven't got to do without me.'

He held her close and though she sobbed still she began to feel comforted.

'I'm sorry I was so beastly to you just now.'

'Oh, my dear.'

'Do you really think I'm a ham actress?'

'Darling, Duse couldn't hold a candle to you.'

'Do you honestly think that? Give me your hanky. You never saw Sarah Bernhardt, did you?'

'No, never.'

'She ranted like the devil.'

They sat together for a little while, in silence, and Julia grew calmer in spirit. Her heart was filled with a great love for Michael.

'You're still the best-looking man in England,' she murmured at last. 'No one will ever persuade me to the contrary.'

She felt that he drew in his belly and thrust out his chin, and it seemed to her rather sweet and touching.

'You're quite right. I'm tired out. I feel low and miserable. I feel all empty inside. The only thing is to go away.'

23

After Julia had made up her mind to that she was glad. The prospect of getting away from the misery that tormented her at once made it easier to bear. The notices were put up; Michael collected his cast for the revival and started rehearsals. It amused Julia to sit idly in a stall and watch the actress who had been engaged rehearse the part which she had played herself some years before. She had never lost the thrill it gave her when she first went on the stage to sit in the darkened playhouse, under dust-sheets, and see the characters grow in the actors' hands. Merely to be inside a theatre rested her; nowhere was she so happy. Watching the rehearsals she was able to relax so that when at night she had her own performance to give she felt fresh. She realized that all Michael had said was true. She took hold of herself. Thrusting her private emotion into the background and thus getting the character under control, she managed once more to play with her accustomed virtuosity. Her acting ceased to be a means by which she gave release to her feelings and was again the manifestation of her creative instinct. She got a quiet exhilaration out of thus recovering mastery over her medium. It gave her a sense of power and of liberation.

But the triumphant effort she made took it out of her, and when she was not in the theatre she felt listless and discouraged. She lost her exuberant vitality. A new humility overcame her. She had a feeling that her day was done. She sighed as she told herself that nobody wanted her any more. Michael suggested that she should go to Vienna to be near Roger, and she would have liked that, but she shook her head.

'I should only cramp his style.'

She was afraid he would find her a bore. He was enjoying himself and she would only be in the way. She could not bear the thought that he would find it an irksome duty to take her here and there and occasionally have luncheon or dinner with her. It was only natural that he should have more fun with the friends of his own age that he had made. She decided to go and stay with her mother. Mrs. Lambert – Madame de Lambert, as Michael insisted on calling her – had lived for many years now with her sister, Madame Falloux, at St. Malo. She spent a few days every year in London with Julia, but this year had not been well enough to come. She was an old lady, well over seventy, and Julia knew that it would be a great joy for her to have her daughter on a long visit. Who cared about an English actress in Vienna? She wouldn't be anyone there. In St. Malo she would be something of a figure, and it would be fun for the two old women to be able to show her off to their friends.

'Ma fille, la plus grande actrice d'Angleterre,' and all that sort of thing.

Poor old girls, they couldn't live much longer and they led drab, monotonous lives. Of course it would be fearfully boring for her, but it would be a treat for them. Julia had a feeling that perhaps in the course of her brilliant and triumphant career she had a trifle neglected her mother. She could make up for it now. She would lay herself out to be charming. Her tenderness for Michael and her ever-present sense of having been for years unjust to him filled her with contrition. She felt that she had been selfish and overbearing, and she wanted to atone for all that. She was eager to sacrifice herself, and so wrote to her mother to announce her imminent arrival.

She managed in the most natural way in the world to see nothing of Tom till her last day in London. The play had closed the night before and she was starting for St. Malo in the evening. Tom came in about six o'clock to say good-bye to her. Michael was there, Dolly, Charles Tamerley and one or two others, so that there was no chance of their being left even for a moment by themselves. Julia found no difficulty in talking to him naturally. To see him gave her not the anguish she had feared but no more than a dull heartache. They had kept the date and place of her departure secret, that is to say, the Press representative of the theatre had only rung up a very few newspapers, so that when Julia and Michael reached the station there were not more than half a dozen reporters and three cameramen. Julia said a few gracious words to them, and Michael a few more, then the Press representative took the reporters aside and gave them a succinct account of Julia's plans. Meanwhile Julia and Michael posed while the camera-men to the glare of flashes photographed them arm in arm, exchanging a final kiss, and at last Julia, half out of the carriage window, giving her hand to Michael who stood on the platform.

'What a nuisance these people are,' she said. 'One simply cannot escape them.'

'I can't imagine how they knew you were going.'

The little crowd that had assembled when they realized that something was going on stood at a respectful distance. The Press representative came up and told Michael he thought he'd given the reporters enough for a column. The train steamed out.

Julia had refused to take Evie with her. She had a feeling that in order to regain her serenity she must cut herself off completely for a time from her old life. Evie in that French household would be out of place. For Madame Falloux, Julia's Aunt Carrie, married as a girl to a Frenchman, now as an old, old lady spoke French more easily than English. She had been a widow for many years and her only son had been killed in the war. She lived in a tall, narrow stone house on a hill, and when you crossed its threshold from the cobbled street you entered upon the peace of a by-gone age. Nothing had been changed for half a century. The drawing-room was furnished with a Louis XV suite under covers, and the covers were only taken off once a month to give the silk underneath a delicate brushing. The crystal chandelier was shrouded in muslin so that the flies should not spot it. In front of the chimney-piece was a fire-screen of peacocks' feathers artfully arranged and protected by glass. Though the room was never used Aunt Carrie dusted it herself every day. The dining-room was panelled and here too the chairs were under dust-covers. On the sideboard was a silver épergne, a silver coffee-pot, a silver teapot and a silver tray. Aunt Carrie and Julia's mother, Mrs Lambert, lived in the morning-room, a long narrow room, with empire furniture. On the walls in oval frames were oil portraits of Aunt Carrie and her deceased husband, of his father and mother, and a pastel of the dead son as a child. Here they had their work-boxes, here they read their papers, the *Catholic La Croix*, the *Revue des Deux Mondes* and the local daily, and here they played dominoes in the evening. Except on Thursday evenings when the Abbé and the Commandant La Garde, a retired naval officer, came to dinner, they had their meals there; but when Julia arrived they decided that it would be more convenient to eat in the dining-room.

Aunt Carrie still wore mourning for her husband and her son. It was seldom warm enough for her to leave off the little black tricot that she crocheted herself. Mrs Lambert wore black too, but when Monsieur L'Abbé and the Commandant came to dinner she put over her shoulders a white lace shawl that Julia had given her. After dinner they played plafond for two sous a hundred. Mrs Lambert, because she had lived for so many years in Jersey and still went to London, knew all about the great world, and she said that a game called contract was much played, but the Commandant said it was all very well for Americans, but he was content to stick to plafond, and the Abbé said that for his part he thought it a pity that whist had been abandoned. But there, men were never satisfied with what they had; they wanted change, change, change, all the time.

Every Christmas Julia gave her mother and her aunt expensive presents, but they never used them. They

182

showed them to their friends with pride, these wonderful things that came from London, and then wrapped them up in tissue paper and put them away in cupboards. Julia had offered her mother a car, but she refused it. For the little they went out, they could go on foot; a chauffeur would steal their petrol, if he had his meals out it would be ruinous and if he had them in it would upset Annette. Annette was cook, house-keeper and housemaid. She had been with Aunt Carrie for five and thirty years. Her niece was there to do the rough work, but Angèle was young, she wasn't forty yet, and it would hardly do to have a man constantly about the house.

They put Julia in the same room she had had as a girl when she was living with Aunt Carrie for her education. It gave her a peculiar, heart-rending sensation, indeed for a little it made her quite emotional. But she fell into the life very easily. Aunt Carrie had become a Catholic on her marriage and Mrs Lambert, when on losing her husband she settled down in St. Malo, having received instructions from the Abbé, in due course took the same step. The two old ladies were very devout. They went to Mass every morning and to High Mass on Sundays. Otherwise they seldom went out. When they did it was to pay a ceremonious call on some old lady who had had a bereavement in the family or one of whose grandchildren was become engaged. They read their papers, and their magazine, did a great deal of sewing for charitable purposes, played dominoes and listened to the radio that Julia had given them. Though the Abbé and the Commandant had dined with them every Thursday for many years they were always in a flutter when Thursday came. The Commandant, with the sailor's downrightness that they expected of him, did not hesitate to say so if something was not cooked to his liking, and even the Abbé, though a saint, had his likes and dislikes. For instance, he was very fond of sole normande, but he insisted on its being cooked with the best butter, and with butter at the price it was since the war that was very expensive. Every Thursday morning Aunt Carrie took the cellar key from the place where she had hidden it and herself fetched a bottle of claret from the cellar. She and her sister finished what was left of it by the end of the week.

They made a great fuss of Julia. They dosed her with tisanes, and were anxious that she should not sit in anything that might be thought a draught. Indeed a great part of their lives was devoted to avoiding draughts. They made her lie on sofas and were solicitous that she should cover her feet. They reasoned with her about the clothes she wore. Those silk stockings that were so thin you could see through them; and what did she wear next to her skin? Aunt Carrie would not have been surprised to learn that she wore nothing but a chemise.

'She doesn't even wear that,' said Mrs Lambert.

'What does she wear then?'

'Panties,' said Julia.

'And a soutien-gorge, I suppose.'

'Certainly not,' cried Julia tartly.

'Then, my niece, under your dress you are naked?'

'Practically.'

'C'est de la folie,' said Aunt Carrie.

'C'est vraiment pas raisonnable, ma fille,' said Mrs Lambert.

'And without being a prude,' added Aunt Carrie, 'I must say that it is hardly decent.'

Julia showed them her clothes, and on the first Thursday after her arrival they discussed what she should wear for dinner. Aunt Carrie and Mrs Lambert grew rather sharp with one another. Mrs Lambert thought that since her daughter had evening dresses with her she ought to wear one, but Aunt Carrie considered it quite unnecessary.

'When I used to come and visit you in Jersey, my dear, and gentlemen were coming to dinner, I remember you would put on a tea-gown.'

'Of course a tea-gown would be very suitable.'

They looked at Julia hopefully. She shook her head.

184

'I would sooner wear a shroud.'

Aunt Carrie wore a high-necked dress of heavy black silk, with a string of jet, and Mrs Lambert a similar one, but with her lace shawl and a paste necklace. The Commandant, a sturdy little man with a much-wrinkled face, white hair cut *en brosse* and an imposing moustache dyed a deep black, was very gallant, and though well past seventy pressed Julia's foot under the table during dinner. On the way out he seized the opportunity to pinch her bottom.

'Sex appeal,' Julia murmured to herself as with dignity she followed the two old ladies into the parlour.

They made a fuss of her, not because she was a great actress, but because she was in poor health and needed rest. Julia to her great amazement soon discovered that to them her celebrity was an embarrassment rather than an asset. Far from wanting to show her off, they did not offer to take her with them to pay calls. Aunt Carrie had brought the habit of afternoon tea with her from Jersey, and had never abandoned it. One day, soon after Julia's arrival, when they had invited some ladies to tea, Mrs Lambert at luncheon thus addressed her daughter.

'My dear, we have some very good friends at St. Malo, but of course they still look upon us as foreigners, even after all these years, and we don't like to do anything that seems at all eccentric. Naturally we don't want you to tell a lie, but unless you are forced to mention it, your Aunt Carrie thinks it would be better if you did not tell anyone that you are an actress.'

Julia was taken aback, but, her sense of humour prevailing, she felt inclined to laugh.

'If one of the friends we are expecting this afternoon happens to ask you what your husband is, it wouldn't be untrue, would it? to say that he was in business.'

'Not at all,' said Julia, permitting herself to smile.

'Of course, we know that English actresses are not like French ones,' Aunt Carrie added kindly. 'It's almost an understood thing for a French actress to have a lover.'

'Dear, dear,' said Julia.

Her life in London, with its excitements, its triumphs and its pains, began to seem very far away. She found herself able soon to consider Tom and her feeling for him with a tranquil mind. She realized that her vanity had been more wounded than her heart. The days passed monotonously. Soon the only thing that recalled London to her was the arrival on Monday of the Sunday papers. She got a batch of them and spent the whole day reading them. Then she was a trifle restless. She walked on the ramparts and looked at the islands that dotted the bay. The grey sky made her sick for the grey sky of England. But by Tuesday morning she had sunk back once more into the calmness of the provincial life. She read a good deal, novels, English and French, that she bought at the local bookshop, and her favourite Verlaine. There was a tender melancholy in his verses that seemed to fit the grey Breton town, the sad old stone houses and the quietness of those steep and tortuous streets. The peaceful habits of the two old ladies, the routine of their uneventful existence and their quiet gossip, excited her compassion. Nothing had happened to them for years, nothing now would ever happen to them till they died, and then how little would their lives have signified. The strange thing was that they were content. They knew neither malice nor envy. They had achieved the aloofness from the common ties of men that Julia felt in herself when she stood at the footlights bowing to the applause of a enthusiastic audience. Sometimes she had thought that aloofness her most precious possession. In her it was born of pride; in them of humility. In both cases it brought one precious thing, liberty of spirit; but with them it was more secure.

Michael wrote to her once a week, brisk, business-like letters in which he told her what the takings were at the Siddons and the preparations he was making for the next production; but Charles Tamerley wrote to her every day. He told her the gossip of the town, he talked in his charming, cultivated way of the pictures he saw and the books he read. He was tenderly allusive and playfully erudite. He philosophized without pedantry. He told her that he adored her. They were the most beautiful love-letters Julia had ever received, and for the sake of posterity she made up her mind to keep them. One day perhaps someone would publish them and people would go to the National Portrait Gallery and look at her portrait, the one McEvoy had painted, and sigh when they thought of the sad, romantic love-story of which she had been the heroine.

Charles had been wonderful to her during the first two weeks of her bereavement, she did not know what she would have done without him. He had always been at her beck and call. His conversation, by taking her into a different world, had soothed her nerves. Her soul had been muddied, and in his distinction of spirit she had washed herself clean. It had rested her wonderfully to wander about the galleries with him and look at pictures. She had good reason to be grateful to him. She thought of all the years he had loved her. He had waited for her now for more than twenty years. She had not been very kind to him. It would have given him so much happiness to possess her and really it would not have hurt her. She wondered why she had resisted him so long. Perhaps because he was so faithful, because his devotion was so humble, perhaps only because she wanted to preserve in his mind the ideal that he had of her. It was stupid really and she had been selfish. It occurred to her with exultation that she could at last reward him for all his tenderness, his patience and his selflessness. She had not lost the sense of unworthiness which Michael's great kindness had aroused in her, and she was remorseful still because she had been for so long impatient of him. The desire for self-sacrifice with which she left England burnt still in her breast with an eager flame. She felt that Charles was a worthy object for its exercise. She laughed a little, kindly and compassionately, as she thought of

187

his amazement when he understood what she intended; for a moment he would hardly be able to believe it, and then what rapture, then what ecstasy! The love that he had held banked up for so many years would burst its sluices like a great torrent and in a flood o'erwhelm her. Her heart swelled at the thought of his infinite gratitude. But still he could hardly believe in his good fortune; and when it was all over and she lay in his arms she would nestle up to him and whisper tenderly:

'Was it worth waiting for?'

'Like Helen, you make me immortal with a kiss.'

It was wonderful to be able to give so much happiness to a human being.

'I'll write to him just before I leave St. Malo,' she decided.

The spring passed into summer, and at the end of July it was time for Julia to go to Paris and see about her clothes. Michael wanted to open with the new play early in September, and rehearsals were to start in August. She had brought the play with her to St. Malo, intending to study her part, but the circumstances in which she lived had made it impossible. She had all the leisure she needed, but in that grey, austere and yet snug little town, in the constant company of those two old ladies whose interests were confined to the parish church and their household affairs, though it was a good play, she could take but little interest in it.

'It's high time I was getting back,' she said. 'It would be hell if I really came to the conclusion that the theatre wasn't worth the fuss and bother they make about it.'

She said good-bye to her mother and to Aunt Carrie. They had been very kind to her, but she had an inkling that they would not be sorry when her departure allowed them to return to the life she had interrupted. They were a little relieved besides to know that now there was no more danger of some eccentricity, such as you must always run the risk of with an actress, which might arouse the unfavourable comment of the ladies of St. Malo.

She arrived in Paris in the afternoon, and when she was shown into her suite at the Ritz, she gave a sigh of satisfaction. It was a treat to get back to luxury. Three or four people had sent her flowers. She had a bath and changed. Charley Deveril, who always made her clothes for her, an old friend, called to take her to dinner at the Bois.

'I had a wonderful time,' she told him, 'and of course it was a grand treat for those old girls to have me there, but I have a feeling that if I'd stayed a day longer I should have been bored.'

To drive up the Champs Elysées on that lovely evening filled her with exhilaration. It was good to smell once more the smell of petrol. The cars, the taxis, the hooting of horns, the chestnut trees, the street lights, the crowd on the pavement and the crowd sitting outside the cafés; it was an enchantment. And when they got to the Château de Madrid, so gay, so civilized and so expensive, it was grand to see once more well-dressed women, decently made-up, and tanned men in dinner-jackets.

'I feel like a queen returning from exile.'

Julia spent several happy days choosing her clothes and having the first fittings. She enjoyed every moment of them. But she was a woman of character, and when she had come to a decision she adhered to it; before leaving for London she wrote a note to Charles. He had been to Goodwood and Cowes and was spending twenty-four hours in London on his way to Salzburg.

CHARLES DEAR,

How wonderful that I shall see you so soon. Of course I am free on Wednesday. Shall we dine together and do you love me still?

Your JULIA.

As she stuck down the envelope she murmured: *Bis dat qui cito dat.* It was a Latin tag that Michael always quoted when, asked to subscribe to a charity, he sent by return of post exactly half what was expected of him.

24

On Wednesday morning Julia had her face massaged and her hair waved. She could not make up her mind whether to wear for dinner a dress of flowered organdie, very pretty and spring-like with its suggestion of Botticelli's Primavera, or one of white satin beautifully cut to show off her slim young figure, and virginal; but while she was having her bath she decided on the white satin: it indicated rather delicately that the sacrifice she intended was in the nature of an expiation for her long ingratitude to Michael. She wore no jewels but a string of pearls and a diamond bracelet; besides her wedding-ring only one square-cut diamond. She would have liked to put on a slight brown tan, it looked open-air-girl and suited her, but reflecting on what lay before her she refrained. She could not very well, like the actor who painted himself black all over to play Othello, tan her whole body. Always a punctual woman, she came downstairs as the front door was being opened for Charles. She greeted him with a look into which she put tenderness, a roguish charm and intimacy. Charles now wore his thinning grey hair rather long, and with advancing years his intellectual, distinguished features had sagged a little; he was slightly bowed and his clothes looked as though they needed pressing.

'Strange world we live in,' thought Julia. 'Actors do their damnedest to look like gentlemen and gentlemen do all they can to look like actors.'

There was no doubt that she was making a proper effect on him. He gave her the perfect opening.

'Why are you looking so lovely to-night?' he asked.

'Because I'm looking forward to dining with you.'

With her beautiful, expressive eyes she looked deep

into his. She parted her lips in the manner that she found so seductive in Romney's portraits of Lady Hamilton.

They dined at the Savoy. The head-waiter gave them a table on the gangway so that they were admirably in view. Though everyone was supposed to be out of town the grill-room was well filled. Julia bowed and smiled to various friends of whom she caught sight. Charles had much to tell her; she listened to him with flattering interest.

'You are the best company in the world, Charles,' she told him.

They had come late, they dined well, and by the time Charles had finished his brandy people were already beginning to come in for supper.

'Good gracious, are the theatres out already?' he said, glancing at his watch. 'How quickly the time flies when I'm with you. D'you imagine they want to get rid of us?'

'I don't feel a bit like going to bed.'

'I suppose Michael will be getting home presently?'

'I suppose so.'

'Why don't you come back to my house and have a talk?'

That was what she called taking a cue.

'I'd love it,' she answered, putting into her tone the slight blush which she felt would have well become her cheek.

They got into his car and drove to Hill Street. He took her into his study. It was on the ground floor and looked on a tiny garden. The french windows were wide open. They sat down on a sofa.

'Put out some of the lights and let the night into the room,' said Julia. She quoted from 'The Merchant of Venice.' ' "In such a night as this, when the sweet wind did gently kiss the trees . . ." '

Charles switched off everything but one shaded lamp, and when he sat down again she nestled up to him. He put his arm round her waist and she rested her head on his shoulder.

'This is heaven,' she murmured.

'I've missed you terribly all these months.'

'Did you get into mischief?'

'Well, I bought an Ingres drawing and paid a lot of money for it. I must show it to you before you go.'

'Don't forget. Where have you put it?'

She had wondered from the moment she got into the house whether the seduction would take place in the study or upstairs.

'In my bedroom,' he answered.

'That's much more comfortable really,' she reflected.

She laughed in her sleeve as she thought of poor old Charles devising a simple little trick like that to get her into his bedroom. What mugs men were! Shy, that was what was the matter with them. A sudden pang shot through her heart as she thought of Tom. Damn Tom. Charles really was very sweet and she was determined to reward him at last for his long devotion.

'You've been a wonderful friend to me, Charles,' she said in her low, rather husky voice. She turned a little so that her face was very near his, her lips, again like Lady Hamilton's, slightly open. 'I'm afraid I haven't always been very kind to you.'

She looked so deliciously yielding, a ripe peach waiting to be picked, that it seemed inevitable that he should kiss her. Then she would twine her soft white arms round his neck. But he only smiled.

'You mustn't say that. You've been always divine.'

('He's afraid, poor lamb.') 'I don't think anyone has ever been so much in love with me as you were.'

He gave her a little squeeze.

'I am still. You know that. There's never been any woman but you in my life.'

Since, however, he did not take the proffered lips she slightly turned. She looked reflectively at the electric fire. Pity it was unlit. The scene wanted a fire.

'How different everything would have been if we'd bolted that time. Heigh-ho.'

She never quite knew what heigh-ho meant, but they used it a lot on the stage, and said with a sigh it always sounded very sad.

'England would have lost its greatest actress. I know now how dreadfully selfish it was of me ever to propose it.'

'Success isn't everything. I sometimes wonder whether to gratify my silly little ambition I didn't miss the greatest thing in the world. After all, love is the only thing that matters.' And now she looked at him again with eyes more beautiful than ever in their melting tenderness. 'D'you know, I think that now, if I had my time over again, I'd say take me.'

She slid her hand down to take his. He gave it a graceful pressure.

'Oh, my dear.'

'I've so often thought of that dream villa of ours. Olive trees and oleanders and the blue sea. Peace. Sometimes I'm appalled by the dullness and vulgarity of my life. What you offered was beauty. It's too late now, I know; I didn't know then how much I cared for you, I never dreamt that as the years went on you would mean more and more to me.'

'It's heavenly to hear you say that, my sweet. It makes up for so much.'

'I'd do anything in the world for you, Charles. I've been selfish. I've ruined your life, I didn't know what I was doing.'

Her voice was low and tremulous and she threw back her head so that her neck was like a white column. Her décolleté showed part of her small firm breasts and with her hands she pressed them forward a little.

'You mustn't say that, you mustn't think that,' he answered gently. 'You've been perfect always. I wouldn't have had you otherwise. Oh, my dear, life is so short and love is so transitory. The tragedy of life is that sometimes we get what we want. Now that I look back on our long past together I know that you were wiser than I. "What leaf-fringed legend haunts about thy shape?" Don't you remember how it goes? "Never, never canst thou kiss, though winning near the goal — yet, do not grieve; she cannot fade, though thou hast not thy bliss. For ever wilt thou love, and she be fair!" '

('Idiotic.') 'Such lovely lines,' she sighed. 'Perhaps you're right. Heigh-ho.'

He went on quoting. That was a trick of his that Julia had always found somewhat tiresome.

' "Ah, happy, happy boughs! that cannot shed
Your leaves, nor ever bid the Spring adieu;
And, happy melodist, unwearied,
For ever piping songs for ever new! . . ." '

It gave Julia an opportunity to think. She stared in the unlit fire, her gaze intent, as though she were entranced by the exquisite beauty of those words. It was quite obvious that he just hadn't understood. It could hardly be wondered at. She had been deaf to his passionate entreaties for twenty years, and it was very natural if he had given up his quest as hopeless. It was like Mount Everest; if those hardy mountaineers who had tried for so long in vain to reach the summit finally found an easy flight of steps that led to it, they simply would not believe their eyes: they would think there was a catch in it. Julia felt that she must make herself a little plainer; she must, as it were, reach out a helping hand to the weary pilgrim.

'It's getting dreadfully late,' she said softly. 'Show me your new drawing and then I must go home.'

He rose and she gave him both her hands so that he should help her up from the sofa. They went upstairs. His pyjamas and dressing-gown were neatly arranged on a chair.

'How well you single men do yourselves. Such a cosy, friendly bedroom.'

He took the framed drawing off the wall and brought it over for her to look at under the light. It was a portrait in pencil of a stoutish woman in a bonnet and a low-necked dress with puffed sleeves. Julia thought her plain and the dress ridiculous.

'Isn't it ravishing?' she cried.

'I knew you'd like it. A good drawing, isn't it?'

'Amazing.'

He put the little picture back on its nail. When he turned round again she was standing near the bed with her hands behind her back a little like a Circassian slave introduced by the chief eunuch to the inspection of the Grand Vizier; there was a hint of modest withdrawal in her bearing, a delicious timidity, and at the same time the virgin's anticipation that she was about to enter into her kingdom. Julia gave a sigh that was ever so slightly voluptuous.

'My dear, it's been such a wonderful evening. I've never felt so close to you before.'

She slowly raised her hands from behind her back and with the exquisite timing that came so naturally to her moved them forwards, stretching out her arms, and held them palms upward as though there rested on them, invisibly, a lordly dish, and on the dish lay her proffered heart. Her beautiful eyes were tender and yielding and on her lips played a smile of shy surrender.

She saw Charles's smile freeze on his face. He had understood all right.

('Christ, he doesn't want me. It was all a bluff.') The revelation for a moment staggered her. ('God, how am I going to get out of it? What a bloody fool I must look.')

She very nearly lost her poise. She had to think like lightning. He was standing there, looking at her with an embarrassment that he tried hard to conceal. Julia was panic-stricken. She could not think what to do with those hands that held the lordly dish; God knows, they were small, but at the moment they felt like legs of mutton hanging there. Nor did she know what to say. Every second made her posture and the situation more intolerable.

('The skunk, the dirty skunk. Codding me all these years.')

She did the only thing possible. She continued the gesture. Counting so that she should not go too fast, she drew her hands towards one another, till she could clasp them, and then throwing back her head, raised them, very slowly, to one side of her neck. The attitude she reached was as lovely as the other, and it was the attitude that suggested to her what she had to say. Her deep rich voice trembled a little with emotion.

'I'm so glad when I look back to think that we have nothing to reproach ourselves with. The bitterness of life is not death, the bitterness of life is that love dies. (She'd heard something like that said in a play.) If we'd been lovers you'd have grown tired of me long ago, and what should we have now to look back on but regret for our own weakness? What was that line of Shelley's that you said just now about fading?'

'Keats,' he corrected. ' "She cannot fade though thou hast not thy bliss." '

'That's it. Go on.'

She was playing for time.

' "For ever wilt thou love, and she be fair." '

She threw her arms wide in a great open gesture and tossed her curly head. She'd got it.

'It's true, isn't it? "For ever wilt thou love and I be fair." What fools we should have been if for a few moments' madness we had thrown away the wonderful happiness our friendship has brought us. We have nothing to be ashamed of. We're clean. We can walk with our heads held high and look the whole world in the face.'

She instinctively felt that this was an exit line, and suiting her movements to the words, with head held high, backed to the door and flung it open. Her power was such that she carried the feeling of the scene all the way down the stairs with her. Then she let it fall and with the utmost simplicity turned to Charles who had followed her.

196

'My cloak.'

'The car is there,' he said as he wrapped it round her. 'I'll drive you home.'

'No, let me go alone. I want to stamp this hour on my heart. Kiss me before I go.'

She held up her lips to him. He kissed them. But she broke away from him, with a stifled sob, and tearing open the door ran to the waiting car.

When she got home and stood in her own bedroom she gave a great whoof of relief.

'The bloody fool. Fancy me being taken in like that. Thank God, I got out of it all right. He's such an ass, I don't suppose he began to see what I was getting at.' But that frozen smile disconcerted her. 'He may have suspected, he couldn't have been certain, and afterwards he must have been pretty sure he'd made a mistake. My God, the rot I talked. It seemed to go down all right, I must say. Lucky I caught on when I did. In another minute I'd have had my dress off. That wouldn't have been so damned easy to laugh away.'

Julia began to titter. The situation was mortifying of course, he had made a damned fool of her, but if you had any sense of humour you could hardly help seeing that there was a funny side to it. She was sorry that there was nobody to whom she could tell it; even if it was against herself it would make a good story. What she couldn't get over was that she had fallen for the comedy of undying passion that he had played all those years; for of course it was just a pose; he liked to see himself as the constant adorer, and the last thing he wanted, apparently, was to have his constancy rewarded.

'Bluffed me, he did, completely bluffed me.'

But an idea occurred to Julia and she ceased to smile. When a woman's amorous advances are declined by a man she is apt to draw one or two conclusions; one is that he is homosexual and the other is that he is impotent. Julia reflectively lit a cigarette. She asked herself if Charles had used his devotion to her as a cover to distract attention from his real inclinations. But she shook her head. If he had been homosexual she would surely have had some hint of it; after all, in society since the war they talked of practically nothing else. Of course it was quite possible he was impotent. She reckoned out his age. Poor Charles. She smiled again. And if that were the case it was he, not she, who had been placed in an embarrassing and even ridiculous position. He must have been scared stiff, poor lamb. Obviously it wasn't the sort of thing a man liked to tell a woman, especially if he were madly in love with her; the more she thought of it the more probable she considered the explanation. She began to feel very sorry for him, almost maternal in fact.

'I know what I'll do,' she said, as she began to undress, 'I'll send him a huge bunch of white lilies to-morrow.'

25

Julia lay awake next morning for some time before she rang her bell. She thought. When she reflected on her adventure of the previous night she could not but be pleased that she had shown so much presence of mind. It was hardly true to say that she had snatched victory from defeat, but looking upon it as a strategic retreat her conduct had been masterly. She was notwithstanding ill at ease. There might be yet another explanation for Charles's singular behaviour. It was possible that he did not desire her because she was not desirable. The notion had crossed her mind in the night, and though she had at once dismissed it as highly improbable, there was no denying it, at that hour of the morning it had a nasty look. She rang. As a rule, since Michael often came in while Julia had breakfast, Evie when she had drawn the curtains handed her a mirror and a comb, her powder and lipstick. On this occasion, instead of running the comb rapidly through her hair and giving her face a perfunctory dab with the puff, Julia took some trouble. She painted her lips with care and put on some rouge; she arranged her hair.

'Speaking without passion or prejudice,' she said, still looking at herself in the glass, when Evie placed the breakfast tray on her bed, 'would you say I was by way of being a good-looking woman, Evie?'

'I must know what I'm letting myself in for before answering that question.'

'You old bitch,' said Julia.

'You're no beauty, you know.'

'No great actress ever has been.'

'When you're all dolled up posh like you was last night, and got the light b'ind you, I've seen worse, you know.'

('Fat lot of good it did me last night.') 'What I want to say is, if I really set my mind on getting off with a man, d'you think I could?'

'Knowing what men are, I wouldn't be surprised. Who d'you want to get off with now?'

'Nobody. I was only talking generally.'

Evie sniffed and drew her forefinger along her nostrils.

'Don't sniff like that. If your nose wants blowing, blow it.'

Julia ate her boiled egg slowly. She was busy with her thoughts. She looked at Evie. Funny-looking old thing of course, but one never knew.

'Tell me, Evie, do men ever try to pick you up in the street?'

'Me? I'd like to see 'em try.'

'So would I, to tell you the truth. Women are always telling me how men follow them in the street and if they stop and look in at a shop window come up and try to catch their eye. Sometimes they have an awful bother getting rid of them.'

'Disgusting, I call it.'

'I don't know about that. It's rather flattering. You know, it's a most extraordinary thing, no one ever follows me in the street. I don't remember a man ever having tried to pick me up.'

'Oh well, you walk along Edgware Road one evening. You'll get picked up all right.'

'I shouldn't know what to do if I was.'

'Call a policeman,' said Evie grimly.

'I know a girl who was looking in a shop window in Bond Street, a hat shop, and a man came up and asked her if she'd like a hat. I'd love one, she said, and they went in and she chose one and gave her name and address, he paid for it on the nail, and then she said, thank you so much, and walked out while he was waiting for the change.'

'That's what she told you.' Evie's sniff was sceptical. She gave Julia a puzzled look. 'What's the idea?'

'Oh, nothing. I was only wondering why in point of fact I never have been accosted by a man. It's not as if I had no sex appeal.'

But had she? She made up her mind to put the matter to the test.

That afternoon, when she had had her sleep, she got up, made up a little more than usual, and without calling Evie put on a dress that was neither plain nor obviously expensive and a red straw hat with a wide brim.

'I don't want to look like a tart,' she said as she looked at herself in the glass. 'On the other hand I don't want to look too respectable.'

She tiptoed down the stairs so that no one should hear her and closed the door softly behind her. She was a trifle nervous, but pleasantly excited; she felt that she was doing something rather shocking. She walked through Connaught Square into the Edgware Road. It was about five o'clock. There was a dense line of buses, taxis and lorries; bicyclists dangerously threaded their way through the traffic. The pavements were thronged. She sauntered slowly north. At first she walked with her eyes straight in front of her, looking neither to the right nor to the left, but soon realized that this was useless. She must look at people if she wanted them to look at her. Two or three times when she saw half a dozen persons gazing at a shop window she paused and gazed too, but none of them took any notice of her. She strolled on. People passed her in one direction and another. They seemed in a hurry. No one paid any attention to her. When she saw a man alone coming towards her she gave him a bold stare, but he passed on with a blank face. It occurred to her that her expression was too severe, and she let a slight smile hover on her lips. Two or three men thought she was smiling at them and quickly averted their gaze. She looked back as one of them passed her and he looked back too, but catching her eye he hurried on. She felt a trifle snubbed and decided not to look round again. She walked on and on. She had always heard that the London crowd was the best behaved in the world, but really its behaviour on this occasion was unconscionable.

'This couldn't happen to one in the streets of Paris, Rome or Berlin,' she reflected.

She decided to go as far as the Marylebone Road, and then turn back. It would be too humiliating to have to go home without being once accosted. She was walking so slowly that passers-by sometimes jostled her. This irritated her.

'I ought to have tried Oxford Street,' she said. 'That fool Evie. The Edgware Road's obviously a wash-out.'

Suddenly her heart gave an exultant leap. She had caught a young man's eye and she was sure that there was a gleam in it. He passed, and she had all she could do not to turn round. She started, for in a moment he passed her again, he had retraced his steps, and this time he gave her a stare. She shot him a glance and then modestly lowered her eyes. He fell back and she was conscious that he was following her. It was all right. She stopped to look into a shop window and he stopped too. She knew how to behave now. She pretended to be absorbed in the goods that were displayed, but just before she moved on gave him a quick flash of her faintly-smiling eyes. He was rather short, he looked like a clerk or a shop-walker, he wore a grey suit and a brown soft hat. He was not the man she would have chosen to be picked up by, but there it was, he was evidently trying to pick her up. She forgot that she was beginning to feel tired. She did not know what would happen next. Of course she wasn't going to let the thing go too far, but she was curious to see what his next step would be. She wondered what he would say to her. She was excited and pleased; it was a weight off her mind. She walked on slowly and she knew he was close behind her. She stopped at another shop window, and this time when he stopped he was close beside her. Her heart began to beat wildly. It was really beginning to look like an adventure.

'I wonder if he'll ask me to go to a hotel with him. I don't suppose he could afford that. A cinema. That's it. It would be rather fun.'

She looked him full in the face now and very nearly smiled. He took off his hat.

'Miss Lambert, isn't it?'

She almost jumped out of her skin. She was indeed so taken aback that she had not the presence of mind to deny it.

'I thought I recognized you the moment I saw you, that's why I turned back, to make sure, see, and I said to meself, if that's not Julia Lambert I'm Ramsay Macdonald. Then you stopped to look in that shop window and that give me the chance to 'ave a good look at you. What made me 'esitate was seeing you in the Edgware Road. It seems so funny, if you know what I mean.'

It was much funnier than he imagined. Anyhow it didn't matter if he knew who she was. She ought to have guessed that she couldn't go far in London without being recognized. He had a cockney accent and a pasty face, but she gave him a jolly, friendly smile. He mustn't think she was putting on airs.

'Excuse me talking to you, not 'aving been introduced and all that, but I couldn't miss the opportunity. Will you oblige me with your autograph?'

Julia caught her breath. It couldn't be that this was

why he had followed her for ten minutes. He must have thought that up as an excuse for speaking to her. Well, she would play up.

'I shall be delighted. But I can't very well give it you in the street. People would stare so.'

'That's right. Look here, I was just going along to 'ave my tea. There's a Lyons at the next corner. Why don't you come in and 'ave a cup too?'

She was getting on. When they'd had tea he'd probably suggest going to the pictures.

'All right,' she said.

They walked along till they came to the shop and took their places at a small table.

'Two teas, please, miss,' he ordered. 'Anything to eat?' And when Julia declined: 'Scone and butter for one, miss.'

Julia was able now to have a good look at him. Though stocky and short he had good features, his black hair was plastered down on his head and he had fine eyes, but his teeth were poor and his pale skin gave him an unhealthy look. There was a sort of impudence in his manner that Julia did not much like, but then, as she sensibly reflected, you could hardly expect the modesty of the violet in a young man who picked you up in the Edgware Road.

'Before we go any further let's 'ave this autograph, eh? Do it now, that's my motto.'

He took a fountain pen from his pocket and from a bulging pocket-book a large card.

'One of our trade cards,' he said. 'That'll do O.K.'

Julia thought it silly to carry the subterfuge to this length, but she good-humouredly signed her name on the back of the card.

'Do you collect autographs?' she asked him with a subtle smile.

'Me? Noa. I think it's a lot of tommy rot. My young lady does. She's got Charlie Chaplin and Douglas Fairbanks and I don't know what all. Show you 'er photo if you like.'

203

From his pocket-book he extracted a snapshot of a rather pert-looking young woman showing all her teeth in a cinema smile.

'Pretty,' said Julia.

'And how. We're going to the pictures to-night. She will be surprised when I give her your autograph. The first thing I said to meself when I knew it was you was, I'll get Julia Lambert's autograph for Gwen or die in the attempt. We're going to get married in August, when I 'ave my 'oliday, you know; we're going to the Isle of Wight for the 'oneymoon. I shall 'ave a rare lot of fun with 'er over this. She won't believe me when I tell her you an' me 'ad tea together, she'll think I'm kidding, and then I'll show 'er the autograph, see?'

Julia listened to him politely, but the smile had left her face.

'I'm afraid I shall have to go in a minute,' she said. 'I'm late already.'

'I 'aven't got too much time meself. You see, meeting my young lady, I want to get away from the shop on the tick.'

The check had been put on the table when the girl brought their tea, and when they got up Julia took a shilling out of her bag.

'What are you doing that for? You don't think I'm going to let you pay. I invited you.'

'That's very kind of you.'

'But I'll tell you what you can do, let me bring my young lady to see you in your dressing-room one day. Just shake 'ands with her, see? It would mean a rare lot to her. Why, she'd go on talking about it the rest of her life.'

Julia's manner had been for some minutes growing stiffer and now, though gracious still, it was almost haughty.

'I'm sorry, but we never allow strangers behind.'

'Oh, sorry. You don't mind my asking though, do you? I mean, it's not as if it was for meself.'

'Not at all. I quite understand.'

She signalled to a cab crawling along the curb and gave her hand to the young man.

'Good-bye, Miss Lambert. So long, good luck and all that sort of thing. And thanks for the autograph.'

Julia sat in the corner of the taxi raging.

'Vulgar little beast. Him and his young lady. The nerve of asking if he could bring her to see ME.'

When she got home she went upstairs to her room. She snatched her hat off her head and flung it angrily on the bed. She strode over to the looking-glass and stared at herself.

'Old, old, old,' she muttered. 'There are no two ways about it; I'm entirely devoid of sex appeal. You wouldn't believe it, would you? You'd say it was preposterous. What other explanation is there? I walk from one end of the Edgware Road to the other and God knows I'd dressed the part perfectly, and not a man pays the smallest attention to me except a bloody little shop-assistant who wants my autograph for his young lady. It's absurd. A lot of sexless bastards. I don't know what's coming to the English. The British Empire!'

The last words she said with a scorn that would have withered a whole front bench of cabinet ministers. She began to gesticulate.

'It's ridiculous to suppose that I could have got to my position if I hadn't got sex appeal. What do people come to see an actress for? Because they want to go to bed with her. Do you mean to tell me that I could fill a theatre for three months with a rotten play if I hadn't got sex appeal? What is sex appeal anyway?'

She paused, looking at herself reflectively.

'Surely I can act sex appeal. I can act anything.'

She began to think of the actresses who notoriously had it, of one especially, Lydia Mayne, whom one always engaged when one wanted a vamp. She was not much of an actress, but in certain parts she was wonderfully effective. Julia was a great mimic, and now she began to do an imitation of Lydia Mayne. Her eyelids drooped sensually over her eyes as Lydia's did and her body writhed sinuously in her dress. She got into her eyes the provoking indecency of Lydia's glance and into her serpentine gestures that invitation which was Lydia's speciality. She began to speak in Lydia's voice, with the lazy drawl that made every remark she uttered sound faintly obscene.

'Oh, my dear man, I've heard that sort of thing so often. I don't want to make trouble between you and your wife. Why won't men leave me alone?'

It was a cruel caricature that Julia gave. It was quite ruthless. It amused her so much that she burst out laughing.

'Well, there's one thing, I may not have any sex appeal, but after seeing my imitation there aren't many people who'd think Lydia had either.'

It made her feel much better.

26

Rehearsals began and distracted Julia's troubled mind. The revival that Michael put on when she went abroad had done neither very well nor very badly, but rather than close the theatre he was keeping it in the bill till 'Nowadays' was ready. Because he was acting two matinées a week, and the weather was hot, he determined that they should take rehearsals easy. They had a month before them.

Though Julia had been on the stage so long she had never lost the thrill she got out of rehearsing, and the first rehearsal still made her almost sick with excitement. It was the beginning of a new adventure. She did not feel like a leading lady then, she felt as gay and eager as if she were a girl playing her first small part. But at the same time she had a delicious sense of her own powers. Once more she had the chance to exercise them.

At eleven o'clock she stepped on to the stage. The cast

stood about idly. She kissed and shook hands with the artists she knew and Michael with urbanity introduced to her those she did not. She greeted Avice Crichton with cordiality. She told her how pretty she was and how much she liked her hat; she told her about the lovely frocks she had chosen for her in Paris.

'Have you seen Tom lately?' she asked.

'No, I haven't. He's away on his holiday.'

'Oh yes. He's a nice little thing, isn't he?'

'Sweet.'

The two women smiled into one another's eyes. Julia watched her when she read her part and listened to her intonations. She smiled grimly. It was exactly what she had expected. Avice was one of those actresses who were quite sure of themselves from the first rehearsal. She didn't know what was coming to her. Tom meant nothing to Julia any more, but she had a score to settle with Avice and she wasn't going to forget it. The slut!

The play was a modern version of 'The Second Mrs Tanqueray,' but with the change of manners of this generation it had been treated from the standpoint of comedy. Some of the old characters were introduced, and Aubrey Tanqueray, now a very old man, appeared in the second act. After Paula's death he had married for the third time. Mrs Cortelyon had undertaken to compensate him for his unfortunate experience with his second wife, and she was now a cantankerous and insolent old lady. Ellean, his daughter, and Hugh Ardale had agreed to let bygones be bygones, for Paula's tragic death had seemed to wipe out the recollection of his lapse into extra-conjugal relations; and they had married. He was now a retired brigadier-general who played golf and deplored the decline of the British Empire – 'Gad, sir, I'd stand those damned socialists against a wall and shoot 'em if I had my way'; whereas Ellean by this time an elderly woman, after a prudish youth had become gay, modern and plain-spoken. The character that Michael played was called Robert Humphreys, and like the Aubrey of Pinero's play he was a widower with an only daughter; he had been a consul in China for many years, and having come into money had retired and was settling on the estate, near where the Tanquerays still lived, which a cousin had left him. His daughter, Honor (this was the part for which Avice Crichton had been engaged), was studying medicine with the intention of practising in India. Alone in London, and friendless after so many years abroad, he had picked up a well-known woman of the town called Mrs Marten. Mrs Marten belonged to the same class as Paula, but she was less exclusive; she 'did' the summer and the winter season at Cannes and in the intervals lived in a flat in Albermarle Street where she entertained the officers of His Majesty's brigade. She played a good game of bridge and an even better game of golf. The part well suited Julia.

The author followed the lines of the old play closely. Honor announced to her father that she was abandoning her medical studies and until her marriage wished to live with him, for she had just become engaged to Ellean's son, a young guardsman. Somewhat disconcerted, Robert Humphreys broke to her his intention of marrying Mrs Marten. Honor took the information with composure.

'Of course you know she's a tart, don't you?' she said coolly.

He, much embarrassed, spoke of the unhappy life she had led and how he wanted to make up to her for all she had suffered.

'Oh, don't talk such rot,' she answered. 'It's grand work if you can get it.'

Ellean's son had been one of Mrs Marten's numerous lovers just as Ellean's husband had been one of Paula Tanqueray's. When Robert Humphreys brought his wife down to his home in the country and this fact was discovered, they decided that Honor must be informed. To their consternation Honor did not turn a hair. She knew already.

'I was as pleased as Punch when I found out,' she told

her step-mother. 'You see, darling, you can tell me if he's all right in bed.'

This was Avice Crichton's best scene, it lasted a full ten minutes, and Michael had realized from the beginning that it was effective and important. Avice's cold, matter-of-fact prettiness had been exactly what he had thought would be so telling in the circumstances. But after half-a-dozen rehearsals he began to think that that was all she had to give. He talked it over with Julia.

'How d'you think Avice is shaping?'

'It's early days to tell yet.'

'I'm not happy about her. You said she could act. I've seen no sign of it yet.'

'It's a cast-iron part. She can't really go wrong in it.'

'You know just as well as I do that there's no such thing as a cast-iron part. However good a part is, it has to be acted for all it's worth. I'm not sure if it wouldn't be better to kick her out and get somebody else.'

'That wouldn't be so easy. I think you ought to give her a chance.'

'She's so awkward, her gestures are so meaningless.'

Julia reflected. She had her reasons for wishing to keep Avice in the cast. She knew her well enough to be sure that if she were dismissed she would tell Tom that it was because Julia was jealous of her. He loved her and would believe anything she said. He might even think that Julia had put this affront on her in revenge for his desertion. No, no, she must stay. She must play the part, and fail; and Tom must see with his own eyes what a bad actress she was. They both of them thought the play would make her. Fools. It would kill her.

'You know how clever you are, Michael, I'm sure you can train her if you're willing to take a little trouble.'

'But that's just it, she doesn't seem able to take direction. I show her exactly how to say a line and then she goes and says it in her own way. You wouldn't believe it, but sometimes I can hardly help thinking she's under the delusion that she knows better than I do.'

'You make her nervous. When you tell her to do something she's in such a dither she doesn't know what she's up to.'

'Good lord, no one could be more easy than I am. I've never even been sharp with her.'

Julia gave him an affectionate smile.

'Are you going to pretend that you really don't know what's the matter with her?'

'No, what?'

He looked at her with a blank face.

'Come off it, darling. Haven't you noticed that she's madly in love with you?'

'With me? But I thought she was practically engaged to Tom. Nonsense. You're always fancying things like that.'

'But it's quite obvious. After all she isn't the first who's fallen for your fatal beauty, and I don't suppose she'll be the last.'

'Heaven knows, I don't want to queer poor Tom's pitch.'

'It's not your fault, is it?'

'What d'you want me to do about it then?'

'Well, I think you ought to be nice to her. She's very young, you know, poor thing. What she wants is a helping hand. If you took her alone a few times and went through the part with her I believe you could do wonders. Why don't you take her out to lunch one day and have a talk to her?'

She saw the gleam in Michael's eyes as he considered the proposition and the shadow of a smile that was outlined on his lips.

'Of course the great thing is to get the play as well acted as we can.'

'I know it'll be a bore for you, but honestly, for the sake of the play I think it'll be worth while.'

'You know that I would never do anything to upset you, Julia. I mean, I'd much sooner fire the girl and get someone else in her place.'

'I think that would be such a mistake. I'm convinced

that if you'll only take enough trouble with her she'll give a very good performance.'

He walked up and down the room once or twice. He seemed to be considering the matter from every side.

'Well, I suppose it's my job to get the best performance I can out of every member of my cast. In every case you have to find out which is the best method of approach.'

He threw out his chin and drew in his belly. He straightened his back. Julia knew that Avice Crichton would hold the part, and next day at rehearsal he took her aside and had a long talk with her. She knew by his manner exactly what he was saying and, watching them out of the corner of her eye, presently she saw Avice nod and smile. He had asked her to lunch with him. With a contented mind Julia went on studying her part.

27

They had been rehearsing for a fortnight when Roger arrived from Austria. He had been spending a few weeks on a Carinthian lake, and after a day or two in London was to go and stay with friends in Scotland. Since Michael had to dine early to go to the theatre Julia went to meet him by herself. When she was dressing, Evie, sniffing as usual, told her that she was taking as much pains to make herself look nice as if she were going to meet a young man. She wanted Roger to be proud of her, and certainly she looked very young and pretty in her summer frock as she strolled down the platform. You would have thought, but wrongly, that she was perfectly unconscious of the attention she attracted. Roger, after a month in the sun, was very brown, but he was still rather spotty and he seemed thinner than when he had left London at the New Year. She hugged him with exuberant affection. He smiled slightly.

They were to dine by themselves. Julia asked him if he

would like to go to a play afterwards or to the pictures, but he said he preferred to stay at home.

'That'll be much nicer,' she answered, 'and we'll just talk.'

There was indeed a subject that Michael had invited her to discuss with Roger when the opportunity arose. Now that he was going to Cambridge so soon he ought to make up his mind what he wanted to do. Michael was afraid that he would drift through his time there and then go into a broker's office or even on the stage. Thinking that Julia had more tact than he, and more influence with the boy, he had urged her to put before him the advantages of the Foreign Office and the brilliant possibilities of the Bar. Julia thought it would be strange if in the course of two or three hours' conversation she could not find a way to lead to this important topic. At dinner she tried to get him to talk about Vienna. But he was reticent.

'Oh, I just did the usual things, you know. I saw the sights and worked hard at my German. I knocked about in beer places. I went to the opera a good deal.'

She wondered if he had had any love affairs.

'Anyhow, you haven't come back engaged to a Viennese maiden,' she said, thinking to draw him out.

He gave her a reflective, but faintly amused look. You might almost have thought that he had seen what she was driving at. It was strange; though he was her own son she did not feel quite at home with him.

'No,' he answered, 'I was too busy to bother with that sort of thing.'

'I suppose you went to all the theatres.'

'I went two or three times.'

'Did you see anything that would be any use to me?'

'You know, I never thought about that.'

His answer might have seemed a little ungracious but that it was accompanied by a smile, and his smile was very sweet. Julia wondered again how it was that he had inherited so little of Michael's beauty and of her charm. His red hair was nice, but his pale lashes gave his face a sort of empty look. Heaven only knew where with such a father and such a mother he had got his rather lumpy figure. He was eighteen now; it was time he fined down. He seemed a trifle apathetic; he had none of her sparkling vitality; she could picture the vividness with which she would have narrated her experiences if she had just spent six months in Vienna. Why, already she had made a story about her stay at St. Malo with Aunt Carrie and her mother that made people roar with laughter. They all said it was as good as a play, and her own impression was that it was much better than most. She told it to Roger now. He listened with his slow, quiet smile; but she had an uneasy feeling that he did not think it quite so funny as she did. She sighed in her heart. Poor lamb, he could have no sense of humour. Then he made some remark that led her to speak of 'Nowadays.' She told him its story, and explained what she was doing with her part; she talked to him of the cast and described the sets. At the end of dinner it suddenly struck her that she had been talking entirely of herself and her own interests. She did not know how she had been led to do this, and the suspicion flashed across her mind that Roger had guided the conversation in that direction so that it should be diverted from him and his affairs. But she put it aside. He really wasn't intelligent enough for that. It was later when they sat in the drawing-room listening to the radio and smoking, that Julia found the chance to slip in, apparently in the most casual fashion, the question she had prepared.

'Have you made up your mind what you're going to be yet?'

'No. Is there any hurry?'

'You know how ignorant I am about everything. Your father says that if you're going to be a barrister you ought to work at law when you go to Cambridge. On the other hand, if you fancy the Foreign Office you should take up modern languages.'

He looked at her for so long, with that queer, reflective

air of his, that Julia had some difficulty in holding her light, playful and yet affectionate expression.

'If I believed in God I'd be a priest,' he said at last.

'A priest?'

Julia could hardly believe her ears. She had a feeling of acute discomfort. But his answer sank into her mind and in a flash she saw him as a cardinal, inhabiting a beautiful palazzo in Rome, filled with wonderful pictures, and surrounded by obsequious prelates; and then again as a saint, in a mitre and vestments heavily embroidered with gold, with benevolent gestures distributing bread to the poor. She saw herself in a brocaded dress and a string of pearls. The mother of the Borgias.

'That was all right in the sixteenth century,' she said. 'It's too late in the day for that.'

'Much.'

'I can't think what put such an idea in your head.' He did not answer, so that she had to speak again. 'Aren't you happy?'

'Quite,' he smiled.

'What is it you want?'

Once again he gave her his disconcerting stare. It was hard to know if he was serious, for his eyes faintly shimmered with amusement.

'Reality.'

'What *do* you mean?'

'You see, I've lived all my life in an atmosphere of make-believe. I want to get down to brass tacks. You and father are all right breathing this air, it's the only air you know and you think it's the air of heaven. It stifles me.'

Julia listened to him attentively, trying to understand what he meant.

'We're actors, and successful ones. That's why we've been able to surround you with every luxury since you were born. You could count on the fingers of one hand the actors who've sent their son to Eton.'

'I'm very grateful for all you've done for me.'

'Then what are you reproaching us for?'

214

'I'm not reproaching you. You've done everything you could for me. Unfortunately for me you've taken away my belief in everything.'

'We've never interfered with your beliefs. I know we're not religious people, we're actors, and after eight performances a week one wants one's Sundays to oneself. I naturally expected they'd see to all that at school.'

He hesitated a little before he spoke again. One might have thought that he had to make a slight effort over himself to continue.

'When I was just a kid, I was fourteen, I was standing one night in the wings watching you act. It must have been a pretty good scene, you said the things you had to say so sincerely, and what you were saying was so moving, I couldn't help crying. I was all worked up. I don't know how to say it quite, I was uplifted; I felt terribly sorry for you, I felt a bloody little hero; I felt I'd never do anything again that was beastly or underhand. And then you had to come to the back of the stage, near where I was standing, the tears were streaming down your face; you stood with your back to the audience and in your ordinary voice you said to the stage manager; what the bloody hell is that electrician doing with the lights? I told him to leave out the blue. And then in the same breath you turned round and faced the audience with a great cry of anguish and went on with the scene.'

'But, darling, that was acting. If an actress felt the emotions she represented she'd tear herself to pieces. I remember the scene well. It used to bring down the house. I've never heard such applause in my life.'

'I suppose I was a fool to be taken in by it. I believed you meant what you said. When I saw that it was all pretence it smashed something. I've never believed in you since. I'd been made a fool of once; I made up my mind that I wouldn't ever be made a fool of again.'

She gave him her delightful and disarming smile.

'Darling, I think you're talking nonsense.'

'Of course you do. You don't know the difference

between truth and make-believe. You never stop acting. It's second nature to you. You act when there's a party here. You act to the servants, you act to father, you act to me. To me you act the part of the fond, indulgent, celebrated mother. You don't exist, you're only the innumerable parts you've played. I've often wondered if there was ever a you or if you were never anything more than a vehicle for all these other people that you've pretended to be. When I've seen you go into an empty room I've sometimes wanted to open the door suddenly, but I've been afraid to in case I found nobody there.'

She looked up at him quickly. She shivered, for what he said gave her an eerie sensation. She listened to him attentively, with a certain anxiety, for he was so serious that she felt he was expressing something that had burdened him for years. She had never in his whole life heard him talk so much.

'D'you think I'm only sham?'

'Not quite. Because sham is all you are. Sham is your truth. Just as margarine is butter to people who don't know what butter is.'

She had a vague feeling of guilt. The Queen in 'Hamlet': 'And let me wring your heart; for so I shall, if it be made of penetrable stuff.' Her thoughts wandered.

('I wonder if I'm too old to play Hamlet. Siddons and Sarah Bernhardt played him. I've got better legs than any of the men I've seen in the part. I'll ask Charles what he thinks. Of course there's that bloody blank verse. Stupid of him not to write it in prose. Of course I might do it in French at the Français. God, what a stunt that would be.')

She saw herself in a black doublet, with long silk hose. 'Alas, poor Yorick.' But she bethought herself.

'You can hardly say that your father doesn't exist. Why, he's been playing himself for the last twenty years.' ('Michael could play the King, not in French, of course, but if we decided to have a shot at it in London.')

'Poor father, I suppose he's good at his job, but he's not

very intelligent, is he? He's so busy being the handsomest man in England.'

'I don't think it's very nice of you to speak of your father like that.'

'Have I told you anything you don't know?' he asked coolly.

Julia wanted to smile, but would not allow the look of somewhat pained dignity to leave her face.

'It's our weakness, not our strength, that endears us to those who love us,' she replied.

'In what play did you say that?'

She repressed a gesture of annoyance. The words had come naturally to her lips, but as she said them she remembered that they were out of a play. Little brute! But they came in very appositely.

'You're hard,' she said plaintively. She was beginning to feel more and more like Hamlet's mother. 'Don't you love me?'

'I might if I could find you. But where are you? If one stripped you of your exhibitionism, if one took your technique away from you, if one peeled you as one peels an onion of skin after skin of pretence and insincerity, of tags of old parts and shreds of faked emotions, would one come upon a soul at last?' He looked at her with his grave sad eyes and then he smiled a little. 'I like you all right.'

'Do you believe I love you?'

'In your way.'

Julia's face was suddenly discomposed.

'If you only knew the agony I suffered when you were ill! I don't know what I should have done if you'd died!'

'You would have given a beautiful performance of a bereaved mother at the bier of her only child.'

'Not nearly such a good performance as if I'd had the opportunity of rehearsing it a few times,' Julia answered tartly. 'You see, what you don't understand is that acting isn't nature; it's art, and art is something you create. Real grief is ugly; the business of the actor is to represent it not only with truth but with beauty. If I were really dying

217

as I've died in half a dozen plays, d'you think I'd care whether my gestures were graceful and my faltering words distinct enough to carry to the last row of the gallery? If it's a sham it's no more a sham than a sonata of Beethoven's, and I'm no more of a sham than the pianist who plays it. It's cruel to say that I'm not fond of you. I'm devoted to you. You've been the only thing in my life.'

'No. You were fond of me when I was a kid and you could have me photographed with you. It made a lovely picture and it was fine publicity. But since then you haven't bothered much about me. I've bored you rather than otherwise. You were always glad to see me, but you were thankful that I went my own way and didn't want to take up your time. I don't blame you; you hadn't got time in your life for anyone but yourself.'

Julia was beginning to grow a trifle impatient. He was getting too near the truth for her comfort.

'You forget that young things are rather boring.'

'Crashing, I should think,' he smiled. 'But then why do you pretend that you can't bear to let me out of your sight? That's just acting too.'

'You make me very unhappy. You make me feel as if I hadn't done my duty to you.'

'But you have. You've been a very good mother. You've done something for which I shall always be grateful to you, you've left me alone.'

'I don't understand what you want.'

'I told you. Reality.'

'But where are you going to find it?'

'I don't know. Perhaps it doesn't exist. I'm young still; I'm ignorant. I thought perhaps that at Cambridge, meeting people and reading books, I might discover where to look for it. If they say it only exists in God, I'm done.'

Julia was disturbed. What he said had not really penetrated to her understanding, his words were lines and the important thing was not what they meant, but whether they 'got over', but she was sensitive to the emotion she felt in him. Of course he was only eighteen, and it would be silly to take him too seriously, she couldn't help thinking he'd got all that from somebody else, and that there was a good deal of pose in it. Did anyone have ideas of his own and did anyone not pose just a wee, wee bit? But of course it might be that at the moment he felt everything he said, and it wouldn't be very nice of her to make light of it.

'Of course I see what you mean,' she said. 'My greatest wish in the world is that you should be happy. I'll manage your father, and you can do as you like. You must seek your own salvation, I see that. But I think you ought to make sure that all these ideas of yours aren't just morbid. Perhaps you were too much alone in Vienna and I daresay you read too much. Of course your father and I belong to a different generation and I don't suppose we can help you. Why don't you talk it over with someone more of your own age? Tom, for instance.'

'Tom? A poor little snob. His only ambition in life is to be a gentleman, and he hasn't the sense to see that the more he tries the more hopeless it is.'

'I thought you liked him so much. Why, at Taplow last summer you just lived in his pocket.'

'I didn't dislike him. I made use of him. He could tell me a lot of things that I wanted to know. But I thought him an insignificant, silly little thing.'

Julia remembered how insanely jealous she had been of their friendship. It made her angry to think of all the agony she had wasted.

'You've dropped him, haven't you?' he asked suddenly.

She was startled.

'I suppose I have more or less.'

'I think it's very wise of you. He wasn't up to your mark.'

He looked at her with his calm, reflective eyes, and on a sudden Julia had a sickening fear that he knew that Tom had been her lover. It was impossible, she told herself, it was only her guilty conscience that made her think so;

at Taplow there had been nothing; it was incredible that any of the horrid gossip had reached his ears; and yet there was something in his expression that made her certain that he knew. She was ashamed.

'I only asked him to come down to Taplow because I thought it would be nice for you to have a boy of that age to play around with.'

'It was.'

There was in his eyes a faint twinkle of amusement. She felt desperate. She would have liked to ask him what he was grinning at, but dared not; for she knew; he was not angry with her, she could have borne that, he was merely diverted. She was bitterly hurt. She would have cried, but that he would only laugh. And what could she say to him? He believed nothing she said. Acting! for once she was at a loss how to cope with a situation. She was up against something that she did not know, something mysterious and rather frightening. Could that be reality? At that moment they heard a car drive up.

'There's your father,' she exclaimed.

What a relief! The scene was intolerable, and she was thankful that his arrival must end it. In a moment Michael, very hearty, with his chin thrust out and his belly pulled in, looking for all his fifty odd years incredibly handsome, burst into the room and, in his manly way, thrust out his hand to greet, after a six months' absence, his only begotten son.

28

Three days later Roger went up to Scotland. By the exercise of some ingenuity Julia had managed that they should not again spend any length of time alone together. When they happened to be by themselves for a few minutes they talked of indifferent things. Julia was not really sorry to see him go. She could not dismiss from her mind the curious conversation she had had with him. There was one point in particular that unaccountably worried her; this was his suggestion that if she went into an empty room and someone suddenly opened the door there would be nobody there. It made her feel very uncomfortable.

'I never set out to be a raving beauty, but the one thing no one has ever denied me is personality. It's absurd to pretend that because I can play a hundred different parts in a hundred different ways I haven't got an individuality of my own. I can do that because I'm a bloody good actress.'

She tried to think what happened to her when she went alone into an empty room.

'But I never am alone, even in an empty room. There's always Michael, or Evie, or Charles, or the public; not in the flesh, of course, but in the spirit, as it were. I must speak to Charles about Roger.'

Unfortunately he was away. But he was coming back for the dress-rehearsal and the first night; he had not missed these occasions for twenty years, and they had always had supper together after the dress-rehearsal. Michael would remain in the theatre, busy with the lights and so on, so that they would be alone. They would be able to have a good talk.

She studied her part. Julia did not deliberately create the character she was going to act by observation; she had a knack of getting into the shoes of the woman she had to portray so that she thought with her mind and felt with her senses. Her intuition suggested to her a hundred small touches that afterwards amazed people by their verisimilitude; but when they asked her where she had got them she could not say. Now she wanted to show the courageous yet uneasy breeziness of the Mrs Marten who played golf and could talk to a man like one good chap to another and yet, essentially a respectable, middle-class woman, hankered for the security of the marriage state.

Michael never liked to have a crowd at a dress-rehearsal, and this time, anxious to keep the secret of the play till the first night, he had admitted besides Charles only the people, photographers and dressmakers, whose presence was necessary. Julia spared herself. She had no intention of giving all she had to give till the first night. It was enough if her performance was adequate. Under Michael's businesslike direction everything went off without a hitch, and by ten o'clock Julia and Charles were sitting in the Grill Room of the Savoy. The first thing she asked him was what he thought of Avice Crichton.

'Not at all bad and wonderfully pretty. She really looked lovely in that second-act dress.'

'I'm not going to wear the dress I wore in the second act. Charley Deverill has made me another.'

He did not see the slightly humorous glance she gave him, and if he had would not have guessed what it meant. Michael, having taken Julia's advice, had gone to a good deal of trouble with Avice. He had rehearsed her by herself upstairs in his private room and had given her every intonation and every gesture. He had also, Julia had good reason to believe, lunched with her several times and taken her out to supper. The result of all this was that she was playing the part uncommonly well. Michael rubbed his hands.

'I'm very pleased with her. I think she'll make quite a hit. I've half a mind to give her a contract.'

'I wouldn't,' said Julia. 'Not till after the first night. You can never really tell how a performance is going to pan out till you've got an audience.'

'She's a nice girl and a perfect lady.'

'A nice girl, I suppose, because she's madly in love with you, and a perfect lady because she's resisting your advances till she's got a contract.'

'Oh, my dear, don't be silly. Why, I'm old enough to be her father.'

But he smiled complacently. She knew very well that his love-making went no farther than holding hands and a kiss or two in a taxi, but she knew also that it flattered him to imagine that she suspected him capable of infidelity.

But now Julia, having satisfied her appetite with proper regard for her figure, attacked the subject which was on her mind.

'Charles dear, I want to talk to you about Roger.'

'Oh yes, he came back the other day, didn't he? How is he?'

'My dear, a most terrible thing has happened. He's come back a fearful prig and I don't know what to do about it.'

She gave him her version of the conversation. She left out one or two things that it seemed inconvenient to mention, but what she told was on the whole accurate.

'The tragic thing is that he has absolutely no sense of humour,' she finished.

'After all he's only eighteen.'

'You could have knocked me down with a feather when he said all those things to me. I felt just like Balaam when his ass broke into light conversation.'

She gave him a gay look, but he did not even smile. He did not seem to think her remark as funny as she did.

'I can't imagine where he got his ideas. It's absurd to think that he could have thought out all that nonsense for himself.'

'Are you sure that boys of that age don't think more than we older people imagine? It's a sort of puberty of the spirit and its results are often strange.'

'It seems so deceitful of Roger to have harboured thoughts like those all these years and never breathed a word about them. He might have been accusing me.' She gave a chuckle. 'To tell you the truth, when Roger was talking to me I felt just like Hamlet's mother.' Then with hardly a break: 'I wonder if I'm too old to play Hamlet?'

'Gertrude isn't a very good part, is it?'

Julia broke into a laugh of frank amusement.

'Don't be idiotic, Charles. I wouldn't play the Queen. I'd play Hamlet.'

'D'you think it's suited to a woman?'

'Mrs. Siddons played it and so did Sarah Bernhardt. It

would set a seal on my career, if you know what I mean. Of course there's the difficulty of the blank verse.'

'I have heard actors speak it so that it was indistinguishable from prose,' he answered.

'Yes, but that's not quite the same, is it?'

'Were you nice to Roger?'

She was surprised at his going back to that subject so suddenly, but she returned to it with a smile.

'Oh, charming.'

'It's hard not to be impatient with the absurdity of the young; they tell us that two and two make four as though it had never occurred to us, and they're disappointed if we can't share their surprise when they have just discovered that a hen lays an egg. There's a lot of nonsense in their ranting and raving, but it's not all nonsense. One ought to sympathize with them; one ought to do one's best to understand. One has to remember how much has to be forgotten and how much has to be learnt when for the first time one faces life. It's not very easy to give up one's ideals, and the brute facts of every day are bitter pills to swallow. The spiritual conflicts of adolescence can be very severe and one can do so little to resolve them.'

'But you don't really think there's anything in all this stuff of Roger's? I believe it's all a lot of communist nonsense that he's learnt in Vienna. I wish we'd never sent him there.'

'You may be right. It may be that in a year or two he'll lose sight of the clo ds of glory and accept the chain. It may be that he'll find what he's looking for, if not in God, then in art.'

'I should hate him to be an actor if that's what you mean.'

'No, I don't think he'll fancy that.'

'And of course he can't be a playwright, he hasn't a sense of humour.'

'I daresay he'll be quite content to go into the Foreign Office. It would be an asset to him there.'

'What would you advise me to do?'

'Nothing. Let him be. That's probably the greatest kindness you can do him.'

'But I can't help being worried about him.'

'You needn't be. Be hopeful. You thought you'd only given birth to an ugly duckling; perhaps he's going to turn into a white-winged swan.'

Charles was not giving Julia what she wanted. She had expected him to be more sympathetic.

'I suppose he's getting old, poor dear,' she reflected. 'He's losing his grip of things. He must have been impotent for years; I wonder it never struck me before.'

She asked what the time was.

'I think I ought to go. I must get a long night's rest.'

Julia slept well and when she awoke had at once a feeling of exultation. To-night was the first night. It gave her a little thrill of pleasure to recollect that people had already been assembling at the pit and gallery doors when she left the theatre after the dress-rehearsal, and now at ten in the morning there was probably already a long queue.'

'Lucky it's a fine day for them, poor brutes.'

In bygone years she had been intolerably nervous before a first night. She had felt slightly sick all day and as the hours passed got into such a state that she almost thought she would have to leave the stage. But by now, after having passed through the ordeal so many times, she had acquired a certain nonchalance. Throughout the early part of the day she felt only happy and mildly excited; it was not till late in the afternoon that she began to feel ill at ease. She grew silent and wanted to be left alone. She also grew irritable, and Michael, having learnt from experience, took care to keep out of her way. Her hands and feet got cold and by the time she reached the theatre they were like lumps of ice. But still the apprehension that filled her was not unpleasant.

Julia had nothing to do that morning but go down to the Siddons for a word-rehearsal at noon, so she lay in bed till late. Michael did not come back to luncheon, having last things to do to the sets, and she ate alone. Then she went to bed and for an hour slept soundly. Her intention was to rest all the afternoon; Miss Phillips was coming at six to give her a light massage, and by seven she wanted to be at the theatre. But when she awoke she felt so much refreshed that it irked her to stay in bed, so she made up her mind to get up and go for a walk. It was a fine, sunny day. Liking the town better than the country and streets more than trees, she did not go into the Park, but sauntered round the neighbouring squares, deserted at that time of year, idly looking at the houses, and thought how much she preferred her own to any of them. She felt at ease and light-hearted. Then she thought it time to go home. She had just reached the corner of Stanhope Place when she heard her name called in a voice that she could not but recognize.

'Julia.'

She turned round and Tom, his face all smiles, caught her up. She had not seen him since her return from France. He was very smart in a neat grey suit and a brown hat. He was tanned by the sun.

'I thought you were away.'

'I came back on Monday. I didn't ring up because I knew you were busy with the final rehearsals. I'm coming to-night; Michael gave me a stall.'

'Oh, I'm glad.'

It was plain that he was delighted to see her. His face was eager and his eyes shone. She was pleased to discover that the sight of him excited no emotion in her. She wondered as they went on talking what there was in him that had ever so deeply affected her.

'What on earth are you wandering about like this for?'

'I've been for a stroll. I was just going in to tea.'

'Come and have tea with me.'

His flat was just round the corner. Indeed he had caught sight of her just as he was going down the mews to get to it.

'How is it you're back so early?'

'Oh, there's nothing much on at the office just now. You know, one of our partners died a couple of months ago, and I'm getting a bigger share. It means I shall be able to keep on the flat after all. Michael was jolly decent about it, he said I could stay on rent free till things got better. I hated the idea of turning out. Do come. I'd love to make you a cup of tea.'

He rattled on so vivaciously that Julia was amused. You would never have thought to listen to him that there had ever been anything between them. He seemed perfectly unembarrassed.

'All right. But I can only stay a minute.'

'O.K.'

They turned into the mews and she preceded him up the narrow staircase.

'You toddle along to the sitting-room and I'll put the water on to boil.'

She went in and sat down. She looked round the room that had been the scene of so many emotions for her. Nothing was changed. Her photograph stood in its old place, but on the chimney piece was a large photograph also of Avice Crichton. On it was written for Tom from Avice. Julia took everything in. The room might have been a set in which she had once acted; it was vaguely familiar, but no longer meant anything to her. The love that had consumed her then, the jealousy she had stifled, the ecstasy of surrender, it had no more reality than one of the innumerable parts she had played in the past. She relished her indifference. Tom came in, with the tea-cloth she had given him, and neatly set out the tea-service which she had also given him. She did not know why the thought of his casually using still all her little presents made her inclined to laugh. Then he came in with the tea and they drank it sitting side by side on the sofa. He told her more about his improved circumstances. In his pleasant, friendly way he acknowledged that it was owing to the work that through her he had been able to bring the firm that he had secured a larger share in the profits. He told her of the holiday from which he had just returned. It was quite clear to Julia that he had no inkling how much he had made her suffer. That too made her now inclined to laugh.

'I hear you're going to have an enormous success to-night.'

'It would be nice, wouldn't it?'

'Avice says that both you and Michael have been awfully good to her. Take care she doesn't romp away with the play.'

He said it chaffingly, but Julia wondered whether Avice had told him that this was what she expected to do.

'Are you engaged to her?'

'No. She wants her freedom. She says an engagement would interfere with her career.'

'With her what?' The words slipped out of Julia's mouth before she could stop them, but she immediately recovered herself. 'Yes, I see what she means of course.'

'Naturally, I don't want to stand in her way. I mean, supposing after to-night she got a big offer for America I can quite see that she ought to be perfectly free to accept.'

Her career! Julia smiled quietly to herself.

'You know, I do think you're a brick, the way you've behaved to her.'

'Why?'

'Oh well, you know what women are!'

As he said this he slipped his arm round her waist and kissed her. She laughed outright.

'What an absurd little thing you are.'

'How about a bit of love?'

'Don't be so silly.'

'What is there silly about it? Don't you think we've been divorced long enough?'

'I'm all for irrevocable divorce. And what about Avice?'

'Oh, she's different. Come on.'

'Has it slipped your memory that I've got a first night to-night?'

228

'There's plenty of time.'

He put both arms round her and kissed her softly. She looked at him with mocking eyes. Suddenly she made up her mind.

'All right.'

They got up and went into the bedroom. She took off her hat and slipped out of her dress. He held her in his arms as he had held her so often before. He kissed her closed eyes and the little breasts of which she was so proud. She gave him her body to do what he wanted with, but her spirit held aloof. She returned his kisses out of amiability, but she caught herself thinking of the part she was going to play that night. She seemed to be two persons, the mistress in her lover's embrace, and the actress who already saw in her mind's eye the vast vague dark audience and heard the shouts of applause as she stepped on to the stage. When, a little later, they lay side by side, he with his arm round her neck, she forgot about him so completely that she was quite surprised when he broke a long silence.

'Don't you care for me any more?'

She gave him a little hug.

'Of course, darling. I dote on you.'

'You're so strange to-day.'

She realized that he was disappointed. Poor little thing, she didn't want to hurt his feelings. He was very sweet really.

'With the first night before me I'm not really myself to-day. You mustn't mind.'

When she came to the conclusion, quite definitely now, that she no longer cared two straws for him she could not help feeling a great pity for him. She stroked his cheek gently.

'Sweetie pie. (I wonder if Michael remembered to have tea sent along to the queues. It doesn't cost much and they do appreciate it so enormously.) You know, I really must get up. Miss Phillips is coming at six. Evie will be in a state, she won't be able to think what's happened to me.'

She chattered brightly while she dressed. She was conscious, although she did not look at him, that Tom was vaguely uneasy. She put her hat on, then she took his face in both her hands and gave him a friendly kiss.

'Good-bye, my lamb. Have a good time to-night.'

'Best of luck.'

He smiled with some awkwardness. She perceived that he did not quite know what to make of her. Julia slipped out of the flat, and if she had not been England's leading actress, and a woman of hard on fifty, she would have hopped on one leg all the way down Stanhope Place till she got to her house. She was as pleased as Punch. She let herself in with her latchkey and closed the front door behind her.

'I daresay there's something in what Roger said. Love isn't worth all the fuss they make about it.'

29

Four hours later it was all over. The play went well from the beginning; the audience, notwithstanding the season, a fashionable one, were pleased after the holidays to find themselves once more in a playhouse, and were ready to be amused. It was an auspicious beginning for the theatrical season. There had been great applause after each act and at the end a dozen curtains calls; Julia took two by herself, and even she was startled by the warmth of her reception. She had made the little halting speech, prepared beforehand, which the occasion demanded. There had been a final call of the entire company and then the orchestra had struck up the National Anthem. Julia, pleased, excited and happy, went to her dressing-room. She had never felt more sure of herself. She had never acted with greater brilliance, variety and resource. The play ended with a long tirade in which Julia, as the retired harlot, castigated the flippancy, the uselessness, the immorality of the idle set into which her marriage had brought her. It was two pages long, and there was not another actress in England who could have held the attention of the audience while she delivered it. With her exquisite timing, with the modulation of her beautiful voice, with her command of the gamut of emotions, she had succeeded by a miracle of technique in making it a thrilling, almost spectacular climax to the play. A violent action could not have been more exciting not an unexpected dénouement more surprising. The whole cast had been excellent with the exception of Avice Crichton. Julia hummed in an undertone as she went into her dressing-room.

Michael followed her in almost at once.

'It looks like a winner all right.' He threw his arms round her and kissed her. 'By God, what a performance you gave.'

'You weren't so bad yourself dear.'

'That's the sort of part I can play on my head,' he answered carelessly, modest as usual about his own acting. 'Did you hear them during your long speech? That ought to knock the critics.'

'Oh, you know what they are. They'll give all their attention to the blasted play and then three lines at the end to me.'

'You're the greatest actress in the world, darling, but by God, you're a bitch.'

Julia opened her eyes very wide in an expression of the most naïve surprise.

'Michael, what do you mean?'

'Don't look so innocent. You know perfectly well. Do you think you can cod an old trooper like me?'

He was looking at her with twinkling eyes, and it was very difficult for her not to burst out laughing.

'I am as innocent as a babe unborn.'

'Come off it. If anyone ever deliberately killed a performance you killed Avice's. I couldn't be angry with you, it was so beautifully done.'

Now Julia simply could not conceal the little smile that curled her lips. Praise is always grateful to the artist. Avice's one big scene was in the second act. It was with Julia, and Michael had rehearsed it so as to give it all to the girl. This was indeed what the play demanded and Julia, as always, had in rehearsals accepted his direction. To bring out the colour of her blue eyes and to emphasize her fair hair they had dressed Avice in pale blue. To contrast with this Julia had chosen a dress of an agreeable yellow. This she had worn at the dress rehearsal. But she had ordered another dress at the same time, of sparkling silver, and to the surprise of Michael and the consternation of Avice it was in this that she made her entrance in the second act. Its brilliance, the way it took the light, attracted the attention of the audience. Avice's blue looked drab by comparison. When they reached the important scene they were to have together Julia produced, as a conjurer produces a rabbit from his hat, a large handkerchief of scarlet chiffon and with this she played. She waved it, she spread it out as though to look at it, she screwed it up, she wiped her brow with it, she delicately blew her nose. The audience fascinated could not take their eyes away from the red rag. And she moved up stage so that Avice to speak to her had to turn her back on the audience, and when they were sitting on a sofa together she took her hand, in an impulsive way that seemed to the public exquisitely natural, and sitting well back herself forced Avice to turn her profile to the house. Julia had noticed early in rehearsals that in profile Avice had a sheep-like look. The author had given Avice lines to say that had so much amused the cast at the first rehearsal that they had all burst out laughing. Before the audience had quite realized how funny they were Julia had cut in with her reply, and the audience anxious to hear it suppressed their laughter. The scene which was devised to be extremely amusing took on a sardonic colour, and

232

the character Avice played acquired a certain odiousness. Avice in her inexperience, not getting the laughs she had expected, was rattled; her voice grew hard and her gestures awkward. Julia took the scene away from her and played it with miraculous virtuosity. But her final stroke was accidental. Avice had a long speech to deliver, and Julia nervously screwed her red handkerchief into a ball; the action almost automatically suggested an expression; she looked at Avice with troubled eyes and two heavy tears rolled down her cheeks. You felt the shame with which the girl's flippancy affected her, and you saw her pain because her poor little ideals of uprightness, her hankering for goodness, were so brutally mocked. The episode lasted no more than a minute, but in that minute, by those tears and by the anguish of her look, Julia laid bare the sordid misery of the woman's life. That was the end of Avice.

'And I was such a damned fool, I thought of giving her a contract,' said Michael.

'Why don't you?'

'When you've got your knife into her? Not on your life. You're a naughty little thing to be so jealous. You don't really think she means anything to me, do you? You ought to know by now that you're the only woman in the world for me.'

Michael thought that Julia had played this trick on account of the rather violent flirtation he had been having with Avice, and though, of course, it was hard luck on Avice he could not help being a trifle flattered.

'You old donkey,' smiled Julia, knowing exactly what he was thinking and tickled to death at his mistake. 'After all, you are the handsomest man in London.'

'All that's as it may be. But I don't know what the author'll say. He's a conceited little ape and it's not a bit the scene he wrote.'

'Oh, leave him to me. I'll fix him.'

There was a knock at the door and it was the author himself who came in. With a cry of delight, Julia went up to him, threw her arms round his neck and kissed him on both cheeks.

'Are you pleased?'

'It looks like a success,' he answered, but a trifle coldly.

'My dear, it'll run for a year.' She placed her hands on his shoulders, and looked him full in the face. 'But you're a wicked, wicked man.'

'I?'

'You almost ruined my performance. When I came to that bit in the second act and suddenly saw what it meant I nearly broke down. You knew what was in that scene, you're the author; why did you let us rehearse it all the time as if there was no more in it than appeared on the surface? We're only actors, how can you expect us to – to fathom your subtlety? It's the best scene in your play and I almost bungled it. No one in the world could have written it but you. Your play's brilliant, but in that scene there's more than brilliance, there's genius.'

The author flushed. Julia looked at him with veneration. He felt shy and happy and proud.

('In twenty-four hours the mug'll think he really meant the scene to go like that.')

Michael beamed.

'Come along to my dressing-room and have a whisky and soda. I'm sure you need a drink after all that emotion.'

They went out as Tom came in. Tom's face was red with excitement.

'My dear, it was grand. You were simply wonderful. Gosh, what a performance.'

'Did you like it? Avice was good, wasn't she?'

'No, rotten.'

'My dear, what do you mean? I thought she was charming.'

'You simply wiped the floor with her. She didn't even look pretty in the second act.'

Avice's career!

'I say, what are you doing afterwards?'

'Dolly's giving a party for us.'

234

'Can't you cut it and come along to supper with me? I'm madly in love with you.'

'Oh, what nonsense. How can I let Dolly down?'

'Oh, do.'

His eyes were eager. She could see that he desired her as he had never done before, and she rejoiced in her triumph. But she shook her head firmly. There was a sound in the corridor of a crowd of people talking, and they both knew that a troop of friends were forcing their way down the narrow passage to congratulate her.

'Damn all these people. God, how I want to kiss you. I'll ring you up in the morning.'

The door burst open and Dolly, fat, perspiring and bubbling over with enthusiasm, swept in at the head of a throng that packed the dressing-room to suffocation. Julia submitted to being kissed by all and sundry. Among others were three or four well-known actresses, and they were prodigal of their praise. Julia gave a beautiful performance of unaffected modesty. The corridor was packed now with people who wanted to get at least a glimpse of her. Dolly had to fight her way out.

'Try not to be too late,' she said to Julia. 'It's going to be a heavenly party.'

'I'll come as soon as ever I can.'

At last the crowd was got rid of and Julia, having undressed, began to take off her make-up. Michael came in, wearing a dressing-gown.

'I say, Julia, you'll have to go to Dolly's party by yourself. I've got to see the libraries and I can't manage it. I'm going to sting them.'

'Oh, all right.'

'They're waiting for me now. See you in the morning.'

He went out and she was left alone with Evie. The dress she had arranged to wear for Dolly's party was placed over a chair. Julia smeared her face with cleansing cream.

'Evie, Mr Fennell will be ringing up to-morrow. Will you say I'm out?'

Evie looked in the mirror and caught Julia's eyes.

'And if he rings up again?'

'I don't want to hurt his feelings, poor lamb, but I have a notion I shall be very much engaged for some time now.'

Evie sniffed loudly, and with that rather disgusting habit of hers drew her forefinger across the bottom of her nose.

'I understand,' she said dryly.

'I always said you weren't such a fool as you looked.' Julia went on with her face. 'What's that dress doing on that chair?'

'That? That's the dress you said you'd wear for the party.'

'Put it away. I can't go to the party without Mr Gosselyn.'

'Since when?'

'Shut up, you old hag. Phone through and say that I've got a bad headache and had to go home to bed, but Mr Gosselyn will come if he possibly can.'

'The party's being given special for you. You can't let the poor old gal down like that?'

Julia stamped her feet.

'I don't want to go to a party. I won't go to a party.'

'There's nothing for you to eat at home.'

'I don't want to go home. I'll go and have supper at a restaurant.'

'Who with?'

'By myself.'

Evie gave her a puzzled glance.

'The play's a success, isn't it?'

'Yes. Everything's a success. I feel on top of the world. I feel like a million dollars. I want to be alone and enjoy myself. Ring up the Berkeley and tell them to keep a table for one in the little room. They'll know what I mean.'

'What's the matter with you?'

'I shall never in all my life have another moment like this. I'm not going to share it with anyone.'

When Julia had got her face clean she left it. She neither

painted her lips nor rouged her cheeks. She put on again the brown coat and skirt in which she had come to the theatre and the same hat. It was a felt hat with a brim, and this she pulled down over one eye so that it should hide as much of her face as possible. When she was ready she looked at herself in the glass.

'I look like a working dressmaker whose husband's left her, and who can blame him? I don't believe a soul would recognize me.'

Evie had had the telephoning done from the stage-door, and when she came back Julia asked her if there were many people waiting for her there.

'About three 'undred I should say.'

'Damn.' She had a sudden desire to see nobody and be seen by nobody. She wanted just for one hour to be obscure. 'Tell the fireman to let me out at the front and I'll take a taxi, and then as soon as I've got out let the crowd know there's no use in their waiting.'

'God only knows what I 'ave to put up with,' said Evie darkly.

'You old cow.'

Julia took Evie's face in her hands and kissed her rad-dled cheeks; then slipped out of her dressing-room, on to the stage and through the iron door into the darkened auditorium.

Julia's simple disguise was evidently adequate, for when she came into the little room at the Berkeley of which she was peculiarly fond, the head waiter did not immediately know.

'Have you got a corner that you can squeeze me into?' she asked diffidently.

Her voice and a second glance told him who she was.

'Your favourite table is waiting for you, Miss Lambert. The message said you would be alone?' Julia nodded and he led her to a table in the corner of the room. 'I hear you've had a big success to-night, Miss Lambert.' How quickly good news travelled. 'What can I order?'

The head waiter was surprised that Julia should be

having supper by herself, but the only emotion that it was his business to show clients was gratification at seeing them.

'I'm very tired, Angelo.'

'A little caviare to begin with, madame, or some oysters?'

'Oysters, Angelo, but fat ones.'

'I will choose them myself, Miss Lambert, and to follow?'

Julia gave a long sigh, for now she could, with a free conscience, order what she had had in mind ever since the end of the second act. She felt she deserved a treat to celebrate her triumph, and for once she meant to throw prudence to the winds.

'Grilled steak and onions, Angelo, fried potatoes, and a bottle of Bass. Give it me in a silver tankard.'

She probably hadn't eaten fried potatoes for ten years. But what an occasion it was! By a happy chance on this day she had confirmed her hold on the public by a performance that she could only describe as scintillating, she had settled an old score, by one ingenious devise disposing of Avice and making Tom see what a fool he had been, and best of all had proved to herself beyond all question that she was free from the irksome bonds that had oppressed her. Her thoughts flickered for an instant round Avice.

'Silly little thing to try to put a spoke in my wheel. I'll let her have her laughs to-morrow.'

The oysters came and she ate them with enjoyment. She ate two pieces of brown bread and butter with the delicious sense of imperilling her immortal soul, and she took a long drink from the silver tankard.

'Beer, glorious beer,' she murmured.

She could see Michael's long face if he knew what she was doing. Poor Michael who imagined she had killed Avice's scene because she thought he was too attentive to that foolish little blonde. Really, it was pitiful how stupid men were. They said women were vain, why they were modest violets in comparison with men. She could

238

not but laugh when she thought of Tom. He had wanted her that afternoon, he had wanted her still more that night. It was wonderful to think that he meant no more to her than a stage hand. It gave one a grand feeling of confidence to be heart-whole.

The room in which she sat was connected by three archways with the big dining-room where they supped and danced; amid the crowd doubtless were a certain number who had been to the play. How surprised they would be if they knew that the quiet little woman in the corner of the adjoining room, her face half hidden by a felt hat, was Julia Lambert. It gave her a pleasant sense of independence to sit there unknown and unnoticed. They were acting a play for her and she was the audience. She caught brief glimpses of them as they passed the archway, young men and young women, young men and women not so young, men with bald heads and men with fat bellies, old harridans clinging desperately to their painted semblance of youth. Some were in love, and some were jealous, and some were indifferent.

Her steak arrived. It was cooked exactly as she liked it, and the onions were crisp and brown. She ate the fried potatoes delicately, with her fingers, savouring each one as though it were the passing moment that she would bid delay.

'What is love beside steak and onions?' she asked. It was enchanting to be alone and allow her mind to wander. She thought once more of Tom and spiritually shrugged a humorous shoulder. 'It was an amusing experience.'

It would certainly be useful to her one of these days. The sight of the dancers seen through the archway was so much like a scene in a play that she was reminded of a notion that she had first had in St. Malo. The agony that she had suffered when Tom deserted her recalled to her memory Racine's *Phèdre* which she had studied as a girl with old Jane Taitbout. She read the play again. The torments that afflicted Theseus' queen were the torments that afflicted her, and she could not but think that there was a striking similarity in their situations. That was a part she could act; she knew what it felt like to be turned down by a young man one had a fancy for. Gosh, what a performance she could give! She knew why in the spring she had acted so badly that Michael had preferred to close down; it was because she was feeling the emotions she portrayed. That was no good. You had to have had the emotions, but you could only play them when you had got over them. She remembered that Charles had once said to her that the origin of poetry was emotion recollected in tranquillity. She didn't know anything about poetry, but it was certainly true about acting.

'Clever of poor old Charles to get hold of an original idea like that. It shows how wrong it is to judge people hastily. One thinks the aristocracy are a bunch of nit-wits, and then one of them suddenly comes out with something like that that's so damned good it takes your breath away.'

But Julia had always felt that Racine had made a great mistake in not bringing on his heroine till the third act.

'Of course I wouldn't have any nonsense like that if I played it. Half an act to prepare my entrance if you like, but that's ample.'

There was no reason why she should not get some dramatist to write her a play on the subject, either in prose or in short lines of verse with rhymes at not too frequent intervals. She could manage that, and effectively. It was a good idea, there was no doubt about it, and she knew the clothes she would wear, not those flowing draperies in which Sarah swathed herself, but the short Greek tunic that she had seen on a bas-relief when she went to the British Museum with Charles.

'How funny things are! You go to those museums and galleries and think what a damned bore they are and then, when you least expect it, you find that something you've seen comes in useful. It shows art and all that isn't really waste of time.'

Of course she had the legs for a tunic, but could one

be tragic in one? This she thought about seriously for two or three minutes. When she was eating out her heart for the indifferent Hippolytus (and she giggled when she thought of Tom, in his Savile Row clothes, masquerading as a young Greek hunter) could she really get her effects without abundant draperies? The difficulty excited her. But then a thought crossed her mind that for a moment dashed her spirits.

'It's all very well, but where are the dramatists? Sarah had her Sardou, Duse her D'Annunzio. But who have I got? "The Queen of Scots hath a bonnie bairn and I am but a barren stock." '

She did not, however, let this melancholy reflection disturb her serenity for long. Her elation was indeed such that she felt capable of creating dramatists from the vast inane as Deucalion created men from the stones of the field.

'What nonsense that was that Roger talked the other day, and poor Charles, who seemed to take it seriously. He's a silly little prig, that's all.' She indicated a gesture towards the dance room. The lights had been lowered, and from where she sat it looked more than ever like a scene in a play. 'All the world's a stage, and all the men and women merely players.' But there's the illusion, through that archway; it's we, the actors, who are the reality. That's the answer to Roger. They are our raw materials. We are the meaning of their lives. We take their silly little emotions and turn them into art, out of them we create beauty, and their significance is that they form the audience we must have to fulfil ourselves. They are the instruments on which we play, and what is an instrument without somebody to play on it?'

The notion exhilarated her, and for a moment or two she savoured it with satisfaction. Her brain seemed miraculously lucid.

'Roger says we don't exist. Why, it's only we who do exist. They are the shadows and we give them substance. We are the symbols of all this confused, aimless strug-

241

gling that they call life, and it's only the symbol which is real. They say acting is only make-believe. That make-believe is the only reality.'

Thus Julia out of her own head framed anew the platonic theory of ideas. It filled her with exultation. She felt a sudden wave of friendliness for that immense anonymous public who had being only to give her opportunity to express herself. Aloof on her mountain top she considered the innumerable activities of men. She had a wonderful sense of freedom from all earthly ties, and it was such an ecstasy that nothing in comparison with it had any value. She felt like a spirit in heaven.

The head waiter came up to her with a ingratiating smile.

'Everything all right, Miss Lambert?'

'Lovely. You know, it's strange how people differ. Mrs. Siddons was a rare one for chops; I'm not a bit like her in that; I'm a rare one for steaks.'